VINTAGE MURDER MYSTERIES

With the sign of a human skull upon its
back and a melancholy shriek emitted when
disturbed, the Death's Head Hawkmoth has
for centuries been a bringer of doom and an
omen of death - which is why we chose it as
the emblem for our Vintage Murder Mysteries.

Some say that its appearance in King George III's
bedchamber pushed him into madness.
Others believe that should its wings extinguish
a candle by night, those nearby will be cursed
with blindness. Indeed its very name, *Acherontia
atropos*, delves into the most sinister realms of
Greek mythology: Acheron, the River of Pain in
the underworld, and Atropos, the Fate charged
with severing the thread of life.

The perfect companion, then, for our Vintage
Murder Mysteries sleuths, for whom sinister
occurrences are never far away and murder
is always just around the corner ...

GLADYS MITCHELL

Here Comes a Chopper

'Here comes a candle to light you to bed,
Here comes a chopper to chop off your head.'

VINTAGE BOOKS
London

Published by Vintage 2014

2 4 6 8 10 9 7 5 3 1

First published in Great Britain by Michael Joseph 1946

Vintage
Random House, 20 Vauxhall Bridge Road,
London SW1V 2SA

www.vintage-books.co.uk

Addresses for companies within The Random House Group Limited can be found at: www.randomhouse.co.uk/offices.htm

The Random House Group Limited Reg. No. 954009

A CIP catalogue record for this book
is available from the British Library

ISBN 9780099582243

The Random House Group Limited supports the Forest Stewardship Council® (FSC®), the leading international forest-certification organisation. Our books carrying the FSC label are printed on FSC®-certified paper. FSC is the only forest-certification scheme supported by the leading environmental organisations, including Greenpeace. Our paper procurement policy can be found at: www.randomhouse.co.uk/environment

MIX
Paper from
responsible sources
FSC® C016897

Typeset in Meridien by Replika Press Pvt Ltd, India

Printed and bound by in Great Britain by
Clays Ltd, St Ives plc

To

DOROTHY ALLEN

'As goddess Isis when she went
Or glided through the street,
Made all that touched her, with her scent,
And whom she touched, turn sweet.'
   ROBERT HERRICK, *A Song to the Maskers*

Chapter One

'And in the wood, where often you and I
Upon faint primrose beds were wont to lie,
Emptying our bosoms of their counsels sweet,
There my Lysander and myself shall meet,
And thence from Athens turn away our eyes
To seek new friends and stranger companies.'

WILLIAM SHAKESPEARE,
A Midsummer Night's Dream

ROGER SHAVED before a mirror which was set, he always thought, in the darkest and most inconvenient corner of the bathroom, and then, in his bedroom, examined the result. It would do for old Bob, he decided. He explored his long lean jaw with a long, lean hand, finished dressing, disregarded his landlady's summons to the early breakfast he had asked for, and checked his holiday luggage.

Mackintosh, spare shoes and socks, shaving tackle, hairbrush, toothbrush, comb, pyjamas, spare shirt, shorts, handkerchief, chocolate, tobacco, second pipe, unopened box of fifty cigarettes, John Donne, the *Eagle and the Dove*, the *Hesperides*, the *Woman on the Beast*. He regarded his possessions with pride and added to them a couple of boxes of matches—he already had a lighter in his pocket—and a small compass.

He breakfasted—kippers, thick bread and butter, strong tea and two cigarettes—packed his modest but satisfactory kit in the rucksack in which it would be carried, added an Ordnance map and an extra sweater, called good-bye to his landlady and set out.

It occurred to him, before he had gone a hundred yards, that he had left his ashplant in the umbrella stand in the hall. He went back for it, and surprised his landlady, who was kneeling on the mat just inside the front door polishing out the marks left by his hiking shoes on her linoleum, by opening the front door almost on to her face. He apologized, seized the stick, glanced at his wristwatch, and began to run down the road.

The bus was on time, and he caught it. As it was an hourly service, be thought he might congratulate himself on this achievement. He was superstitious about it, however, for it was within his experience that if matters went too well at the beginning they were apt to fall short towards the end. All the same, he felt glad he had returned for the ashplant. It was a trusted friend, and he would have missed it on the kind of holiday which he and Bob had planned.

Roger enjoyed riding on buses. This one was a

single-decker. He contrived to get the back seat, and there was able to enjoy his first pipe of the day. The route lay along a country road, and he was almost sorry when it was time to get out. There were few people travelling his way, for it was the Thursday before Good Friday, and most people had not begun their Easter holiday. It was not, in any case, a very promising day, and he was glad he had brought the mackintosh, a neat roll at the top of the rucksack.

He paid his fare, leaned back, and, at the end of an hour, looked out for Bob as they approached the bus stop, but Bob was not to be seen. This was somewhat surprising, for Bob was always first, and Roger had grown to expect that this would continue. He hitched the rucksack on to his shoulders—he had taken it off to sit down—knocked out his pipe and refilled it, then set down the ferrule of his ashplant and rose to his feet to get out. Waiting at the bus stop was a girl. She barred his way.

'Don't get out if you're Roger Hoskyn,' she said. 'Get in again. I've come about Bob.' She spoke quietly and with pleasant friendliness, and, Roger retreating before her, she took a seat in the bus. '*Are* you Roger Hoskyn?' she continued. 'I'm sorry, but Bob can't come. He sprained his ankle when he fell over the cat last night. It was too late to let you know, so I promised I'd meet you and tell you.'

'Oh?' said Roger blankly, removing his pipe. He was sorry for Bob, but sorrier still for himself. The holiday plans were finished. So much was clear.

'I'm so sorry,' the girl said again. 'He would have let you know, but we couldn't get you on the 'phone.'

The bus changed its driver and conductor. This took some little time.

'No, my digs are not on the 'phone, worse luck,' said Roger. 'Oh, Lord! What a mess it all is!' He stared gloomily out of the window.

'He said you'd be annoyed,' said the girl. 'But we couldn't think of anything to do.'

It occurred to Roger that the girl—she could not be more than about nineteen, he thought—had put herself to considerable trouble to come and bring him the news. He felt much ashamed of his reactions.

'Poor old Bob!' he said, turning towards her and smiling. 'After all, it's worse for him than it is for me. I say, it was awfully good of you to come. Couldn't we have lunch or something?'

The girl appeared to regard this offer doubtfully; so much so that Roger was piqued.

'I shan't eat *you* for lunch,' he said.

'It isn't that,' said the girl. 'But I have to be rather careful where I go.'

'Oh? On a diet or something?'

'No. A dream.'

The conductor rang the bell. Roger said:

'I beg your pardon?' The bus was rather noisy and he did not think he could have heard her.

'I expect it's silly, and I don't suppose you believe in such things,' said the girl who, although Roger had been very slow to notice it, was most becomingly dressed and was also delightfully pretty. 'I had a dream last night about a plane crash. It was horrible, and it's left me with the feeling that something awful will happen today.'

'Well, it's happened. Old Bob sprained his ankle.'

'That was last night, and doesn't count.'

'It counts to me all right.'

'Yes, I know. He's most frightfully disappointed, and I expect you are, too. It's too rotten!'

'Well, I'm not feeling so bad as I thought I should,' said Roger, beginning to deplore his flannel trousers and old tweed jacket, and the fact that his shaving had been very far from perfect. 'Look here, why not sit on this side?'

They had been talking across the bus. He moved out, gave her the inside seat, slung his rucksack on to the place she had just vacated, and transferred various bulges in the shape of a tin of tobacco, a small electric torch and a stiff-covered notebook from the pockets next to the girl to the pockets next to the gangway, and settled down again.

'There! That's better,' he said. He looked at the conductress to invite her to come for the fares. 'Where shall we go from here? I was going to get out where I met you.'

'I don't mind a bit,' said the girl.

'If I was you,' said the conductress, regarding them sentimentally, for she was married and liked to do her best for those who had not yet achieved the blessed state, 'I should get orf at Rowberry Corner. There's nice walks from there, so they tell me.' She clipped the tickets without awaiting instructions, and handed Roger his change. 'From the *Cow and Horses*, wasn't it? Two fives.'

She retired to the front of the bus and indulged in her own thoughts, which included the shrewd surmise that Roger would not be everybody's choice, but that she supposed girls knew their own business best. 'Bit of a weary willie,' was her verdict, for, like other unobservant and ignorant persons, she was inclined, from the young man's aesthetic air, untidy appearance, pallor and apparent thinness to underestimate his physique and his mental qualities. 'One of them artists, most like.'

Roger, accustomed to a certain amount of homage from his circle, never dreamed of these disparaging opinions.

'Talking of superstitions,' he began.

'Oh, you must think I'm mad,' said the girl quickly.

'On the contrary, I think you're pretty marvellous. Do you know——?' He recounted the tiny incident of the ashplant and mentioned that he had caught the bus they were on by the skin of his teeth. 'And that alone was enough to warn me that something would happen,' he said. 'Still——' he looked at her and smiled—'I don't mind now about old Bob, although I'm awfully sorry he's done in his foot. He always was an old idiot.'

'And did you feel,' asked the girl, 'when once you'd remembered the ashplant, that you'd got to go back for it, whether you wanted to or not?'

'Oh, yes, I did. It would have worried me to

death not to go. But fancy your understanding that! It's really rather extraordinary. We must be co-efficients, or soul-mates, or something don't you think?'

'I think,' said the girl, who had been thought a soul-mate before and knew what it led to, 'that when we get out of this bus we ought to walk miles and miles. It's just the day for it, as long as it doesn't rain. Couldn't we get on to the route that you and Bob were going to take? Then you could go on tomorrow, just as you'd planned, and this evening I could go back by train.'

'But Bob and I had planned twenty miles a day.'

'Well, I can walk twenty miles.'

'Oh, rot! And, if you could, I shouldn't let you! Whatever next!'

'All right. I'll go home after lunch.'

This was not to Roger's taste either.

'All right. We'll see,' he said. The girl laughed, and he changed the subject clumsily. 'Bob always mentioned a *kid* sister—named Dorothy, by the way. I'd thought of someone not more than twelve or thirteen.'

'I was twenty-one last August.'

'Well, I should hardly have thought that, you know. And I'm considered a pretty good judge. I'd have said not more than nineteen. I say, I wish I'd known about the birthday.'

'We had quite a good party, but Bob said he didn't think you'd come, so we didn't invite you.'

'Well, I'm damned!'

The conductress looked round disapprovingly. She did not have 'language' on her bus.

'Rowberry Corner. And not too soon,' she said. Roger hitched his rucksack over one arm and helped Dorothy out. The country road was firm beneath their feet, the sky, which had been cloudy, began to look brighter, they were both very young and it was spring.

'This is quite good,' said Roger. They tramped lightheartedly along, and stride for stride, until Roger looked at his watch. It was past midday. The bus ride had been a fairly long one.

'Grub,' he said. 'I wonder where there's a place?'

They came to an inn, a startlingly decorated roadhouse. 'Looks pretty foul, doesn't it?' he added. 'Here's hoping, anyway.' He entered.

'Lunch?' said the blonde behind the counter. 'Only for regulars, dearie.'

'But you can give us something, surely?' suggested Roger.

'Sandwich and a glass of beer. No lunches except for regulars,' repeated the lady, diverting her attention from the hungry to the thirsty, and pulling half a pint of mild and bitter for a yeoman in loud checks. This man drained away the fluid, wiped his mouth on the back of his hand, looked at the foam-rimmed glass, pushed it towards the blonde, and then volunteered information.

'Might do you something at the *Crown*, mate.'

'The *Crown*? Where's that?' enquired Roger. The blonde condescended to reply. Lifting a shapely arm, she indicated the middle pane of the window of the saloon bar, and briefly replied:

'Over there.'

'What about it?' asked Roger, turning his head. 'Shall we have a drink here, and go on?'

'Can't serve anybody under eighteen,' said the blonde, gazing with deep suspicion at Roger's companion.

'Who's asking you to?' asked Roger, irritated.

'Never mind,' said Dorothy, soothing him. 'The *Crown* will be very much better.'

They did not find the *Crown*. Opposite the roadhouse was a turning along which they walked for about a couple of miles. It ended at last in an open grassy space and a clump of trees.

'The village green,' said Dorothy, pausing to watch some ducks which were splashing across a small brook.

'Can't be. No pub, no church, no cricket pitch, no war memorial,' said Roger sapiently. 'I say, this is a bit thick! Do you think we've come the way they meant?'

'I shouldn't think so. Let's go on a bit, and see what happens.'

'Let's take this turning to the left, then. It ought to bring us back on to our road, and then I suppose we had better ask again, unless in the meantime we come to something else that can do us a meal.'

They took the turning, but it seemed to wind deeper into what has been rightly called the rural heart of England. It showed them hazel and willow, the first green of the alder, quickening twigs in the hedges and the bright lesser celandine beneath. There were streams, some with early cresses, and above the streams were the first deep pink of the apple, the already full blossom of the pear, some half-grown lambs in the fields, the brilliant leaf-buds of hawthorn and the wide-open flowers of the elm; there were birds and the sleeping oak trees, the long, strange catkins of the poplar and everywhere the grass springing green.

But the beauties of earth and sky do not fill the void reserved in the human frame for beef and beer, and Roger began to suffer the pangs of bitter frustration and regret as well as of hunger.

'I can't think now why we refused a perfectly good offer of sandwiches at that wretched roadhouse,' he groaned. They had long ago eaten all the chocolate he had brought in his rucksack. 'Why on earth didn't we sit down and begin when she gave us the chance?'

'She wasn't a nice barmaid, and it wasn't a nice place,' said Dorothy. She spoke firmly. She was young enough to be annoyed when people thought her under the legal age for drinks. 'I should hate to have had anything there. I'm sure we'll find somewhere quite soon.'

'If we don't, you'll have a corpse on your hands,' said Roger. Before them appeared the line of the roofs of some houses. With renewed hope they stepped out more briskly, and entered a village. Down the middle of the village street marched a line of ducks. They bobbed, with clumsy, amusing and rather touching purposefulness, one behind another, like a file of stout, heavy women all going to market. Roger and Dorothy followed. Suddenly Roger said softly:

'Don't look now, but, when you do, see if you see what I see. Although I really think it's a mirage.'

Dorothy smiled.

'I saw it before you spoke. I think it's a pub.'

It was a pub. It sported a large green board which advertised beers. Its own sign proved to be that of the *Dog and Duck*. It was not impressive to look at, although it was freshly painted and very clean. It was small, low-roofed, and was set well back from the road.

'They'll have to give us something,' said Roger, stalking into the public bar whilst Dorothy remained on the doorstep. The small, narrow room contained, besides the bar counter, two men, a woman, a baby in a pram, the landlord (who was wearing a yellow waistcoat) and a small black and white dog which whined and quivered, apparently with impatience, for one of the men said, 'All right! All right! I'm a-comin'.'

Roger's enquiries were satisfactorily answered. The landlord provided him with a glass of rum and Dorothy with some sherry. Then he sent them round to the saloon bar. This was really the bar parlour, but it had a counter on to the public bar. It was furnished with three small tables, a set of good prints, and a yard or so of embroidery enclosed in a mahogany picture frame.

'Well!' said Roger, bestowing his blessing on the

place. The landlord himself served them, placing on the counter bread, cheese, butter, meat pasties and tankards of beer. They fell to, relaxed and happy. They smiled at one another across the little square table. By the time the meal was over they felt as though they had known one another since childhood. There is magic in bread and cheese and beer.

When the meal was over, Roger carried back to the counter the cutlery, plates and tankards, returned to his place, lighted a cigarette for Dorothy and a pipe for himself, and spread out the map on the table.

It showed what they thought was the roadhouse, and from it they traced their route to the *Dog and Duck.*

'Here we are,' said Roger. 'Now, then, where shall we go?'

They discussed the possibilities for twenty minutes or so, and then, having mapped out their route and paid the score, they walked up the village street and came on to a by-pass road. It ran between fields with green hedges. They crossed the road and entered a high, narrow lane. Among the ground-ivy and wood anemones were dog violets. Roger, picking them carefully so as to have the stalks as long as possible, gathered a handful and gave them to the girl. Beneath their feet was the soft brown decadence of leaf-mould, spongy with rain. On one side a hill dropped down to a valley with a stream, and then the land rose in another rounded slope beyond the water. The top of the hill was crowned absurdly with holly, and farther on were beech-woods, their trunks austere, their long buds gleaming copper-coloured and having points like spears.

There was plenty to see: the many-feathered birds, a grey horse harrowing the hillside, the rich brown turn of the soil; in the distance the quick green of larches springing like fire in the smoky, dim brown of the taller trees behind them.

The two walked, paused and loitered, and then at last stepped out. The path dropped to fields hedged with hawthorns, and passed a cow-byre with four young, sleepy Alderneys. Farther on was the farmhouse. The farmyard was powerfully heralded by its midden, a knee-deep mass of manure and filthy straw. On the opposite side of the path a dilapidated notice-board, surmounted by the shape of a hand cut in wood, seemed to indicate some sort of sign-post, but nothing in particular could be learned from it, and the path it pointed out was narrower, more overgrown and more muddy than the one they were already following.

Roger took out the map once more, and Dorothy looked at her watch. It was past five o'clock, and the lane showed no sign of terminating. Apart from the isolated farmhouse, they had passed no buildings for three hours.

'We ought to be within sight of Dorsey,' said Roger, 'but I'm hanged if we are. We ought to have crossed More Heath common half an hour or more ago. Curse this confounded map! It must be wrong.'

'It doesn't matter,' said the girl. 'Let's follow the path as far as that gate down there, and then, if it still seems wrong. we'll come back to this other little path.'

Roger took out his pocket compass and stared at it in perplexity.

'I can't understand it,' he said. 'We've gone wrong somewhere. We ought to be walking north-east, but we're not. We've veered round to north-west. I'll tell you what I think, and you can call me names if you like. I think I picked the wrong footpath to take from that village. You know—where we stopped for grub. I'm sure now that this is the one we should have taken.'

He pointed with the stem of his pipe.

'Oh, well, never mind. It's been just as good a walk, I expect,' said Dorothy.

'That's one way to argue, but I do dislike to be wrong. Besides, the further we go along here, the further we get off our route.'

'We can get on to some other route, then. I don't think it really matters.'

'That's all very well. Still, perhaps we'd better carry on, as we've come this far. It looks to me as though that gate of yours bars our way. Doesn't it seem to you as though it's right across the path?'

This did not prove to be the case. The lane made a sharp bend, and this brought the gate into full view. It opened on to unpromising, bramble-entangled land which scarcely seemed worth the fencing, but the path continued downhill.

Just as the couple reached the gate, a prospect

opened which made them feel more cheerful. Bracken, the new shoots just beginning to show, small hawthorn bushes (sinister to eyes which had read George Allingham's poem), heather tufts, and some plants of wild strawberry, indicated a change in the soil, and away to the left the land rose, noble and spare.

'This looks better,' said Roger, as they turned aside to a ride of Downland turf. 'Let's sit down for a bit and take the weight off our feet, and then it ought to be easy going on this grass.'

Very faintly, from far, far away, they could hear the sound of a bell. Then, near them, was the thudding of hoofs, and three fine horses swept by. One was ridden by a tall, big man, black-haired, flat-shouldered and handsome. A very beautiful, red-haired woman, neither young nor old, rode the second; and on the third was a lively boy with thick, fair hair, flushed cheeks, and a look of pride and happiness very pleasant to see.

The impression, most stirring, was fleeting, for in less than a minute the riders, silhouetted for a moment against the sky at the top of the hill, thundered over the crest and were lost.

'Father, mother and son, I suppose,' said Dorothy.

'Hardly likely,' answered Roger. 'Possible, of course, because the boy might be a recessive, but if that man and woman had children they'd be likely to have red hair.'

This pseudo-scientific statement silenced Dorothy. She lay and meditated, a slender, roundlimbed hamadryad, and Roger, watching her, said suddenly:

'I say, I should like to kiss you. I suppose that would spoil your day?'

'Yes, it would,' she replied, without moving. 'But if it would spoil yours not to, you'd better do it, and get it over.'

Roger spoke moodily, baffled by this reasonable answer.

'I suppose most people want to?'

'Yes, quite a lot of them do.'

'Anybody in particular?'

'Well—I suppose so. Yes.'

'Oh? May I ask——?'

'Yes, of course you may, but I don't suppose I shall tell you.'

'Why didn't he come along with you today?'

'I don't think there's any particular reason. I thought you were going to ask his name.'

'Oh, I see. Well, I don't suppose I know him. I'll give you some advice, if you like.'

'I hardly ever take advice. I get too much from my people.'

'I don't suppose you'll take mine, but I do happen to know just this one thing, or I wouldn't inflict it on you. Have you had a row with this bloke?'

'I don't see why you ask that, and it isn't your business.'

'Well, girls won't admit it, of course, but, when you come to analyse it, rows are always—or almost always—their fault.'

'Really! I like that! If you only knew——'

'But, my dear child, I do know. Don't forget that I'm three years older than you! Three and a half years, actually. Further to that, I am a man, out in the world, earning my own living——'

'Two terms teaching little boys at a prep. school! I know, because Bob told me! He said you were bad at it, too!'

'Look here!' They glowered at one another until Dorothy lay back and laughed. Roger, bending over her, took her suddenly in his arms, held her very close and kissed her. The girl submitted to the kisses but did not return them.

'Look out, silly! There's somebody coming,' she said, when she could speak.

'Oh, damn!' said Roger, letting her go, sitting up and trying to straighten his tie. Two women, appearing from nowhere, were coming behind him up the path. He did not turn his head, but could hear them talking. 'Oh, *damn!* Do you think they could see us?'

'Yes, of course they could! Who could help it? But perhaps they can tell us where we are.'

'I should hardly think so.' He looked austerely at the women as they passed. 'Still, I can ask them, if you like.'

'Well, *we* don't know where we are, and—I want my tea.'

'You poor kid!' He leapt to his feet and went running after the women. He came back looking gloomy, and sat down again. 'They're employed at some big house at the foot of the hill. Apart from this house, which is miles from the nearest bus route and even more miles from a station, we are completely marooned. The best way, they say, is to keep on over the common until we see the spire of a church. We're to keep the spire on our right—that's if they know right from left, which I somewhat doubt—and in the end we shall come to the railway station. They say it's a very long way, but I think we'll have to try it, unless we go back by the way we've come. It might be the better plan, of course.'

'I'd hate that. I hate going back.'

'Good. So do I. Where's the map?'

They studied it closely, Roger pointing out landmarks with the aid of a stem of long grass.

'Here we are, I suppose,' said he. 'This is the pub, and this is our track, and that's where we gathered the violets. These contours must be that steep slope—you know, where we saw the cowslips—and this place here is the farm. Now where's this church they mentioned? Here we are. We're to keep it on our right, and—where's the station? Oh, yes. It does seem a good long way. I make it——' He measured.

'Seven miles,' said Dorothy, watching.

'A conservative estimate, and only as the crow flies, at that. I'd say a lot nearer ten!'

'Oh, no, I don't think so. Come along.'

'Yes, we'd better get a move on.' He put away the map and hauled her up. 'How would you like to borrow my ashplant for a bit?'

'Not at all, thank you. I'm very much happier without it.'

'Just as you like. Hullo!'

There was the sound of hoofs again, and this time the boy they had previously seen went by like a Cyclops, his horse, on a loose rein, thundering. Of the man and the red-haired woman there was no sign. The boy did not pass very close. He galloped away across the common in the direction they intended to take, but, a hazel wood opening to leave a broad avenue of turf, he turned his horse towards it, and was soon out of sight and out of hearing.

Roger and Dorothy stepped out briskly in his wake, and, pausing only to look at a rabbit which was sunning itself in the clearing—for the early evening had turned mellow—they took the broad path through the hazels and climbed rapidly up the slope to the top of the hill.

'We shan't be long now,' said Dorothy. Roger, shifting the rucksack upon his shoulders, glanced at her but said nothing. 'Well, do you think so?' she asked.

'I think we shall have had enough of it by the time we get to that station,' he replied.

Chapter Two

'Call for the best the house may ring,
Sack, white, and claret, let them bring,
And drink apace, while breath you have;
You'll find but cold drink in the grave:
Plover, partridge, for your dinner,
And a capon for the sinner. . . .
Welcome, welcome, shall fly round,
And I shall smile, though under ground.'
    JOHN FLETCHER, *The Dead Host's Welcome*
        (possibly Shirley or Massinger)

FROM THE top of the hill they could see the spire of the church. Obedient to the counsel of the women, they kept it resolutely on their right, and walked for some time on level turf, for the top of the hill proved to be a grassy plateau with a very fine view to the south.

Woods then bordered the track which they were following, and the sun, which had come out only at the approach of evening, slanted through the trees in a red-gold glow. Roger discovered that he was holding Dorothy's hand, but, having made the discovery, he kept it to himself, and they walked on, having the church in view, until the woods ended on a common and the track petered out on to grass and was discoverable only as rabbit-runs among the low-growing gorse. In trying to pick it out again, they came upon a burnt-out car.

'A relic of the war,' said Roger, inspecting it. 'The army had all this land, I believe. I suppose they used this car for target practice. Seem to be taking it to bits now.'

Dorothy was not particularly interested, and said nothing. They walked on. The ground became uneven, and walking was difficult. There were lumps and bumps, and the church, now far to the right, and a mile or more behind them, ceased to be a landmark. The sun had almost set, and it occurred to both the walkers that the common was desolate and that they were becoming uncomfortably hungry.

'I say, I wish I could see some sign of that station,' said Roger. 'Are you very tired?'

'No. I could walk for hours longer.'

'I don't believe it. My legs ache, so yours must.'

'They don't, a bit.'

'Can *you* see any sign of the station?'

They halted and looked around. Behind them the little lost church showed nothing but the top of its spire above the trees. To the left was the edge of the plateau, a down-dropping brownish slope, green at the foot and stretching away to the faint pink and purple of woods and the round-backed Downs.

In front of them the broken ground began to give place to more trees, and traces of a path invited them to descend through birch and pine woods. The distances were blue and misty with evening. The sun soon set, and the sky, although flushed, was fading to the cloudy colours of night. Roger was genuinely anxious, and glanced often at his companion, but Dorothy stalked beside him like Artemis, her chin up and her mouth half-smiling, as though fatigue and anxiety were beyond her comprehension. With some suddenness he discovered that he was in love with her.

'Look!' he said, at last. Below them they saw a house. It stood, ghostly white, in a clearing of the woods. It had a lawn in front and bushes on either side. It was like a house in an eighteenth-century drawing. There were the severely-classical pillars and round-headed windows of the period, the squat, square door, the porch with its uncompromising, beautifully spaced supports, and, dominating all detail, the extraordinary and impeccable symmetry of a building designed for the taste of an era in which no servant problem existed, and in which a lasting civilization was (unwarrantably) taken for granted.

'I think we must be on private land,' said Dorothy. 'I've thought so for about the last mile.'

'I know.' Roger looked unhappy. 'But I think we'll have to risk that. If those women told the truth—and I'm sure they did—we're still some miles from the station. I propose I ask at that house. Who knows? They might even offer us a lift, and I shouldn't feel inclined to refuse it.'

'I don't think they will,' said Dorothy, who, within the limits set by her youth, knew her world. 'Especially if these woods are preserved. They're more likely to set the dogs on us, I should say.'

'Look here,' said Roger, struck by a new and immensely more serious thought, 'what are we going to do if you can't get home?'

'What would you and Bob have done?'

'Oh—anything. In any case, we weren't going home, so it wouldn't have mattered.'

'Well, it doesn't matter now. It might if my people were at home, but there's only Bob, and he won't worry, if I know him.'

'Oh, well, that's something,' said Roger, not at all sure that it made much difference. 'But, still—I say, what a glorious old house it is!'

They stopped to look at it again. Its beautiful proportions were its charm. They could now see that it had a central portico approached by a flight of broad steps, and that its four Doric columns supported an entablature and a pediment which had a wreath designed in stone. The central doorway, broadly panelled and painted white, was surmounted by a wide, square window, and the other windows of the house were similar in form, but a little narrower and longer. Only the basement windows were round-headed, and, of these, there were four to be seen.

The impression of the white stone, the white-painted doorway and window frames, and certain enchantments lent by distance and the closing day, was of the ghost of a house, but of a ghost in the grand manner, beautiful, evocative and with nothing fugitive about it.

'First decade of the eighteenth century; or at any rate, not a day later than 1713,' said Roger, becoming prosaic. 'I wonder if it's where those two women are in service? I should think it must be. There doesn't seem to be anywhere else.'

They began to descend the hill. In front of the house was a semi-circular lawn flanked by bushes. There was an iron railing round the lawn, pierced by wrought-iron gates. On the lawn were four archery targets, great round shields on tripods, and at the edge of the lawn was a little green-painted summer-house by the side of which some steps led up to a terrace of which very little could be seen because of the bushes that bounded it.

'Well, here goes,' said Roger. He pushed open one of the gates and walked up the broad, curved drive. Dorothy, after a moment of hesitation, joined him. 'I'll ask, if you don't want to come,' he said, sensing that she was nervous.

'I don't mind asking, but I don't want to stay out there alone,' she answered, with a shiver. Roger stared.

'There's no one about, and it isn't late,' he said. She smiled.

'I know. Go along and ask.' But she went with him up to the door. It was answered by a benevolent butler, who held the door wide open.

'Please come in, madam,' he said. Dorothy drew back, but the kindly man repeated his request.

'Look here,' said Roger, grinning, 'this isn't the Dover Road, is it?'

'No, sir,' the butler replied, 'but you wouldn't disappoint Master George.'

He held the door open and hypnotized the two into entering. They stood, ill at ease, in the hall.

'If you will excuse me, madam, I will inform her ladyship that you are here. What name shall I say, madam, please?' He stood regarding them as an angler might look upon a couple of very fine trout, that is to say, with an appraising but sparkling eye.

'Miss Woodcote and Mr Hoskyn,' replied Dorothy, fascinated by the butler's expression. It reminded her of that of a cannibal king whose picture she had at home.

'Mr *Roger* Hoskyn,' said Roger, asserting himself in the only way that occurred to him at the moment.

'Very good, sir.'

'They may know my little book,' said Roger hopefully, as the butler went away. 'I say, though, I think they're expecting somebody, and he thinks we're them.'

As this seemed obvious, Dorothy made no reply, and they waited in the broad, almost tub-shaped hall, until the butler returned. But on his seraphic countenance there was not a trace of apology or surprise.

'Will you come this way, sir, please? Shall I take
your things? Will you go with Elsie, madam, please?
Dinner will be served in just twenty minutes from
now,'

Roger handed over his rucksack, mackintosh
and ashplant, and, a neat maid appearing from
the end of the hall, Dorothy, with a comical glance
of despair at her now inarticulate escort, went
with the maid upstairs. It was with a feeling of
adventure that she took the bath drawn by the
maid in a bathroom which had been converted
from a Georgian ante-room. With a light-hearted,
almost light-headed, swiftness she resumed her
clothes, repaired her face, and gave herself a last
look over in a long mirror.

The bedroom in which she had dressed adjoined
the bathroom. It was large and handsome,
rectangular in the proportions of two to one, and
the ceiling bore a heavy decoration in plaster of
roses and curling acanthus. The fireplace, small,
and with a modern grate in which a cheerful little
fire was crackling, had a white marble surround in
the form of a broken architrave, and in the break
there was a marble bust, the head of a man, on
a fairly high pedestal, so that the top of the head
came to where the architrave would have closed
in to the point of its arch had it not, in the conceit
of the time, been left unfinished.

Dorothy was still studying the bust when the maid
brought back her shoes most beautifully cleaned
and polished.

'Her ladyship is so pleased, madam,' she said,

'and little Master George is quite excited. It would have spoilt his day, unless.'

As Dorothy was unable to find any meaning in these remarks, she smiled shyly and said that she was glad. At this moment the gong was sounded, and, the maid proposing to show her the way to the dining-room, she went down a staircase with twisted balusters, close strings and square newels, into a fine, large room lined with oak panelling in fluted Corinthian pilasters. Like the rest of the house, it was spaciously and beautifully proportioned, and had an even more ornate and heavily-plastered ceiling than the bedroom to which she had been assigned.

The fireplace here was surmounted by some wood-carving of apples, grapes and sunflowers, heavy and dark, having a flat panel in the centre which formed a surround for a portrait. The room was furnished, in a harmonious mixture of styles, more from the viewpoint of comfort than of period, and a thick carpet covered the floor.

In these august and extremely pleasant surroundings were gathered what seemed, at first sight, to the visitors, a vast concourse of people, and two of these, both men and both tall and young, immediately picked themselves out from the rest and came towards Dorothy, each bearing a glass of amber-coloured fluid.

'Just in time for some sherry,' said the first.

'You have some,' said the second, transferring his offering to Roger.

Dorothy and Roger took the sherry, looked at

each other, smiled and sipped, and then, under cover of the general conversation, Roger muttered, in a tone which was, however, more audible than he intended:

'I say! I don't know what to make of this. What do you think we ought to do?'

'Stay to dinner. I think it's lovely,' answered the girl. 'Besides, I'm hungry.'

Roger glanced at his empty glass and cautiously looked round the room. There were a dozen other people present, including an old lady much like a lizard, and the handsome little boy and the remarkably beautiful woman with Titian hair whom they had already seen on the common.

'It seems she got home all right, then, although we didn't see her. How old do you think she is?' demanded Dorothy, immediately following Roger's eyes.

'Drawing her old-age pension without a doubt,' replied Roger, with great presence of mind, transferring his gaze to the little old woman, who grinned at him in a mirthless and terrifying manner.

'I mean the red-haired one, idiot! The one we met out riding on the common.'

'Oh, her! The boy's here, too. Wonder what's happened to the bloke?'

They were interrupted by a tall man wearing a monocle.

'My name is Ranmore. I'm the hostess's nephew. That is my aunt, just come in. Let me introduce you, may I?' he observed.

An elderly and unnecessarily stately woman had come into the room, glanced round, and immediately picked up her nephew's almost imperceptible signal.

'This is so sweet of you,' she said. 'Such a very last-minute invitation. Never mind about anything now. I wish Bugle would sound for dinner. Poor little George is nearly dead. Such a good thing you were able to save his life. Such a lovely party. I suppose you have names, but Ranmore never mentions names to me, so never mind now. I've put you next to Mrs Bradley,' she went on, turning to Roger, 'in that stupid Harry Lingfield's place. Don't try to talk to her. She's clever.'

She admonished him thus with a smile and an imperious little tap on his arm. 'Don't bother about Mrs Dunley. She doesn't matter,' she added. Roger bowed and could not help grinning. Soon the gong sounded again, and he found himself thrust into the company of the elderly lizard, who cackled harshly as she claimed him. Dorothy went in with the hostess's nephew, the monocled and polished Ranmore.

'This is by way of being a birthday party, so it's mostly the family,' he said. 'I'm afraid I'm old-fashioned. I rather like family parties.'

He had smiling dark eyes, a small moustache clipped short in the military manner, large, flexible hands and a kindly, somewhat fatherly voice. Dorothy disliked him very much.

Roger found himself third down the table from its head. The elderly lizard placed him in position as though he were an amusing but unimportant exhibit in a show-case, and then prepared to abandon him to strangers.

'We're not really partners,' she said, with a leer which made him flinch. 'You have to look after Mrs Dunley.'

'But *she* doesn't matter,' said Roger. 'I don't have to worry about *her*. I've already been told so.' He was still young enough to misjudge the carrying powers of his own voice, and a heavy-faced woman who had seated herself on the other side of him suddenly and disconcertingly replied:

'Of course you don't, my poor boy. I'm tired, and, when I'm tired, I really can't bear young men. I'm quite sure, somehow, you don't mind my saying so.'

The elderly lady cackled, a sound which brought all eyes in their direction. The pause was followed by a remark from the handsome little boy. He sat next to the hostess on her right.

'What do you say, Grand-Aunt Bradley?'

'That fish stinks, flesh is as grass, old fowl are tough, and good red herring is a myth,' replied the terrifying reptilian promptly. 'And now,' she added to Roger, 'you are wondering why you are here. To be frank, it is, to our hostess, Lady Catherine Leith, a story of some importance.'

Roger, who had taken an immense, immediate liking to her, exclaimed:

'This is awfully good! Please tell me.'

'It is little George's birthday party, you see, and the host, Mr Lingfield, is missing. He went out to ride, but remained, it appears, to quarrel, and, being temperamental and, I fancy, thwarted, has now gone off in a huff.'

'Oh, dear! What a sickener for everybody!'

'Not particularly so. He made us thirteen at table. But all is well, and you and your young friend have put it right, even if he returns. And now let's forget all about it, and settle down to enjoy ourselves. Do you know anybody here?'

'I think I've seen the red-haired woman before.'

'Claudia Denbies?'

'Oh, well, a photograph, then. And we saw her out riding this afternoon. I wonder she risks it. Her hands must be worth a fortune.'

'She may play to us after dinner. You must certainly stay long enough to hear her.'

'I say, I'd love to. I went to one of her concerts in London last winter. She's pretty wonderful, isn't she?' He sat and studied her. The red-haired woman had surprisingly muscular arms which showed to no advantage whatever under the short puffed sleeves of a dinner gown of black and silver. Her eyes were amber, and were very large and set wide apart in her head. Her red hair, curled and dressed in a fashion not of the fashion but curiously becoming to her pale, square, resolute, charmingly impudent face, was neither long nor short, but, parted in the middle, fell, with carelessly picturesque effect, not quite to the nape of her neck. Her mouth was too wide and the lipstick on it much too vivid for beauty. She wore neither rings nor a necklace, yet the effect she created was zestful, barbaric and stimulating. In spite of all this savagery, however, her smile was slightly nervous and very charming. Her wrists and hands were beautiful.

'Eat your dinner,' said his companion. 'It's rude to stare like that.'

She cackled and Roger laughed.

'And now, who are you?' she asked. He told her his name, and, to his great delight, she mentioned his book of poems and complimented him upon it. 'And your young friend?'

'Dorothy Woodcote. As a matter of fact, I was going to ask you——' He hesitated. Mrs Bradley cackled again, but the laugh made, despite its harshness, a very encouraging sound. Moreover, he had a feeling that she knew what he was going to ask her. He plunged. 'I was going to ask you—I thought you were going to tell me—why we're here. I mean, I understand about the thirteen at table, but Dorothy and I—well, I'm rather interested in this very odd sort of ending to our day. You see, we began on a walking tour—at least, *I* did—and the man who'd promised to meet me couldn't come.'

He gave a detailed account of his day, and mentioned the superstitions of the morning. Several people listened appreciatively, laughed, and glanced once or twice at Dorothy.

'We saw you coming,' said one, 'and Bugle was sent to the door to lure you in. Lady Catherine could not bear to sit down thirteen at table. She—this is not her house, but she acts as hostess for her cousin, this Mr Lingfield who is missing—she lives here six months of the year. If Mr Lingfield had been present, we should have been thirteen at table, without you two, and that would have been unsatisfactory. As it is, it is very fortunate that you were able to come along.'

'It is indeed,' said the woman on Roger's left. She spoke drily.

'Well, we didn't so much come along,' said Roger, grinning. 'We were walking, and had lost our way.'

'Do you mean to say you've been kidnapped?' She turned to her neighbour, a young man of about Roger's age, and said, loudly enough for the majority of those at table to hear, 'Do you hear that, Humphrey Bookham? The last two guests have been kidnapped.'

'Kidnapped? Yes, I know. I had my orders, and Bugle carried them out.' He leaned across her and grinned at Roger. 'Good old Bugle! Stout fellow, that fellow.'

From the foot of the table Captain Ranmore looked at him and nodded.

'You've done us proud, my dear Humphrey. I congratulate you on your perspicacity. You tutors are always sly dogs!'

'Perspicacity and slyness are not the same thing,' said Humphrey Bookham, looking annoyed and speaking sharply. He was the young man who had handed Dorothy her glass of sherry.

'I wonder what old Piggie thinks of it all?' said Captain Ranmore in an undertone. He indicated the woman on his right. She sat between him and the tutor, and, so far, had made no remark at the table. She was a thick-set, dark and heavy woman in spectacles. She made no conversation, and seemed anxious only to get on with her dinner. This was not particularly surprising, for the food was remarkably good. Barley cream soup (correctly made with butter, egg and sherry), halibut, braised sweetbreads with mushrooms, roast chicken, cauliflower, creamed potatoes, Christmas pudding and, at the end, ice-cream, made up a substantial, and, to most English people, a highly desirable meal. 'And Bugle, of course,' he added.

'Bugle?' said Dorothy. 'Isn't that——'

'The butler. I expect he let you in. Sort of secretive, selective, rather seal-like cove. And Mrs Bradley, of course. Although I believe she was privy to the idea. Very much in young George's confidence, you know, although she only arrived so very recently. Still, she fastened on George like a leech. A very fly old party, I believe.'

'Oh, yes? You know, the whole thing is rather a mystery. We were walking, Roger and I, and lost our way——'

'I know. We spied on you. We willed you to come to the door. Without you, we might have been thirteen at table. That, to my aunt, is an unthinkable state of affairs. It is not so much that she herself is superstitious—she is, of course—but that among our guests we have people who would have refused to sit down at all rather than risk being the first of thirteen to rise.'

'Yes, I see. I'm superstitious myself.'

'Really? I suppose most people are, when one comes to think. Hackhurst was one of the first. Fellow sitting next to my aunt on the right. Poet, you know. He declared—a lie, of course—that *he* wasn't superstitious but that so many people *were* that he would go without his dinner rather than occasion alarm and despondency. All that sort of thing. He was rather eloquent in an ineffective, poetic sort of way. Besides, he thinks Lingfield is dead. It was Lingfield who made the thirteenth.'

'He doesn't *look* superstitious.'

'Do you think one can tell a thing like that merely from looking at people?'

'Yes, I do.'

'Of course, you're young.' He smiled. His short moustache lifted at the corners of his firm mouth and his eyes were kind.

'Oh!' said Dorothy, annoyed. He laughed.

'Mrs Bradley, next to Hackhurst, doesn't care a hoot. *She* says that superstition is impious, redundant, unintelligent but important.'

Dorothy gazed at Mrs Bradley, and considered not only the remarkable woman herself but her equally remarkable adjectives. She then glanced at the captain and wondered how it was that his memory had retained, apparently without effort, the bulk of Mrs Bradley's remarks. He did not look particularly intelligent, and, up to that point, had not sounded it.

TABLE I

Lady Catherine Leith

George Merrow	John Hackhurst
Claudia Denbies	Mrs Bradley
Gareth Clandon	Roger Hoskyn
Marjorie Clandon	Clare Dunley
Mary Leith	Humphrey Bookham
Dorothy Woodcote	Eunice Pigdon

Captain Ranmore

The Dinner Party given for George Merrow on his thirteenth birthday, at Whiteledge, in the County of Surrey, on Maundy Thursday, March 29th. Fourteen persons at table.

'To continue our tour of the table,' continued the captain, who seemed determined to monopolize the conversation, 'your friend Mr Hoskyn—I think he was introduced as Hoskyn?—does not enter into our calculations, since his is the position of *deus ex machina*. Clare Dunley, whom you may or may not know as the archaeologist who has dug up the site at Duna, is not superstitious at all. That's the woman on Hoskyn's left. Next to her comes Humphrey Bookham, young George's tutor. He, poor young devil, isn't paid to be superstitious. As for Piggie'—he indicated again the thick-set, heavy woman on his right—'she's a pillar of the church, and wouldn't dream of being superstitious. Would you, Piggie dear?' he added, turning towards her with some suddenness.

'It's more than my job's worth *not* to be,' said the

dark woman, Eunice Pigdon, speaking abruptly but with good humour. 'You know that, Grannie. Don't tease.' She had removed her spectacles upon seating herself at the table, and now resumed them.

'She's my aunt's secretary,' Captain Ranmore continued, disregarding this mild rebuke, 'and what she says goes, even among this somewhat mixed bag of relatives and friends. Well, then there are the two Clandons and, of course, Claudia Denbies.' He paused, and his gaze rested unfathomably upon the red-haired woman. 'I don't know whether she's superstitious or not, but, as she's a celebrity, she probably is. Celebrities mostly are, I've noticed. They probably put down their success to luck, knowing it to be undeserved.'

'Oh, but,' said Dorothy quickly, 'you wouldn't call Miss Denbies' success undeserved?'

'*Mrs* Denbies is certainly gifted,' said Captain Ranmore; but he did not answer the question. Instead, he went on, without a pause, 'By the way, if you want to telephone your people, here's your chance. There are going to be family speeches. Perish the thought, but don't say I didn't warn you!'

'Oh, thank you!' said Dorothy, grateful to him at last. 'If you're certain it wouldn't look funny——'

'Of course not. I see that your companion and stable-mate is trying very hard to catch your eye. He has summed up the situation accurately. And, look! Bugle is bringing round the crackers. Take advantage of the hubbub and slip out. No one will notice you've gone, and, if they do, it still won't matter, take my word for it.'

Dorothy took his advice. As soon as the butler had passed her, leaving a Christmas cracker beside her plate, she nodded to Roger, got up and slipped away. He joined her in the hall, where they encountered the footman carrying in a silver salver of presents.

'The telephone, madam? You will find one in the room on your right. I beg your pardon, madam, but, if more convenient, Mr Bugle would soon have Sim round with the car if so be you will give me leave to go in first with Master George's anniversary offerings, and give Sim the word of warning.'

'The car? Oh, that would be simply marvellous,' said Dorothy.

'I shall explain to Lady Catherine, sir, that you had your train to catch,' said the butler, coming out to them. 'That will be quite the best thing, sir. So, if may be you would care to get your things, madam, Sim will be round immediate.'

'What do you think?' asked Roger, as soon as the butler had gone. 'Isn't it just a bit cool to shove us off home like this? Hang it all, we've done them a favour!'

'We've had a good dinner and a bath, and a nice long rest, and I don't suppose they want us any longer. Captain Ranmore seemed to think we ought to go.'

'That's true, too. Oh, well, see you later. Don't be long!'

'I won't! I don't like it here much!'

She went on up the stairs and he to the cubby-hole cloak-room on the right of the entrance hall.

He retrieved his ashplant and rucksack, and, what was more to his liking, his friendly pipe. He lighted this whilst he was waiting. Dorothy soon rejoined him, and, as she descended the stairs, the butler came out from the dining-room and they heard the car coming round.

'Here,' said Roger, handing Bugle five shillings.

'Thank you very much, sir. A pleasant journey, sir, and I hope you have not been inconvenienced,' said Bugle.

'Not so that we noticed it,' said Roger. 'Please pay my respects to Mrs Bradley.'

The butler opened the front door, the chauffeur opened the door of the car, Roger handed Dorothy in, and in another moment the car door was shut and they had sunk back against the comfortable upholstery and were being driven at a decorous pace along the drive and out into the woods.

The woodland ride sloped steeply downwards and the chauffeur engaged his bottom gear. Roger slid his arm round Dorothy. She did not offer resistance to this manoeuvre. After the encounter with so many strangers she felt she knew him well. His nearness and his protective arm were comforting.

She lay against him, rested her head on his shoulder and closed her eyes. The chauffeur changed gear, the car gathered speed, and, in less time than Roger thought quite fair, the car drew up and he had no more than time to release Dorothy before the chauffeur opened the door.

'The station, madam.'

'Thanks very much,' said Roger, giving him half a crown.

'Thank you very much, sir,' said the chauffeur. 'You will find a down train in fifteen minutes, sir, and an up train in six minutes, madam. Whichever you might be wanting. A very good night, sir.'

He climbed back into the car but did not start the engine. Roger, who did not lack intelligence, and Dorothy, who possessed the powers of intuition attributed (often absurdly) to her sex, gazed after him.

'I suppose there's nothing *rummy* about that bloke?' said Roger slowly. 'No, of course there isn't! Come on. Let's get the tickets. All the same, I thought he had a very funny look in his eye. What did you think?'

Chapter Three

'What need I travel, since I may
More choicer wonders here survey?
What need I aye for purple seek
When I may find it in a cheek?
Or sack the Eastern Shores? There lies
More precious diamonds in her eyes.'

JOHN CLEVELAND
(possibly John Hall of Durham),
Not to Travel

'I DON'T know,' said Dorothy, answering the last question as they approached the booking office from which shone out a gleam of kindly light by which a thin-faced booking clerk was reading an evening paper. 'However, thank you very much, and—good night.'

'What?' said Roger. 'I'm going to see you home, whatever happens.'

'But that's silly. You're still on your walking tour.'

'It's too late to think of that now. Anyway,

it doesn't matter, and, also, I've nowhere to stay.'

'Ask the booking clerk. He's sure to know somewhere where you can put up for the night. Then tomorrow you can go off again, and enjoy your holiday. I'd simply hate to think I'd spoilt it for you.'

'Oh, rot,' said Roger, decisively. 'Whatever happens, you haven't done that!' He turned towards the booking office, and spoke through the aperture. 'Two singles to Pulteney Junction, please.'

'Platform four, train in ten minutes,' said the booking clerk, waking up and reaching for the tickets.

'How long does it take from here?'

'Matter of an hour and a half. Change at Shepton End. About forty minutes to there.'

'Oh, Lord!' said Roger, exasperated.

'No through trains until the morning,' said the booking clerk with great satisfaction.

'Oh, well, it can't be helped, then.' Roger led the way on to the platform. There were one or two other passengers standing about. The station was far from presenting the deserted appearance which Dorothy, in her heart, had begun to dread, and her conscience troubled her. She felt that she was ruining Roger's plans.

'You see,' she said, 'I shall be quite all right. Really, there's no need for you to come. I really wish you wouldn't. I do know the way to go home.'

'Shut up! I'm coming,' he replied. The train came in to time, and they secured a compartment to themselves. He unslung his rucksack to put it up on the rack. Suddenly, to his great astonishment, three half-crowns fell out and lay on the seat that backed towards the engine. He shoved the rucksack into position, then picked up the coins and stared at them. A jerk, as the train pulled out, caused him to seat himself hastily almost on Dorothy's lap, but, regardless of this, he spread out the coins and studied them very closely.

'Well, that's a rum go,' he observed.

'What is? Haven't you seen half-crowns before?'

'Don't rot, my child. It *is* a rum go. These must be the coins I handed to the butler, Bugle, and, respectively, the chauffeur Sim. He had a peculiar manner. Bugle, too. Sinister is the word. What do you think their game is? Didn't I give them enough, and is this their delicate hint to that effect? If so, damn their eyes! Impertinent louts!'

'Oh, I'm sure it's not that!' said Dorothy, 'It's like——'

'It's like Benjamin's sack, and I can't explain it any more than *he* could,' said Roger, transferring the coins to his pocket. 'But, of course, it was all on the weird side, wasn't it? From beginning to end I thought that.'

'I'm glad we didn't stay,' said Dorothy, 'We didn't belong, and I'm sure they didn't want us. Once the dinner business was settled we were rather in the way, I expect. Don't let's talk about them any more. Tell me about your job.'

'My job is not one of the subjects that you and I discuss. I'm still smarting under this morning's apt comment. Remember?' He moved a little further off, and then smiled into her eyes. 'I teach little boys in a prep. school, and am not even very good at that.'

She blushed, looked contrite, and smiled.

'I'm sorry for saying that. I was a pig.'

'No, you weren't. It was perfectly true. I say, will you come and see me play in the Seven-a-Sides on Saturday week?'

'Where?'

'At Twickenham. We'll be knocked out first round, of course.'

'I'd love to come.'

'That's a date, then. I'll send you a ticket. Wonder whether old Bob will be able to make it? He wanted to come, I know, but I bet he won't be able to, with that ankle.'

'Oh, I expect he'll be all right by then. And that reminds me. You'd better stay the night at our house.'

Roger had been considering the question of his night's lodging, and had hoped for this invitation.

'That's awfully good of you,' he said. 'Are you sure it will be all right?'

'I don't see why not. I'm the housekeeper while Mother's away. If I want to invite you I can.'

'Oh, I see. Well, then, thanks very much.'

'And then, tomorrow, you can make a fresh start.'

'Yes, I could do that. I say, fancy Claudia Denbies in that house!'

'John Hackhurst, too. I wonder, really, what sort of people they are? Lady Catherine, and all her relatives, I mean.'

'Well, I think they've got pots of money. The old lady had a secretary—that Pigdon woman—and the kid had a tutor, and the butler repudiated my five bob, it seems . . .'

'I still think that's awfully queer. I'd like to know more about that. Do you think the whole lot of them were *honestly* glad to see us?—from the point of view of the number at table, I mean?'

'I expect so, although—well, perhaps you didn't notice. Still, people are odd about the number thirteen. I remember going to an Old Boys' dinner the year before last. At the last minute a fellow named Morrison absolutely refused to sit down at table because he spotted that if he did it would make thirteen.'

'What happened? Didn't he have any dinner?'

'Oh yes. He had a small table all to himself. It was really a desk with a table napkin or a tray-cloth or something on it. He was ragged about it afterwards, of course, but nothing would budge him. You can't really defend superstition, but you have to give in to it sometimes, and everybody knows about thirteen. Rather odd that you and I should have talked about omens, and bad luck, and so on, this morning.'

'Yes; and that reminds me of a very queer remark Captain Ranmore made to me at dinner. He said

John Hackhurst thought that Mr Lingfield—the host, you know, who didn't turn up—was dead. Of course, it must be a joke, but it wasn't really very funny. I suppose, actually, Mr Lingfield and Mrs Denbies must have quarrelled . . .'

'After they had sent the boy ahead. Remember we spotted him riding home alone? I suppose he was in a hurry to get back for his birthday dinner.'

'Yes, he must have wanted to be back in time for that . . .'

'And then the two of them set to and had a scrap . . .'

'And the man was upset and wouldn't meet her again.'

'But, funny, that, don't you think? I don't actually know of any blokes who would turn sulky in that sort of way. I should have thought he would simply have consigned her to the devil, don't you know, and tried to carry on as though nothing had happened. It's women who get all het up at the end of a show-down and go to their rooms and cry. At least, that's my experience.'

'I'm sure they don't!'

'Well. I have known cases. Really I have. Various girls.'

'Not many!'

'Well, I haven't—I mean, I don't go through life having scenes with women, of course. But don't let's scrap about that. It's quite likely the fellow, having a horse and what-not, galloped away in a stew and went much too far—quite literally, I mean—and was too late, then, to show up at dinner, that's all.

Rather thick, though, as he was the host. Still, it must have happened like that.'

Dorothy could not find herself in agreement with this reasoning. She was silent, and then said;

'I wonder what they quarrelled about? We're taking a lot for granted. They may not have quarrelled at all.'

'Well, in that case, surely, Mrs Denbies would have brought a message. It was quite clear, I thought, from what was said, that old Lady Catherine had been expecting him up to the last minute. It was he who made number thirteen.'

'Oh, yes, that's true. They were on the look-out for someone to save the situation, but, even if Mrs Denbies rode straight back, she couldn't have been there so very long before us. I wonder what explanation she gave for coming back by herself, though?'

'Talking of explanations, I'd like an explanation of how my half-crowns got put back into my rucksack. It makes me feel rather an ass.'

'I expect the servants are forbidden to take tips from visitors, that's all.'

'But nobody would have known. There was no one else near when I slipped them the money, was there? No, I expect they're used to millionaires—the servants, I mean—and the money wasn't enough.'

'They didn't seem a bit like that to me. It was a good dinner, though, wasn't it? I enjoyed it.'

'Wizard, I thought. What was the nephew like? I hardly met him.'

'Captain Ranmore? I didn't like him much. Of course, he's old—quite forty. I should think he'd make quite a nice father.'

'Is George his son?'

'I shouldn't think so. It didn't seem like that—and you know what you said about fathers, before we got to the house. There were lots of relations, though, weren't there? I didn't get them all sorted out. Captain Ranmore was telling me about them, but we didn't get to the end. We were going all round the table, and then it came to the crackers. Oh, except that, funnily enough, he missed over the woman next to me, although he mentioned the man and girl on the other side of her—you know, the young ones. The girl was in pink. They were brother and sister. Name of Clandon.'

'I think they're twins.'

'I thought they might be. I rather liked the look of him. Did you?'

'Clandon? Oh, yes, he looked all right. So you don't know who the woman was on your left? She was certainly an odd-looking wench. Repressed or something, I should say. Perpetual spinster, or family breadwinner, perhaps. Under the weather, anyhow.'

'Perhaps she is Lady Catherine's companion. I should think that might be rather wearing.'

'Lord, yes! Although I think I preferred Lady Catherine to that female I got stuck with. Not Mrs Bradley. I liked her very much. I mean the other one. You know, the digger-up of unconsidered trifles—the archaeologist woman.'

'Oh, was she? I'm not sure whether Captain Ranmore mentioned her or not. The tutor seemed nice, I thought.'

'Yes, quite a good chap. Who was the heavy-weight next to Ranmore on his right?'

'Miss Pigdon, Lady Catherine's secretary.'

'Would she have a secretary *and* a companion? I thought they were jobs for one person.'

'They ought to be, anyway. Perhaps the other girl, the queer one, is some sort of poor relation.'

'Yes, I should think she must be. That would account for her, wouldn't it? The monumental depression, and that sort of thing. And, talking of depression, is this bally train going to stop at every station?'

It was a tiresome, crawling journey. Dorothy, who had taken a corner seat, leaned back and closed her eyes. Roger crossed over and sat beside her. He looked at her brown, small, childish hands, and, as he was speculating upon them, the train, like a tired horse approaching its stable, gave a sudden snort, gathered speed, and, as suddenly, jerked on its brakes with a hideous, involuntary squeal and pulled up sharply.

'Now, what?' said Roger. 'I suppose we've lost a couple of wheels or something, or left a coach behind.'

Dorothy sat up, now wide awake, and looked out of the window.

'We're not at a station,' she said.

'That's nothing to occasion surprise on this line,' Roger remarked. 'I should think we must have stopped half a dozen times already outside stations.'

'You really ought to have let me come back alone. It would have been ever so much better,' said Dorothy, trying to see into the gloom.

'I could never have faced old Bob,' said Roger, grinning. 'I say, what are those fellows playing at?' He got up, let down the window and stuck his head out. 'They're going up and down the train with a lantern. I hope we're not going to miss our connection through this!'

He withdrew his head as, apart from the movements of the guard and the fireman with the lanterns, there was nothing to see. In about five minutes, however, the guard came past the window which Roger had left open wide, and asked, but not very hopefully, whether there was a doctor on the train.

'I can do a bit of binding-up, but no diagnosis,' said Roger. 'Anything wrong?'

'We don't quite know, sir. Would you come and have a look at the driver? Had a shock, he has, and his wife expecting tonight. Bad luck he should be on duty, but the influenza's that bad he couldn't be spared.'

'Do you mind?' asked Roger. Dorothy said that she did not mind at all. He opened the door and dropped on to the line—a surprising distance—aided by the light of the lantern. He returned in about ten minutes.

'Fellow appears to have had a shock all right,' he said, when he resumed his seat beside Dorothy.

'Comfort he doesn't have to steer, for I don't think he's capable of it.'

'What's the matter with him, then?'

'Oh, his wife's going to have a baby, and it seems to have got on his nerves.'

'In what way?'

The train, with a good deal of noise, steamed on again.

'Oh, I don't know. Signs and wonders, and all that. Anyhow, he's prepared to carry on. Personally, I shall be glad when we get to our station. I don't much care to be behind a driver who sees headless corpses where no headless corpses should be.'

'Oh, heavens! Is that what he said?'

'It is. However, we've soothed him. Funny thing, though. I smelt his breath. He's dead sober. Ah, here's our station! Now I wonder how long we've got to wait?'

The train was already slowing down. The lights of the station came into view. Roger hauled down his rucksack and slung the straps over his arm. He picked up his ashplant, opened the carriage door, got out, and helped Dorothy out. There was an empty seat on the platform under a lamp. He guided her to it, slung down his luggage beside her, and went off to find a porter.

'This platform, but we've got an hour and a half to wait,' he said, with a groan, on his return. 'We've missed the connection. I'm really terribly sorry. Old Bob will have my blood! I say, are you hungry again, as well as sleepy?'

'Good heavens, no! I couldn't eat a thing! And, anyway, I'm not sleepy now.'

'Do you mind if I smoke?'

'Please do.'

'Cigarette?'

'Thank you.'

Scarcely had they lighted the cigarettes when the chauffeur Sim came through a side gate on to the platform.

'I thought I might find you here, sir,' he observed. 'I've got the car outside. I'm very sorry, sir, but I did not have orders to take you further than the station. However, I've come now, sir, to drive you home.'

'Well, thanks very much,' said Roger, getting up. 'Anything's better than waiting an hour and a half on this beastly station.'

Sim seemed to know the route well, and drove very fast through the darkness. He had not even asked for an address. This was all explained when, two hours after they had left it, they found themselves at the mysterious house again.

'Here, what the devil!' said Roger, as soon as he stepped out of the car.

'I'm very sorry I had to deceive you, sir,' said the chauffeur. 'But my orders were at all costs to get you back here.'

The guests were still at table. Conversation was general, but there was an air of strain about the party. Lady Catherine greeted the arrivals very cordially, and asked them to sit down at once as the party was thirteen at table. Roger, who had halted in the doorway with Dorothy just behind him and looking over his shoulder by standing on tip-toe, merely glowered at the party.

'Do you mean to say,' he said, when, sweetly but peremptorily, she had repeated her request, 'that you've all had to sit and sit because nobody had the sense to get up and break the spell?'

'Lady Catherine was so much distressed at the idea that somebody should bring death upon himself within the year by rising first from the board, that we felt we had to give in,' Mrs Bradley responded. 'And, further, dear child, in ten minutes more we are promised a violin solo to reward us for our exemplary behaviour. Won't you stay and listen? It is so very late for you now, that another half hour won't signify anything particular, and, after that, I myself will drive you home.'

'I certainly should like to hear Mrs Denbies play,' said Dorothy, over Roger's shoulder. 'Go on, silly! Sit down,' she added into her fuming protector's left ear.

So they seated themselves, and, at a motion of Lady Catherine's hand, the whole company rose. George, who had fallen asleep, was lifted up by Bugle and carried away, and the others went into a large chamber on the ground floor in which there was a grand piano on a low platform.

Claudia Denbies tuned her violin, played Bach's *Partita in E Minor* on it, and then, on the 'cello, Andrea Caporale's *Sonata in D Minor* and Fauré's *Elégie*.

'I've strained my back, I think,' she said, in response to a demand from Captain Ranmore for another piece on the violin, 'and find the 'cello a bit easier to manage tonight because I can sit down to it. I hate sitting to play the fiddle.'

'I knew you shouldn't have gone out riding this afternoon,' said Lady Catherine. 'I said at the time it was ridiculous.'

'Oh, I don't think I did it out riding,' replied Claudia Denbies, 'But I must get it right before my London recital. Besides, I've promised Captain Ranmore to shoot at the butts with him tomorrow.'

'And now,' said Mrs Bradley, 'these children must go, Lady Catherine, or they'll get no sleep tonight.'

'Sim is quite ready,' said Lady Catherine, graciously. 'Will you see to them, Eunice?'

'Of course,' said Eunice Pigdon. She took them out to the car which was at the front door. 'I do hope you weren't annoyed at being asked to come back,' she added, as the three of them walked on to the gravel. 'Lady Catherine is very peculiar over the number thirteen.'

'But, surely,' said Roger, voicing the thought which had been in his mind for the last hour, 'it wouldn't have mattered who got up first after we left, as we hadn't sat down thirteen? Besides, we didn't leave thirteen at table. I don't see any sense in it. The first one of the house-party who got up after we left would have been the third of fourteen people, not the first of thirteen. Where's

Lady Catherine's logic? You would have been thirteen *with* Mr Lingfield, not without him. The whole business makes no sense.'

'I know,' Eunice Pigdon agreed. 'Oh, well, it's a good thing you were kind enough to come back, or I'm sure we'd have been sitting there still. Lady Catherine is never gainsaid. It doesn't do. Poor Mary Leith and I have trouble enough as it is. Oh, you won't want this car. Sim, take it back.'

'You could all have got up together,' suggested Dorothy. Eunice Pigdon agreed, but with more politeness than heartiness. She made way for Mrs Bradley and walked slowly back into the house. The chauffeur brought Mrs Bradley's car.

The journey by car seemed short. Nevertheless, it was well after midnight before they drew up at the gates of Dorothy's home. Mrs Bradley would not come in, and favoured them with a leer as she said good night. She drove away immediately, and Roger, taking the key from Dorothy as soon as they reached the front door, opened up for her and was invited in.

It was the first time he had ever seen Bob's home. It seemed spacious after his lodgings. Dorothy took him into the dining-room.

'Thank goodness it's fairly warm in here,' she said. The drive had proved cold, and would have been colder but for the comfort of Roger's breast and arm. The fire, although low, was not out. 'Oh, there's some hot milk,' she added. 'Would you like it?'

'No, really, thanks.'

'Oh, well, there's some whisky in the sideboard. Help yourself. I won't be very long.'

She took off her coat in the hall and went upstairs. Bob was reading in bed. He put down his book when she came in, and regarded her sternly.

'Where on earth have you been?' he demanded. 'Jerry's been here, and he kicked up no end of a stink when he heard you were out and I had to tell him I didn't know where.'

'How's the ankle?' asked Dorothy tactfully, seating herself on the bed.

'None the better for having you sit on it,' retorted her brother, who seemed to be greatly moved. 'Look here, where the devil *have* you been? Do you know what time it is, and what time you left the house this morning?'

'Oh, don't be a heavy father,' retorted Dorothy. 'If you want to know, I've been having a thrilling time, a glorious walk, a marvellous dinner, and quite a lot of adventures.'

'Who with?'

Dorothy checked the names on her fingers. With her long, thick hair, grey eyes, broad brow and confident chin she looked altogether so young that her brother's heart was softened. He loved his young sister, and was secretly proud of her beauty. Her lissome body was in contrast to his own strong, sturdy frame, thick shoulders, and long, strong arms, and people who did not know the family were usually very much surprised to learn that they were related. Bob had protected and fought for Dorothy from the time when they both very young. He had experienced secret, deep, substantial pleasure when she came to his school on sports days, although he had regarded her then, and he regarded her still, as a child. He spoilt and bullied her, kept her out of trouble with their parents, acted as her chaperon, banker, swimming coach and watch-dog, and, generally speaking, obtained much satisfaction out of managing her and being managed by her, teasing her, taking care of her, and showing her off to his friends.

'Heavy father be damned!' he said, before she could begin her list of names. 'Although you probably ought to be tanned. I'll subscribe to that, if that's being a heavy father.'

'There were Lady Catherine, Captain Ranmore, John Hackhurst (the poet, you know), Mr Bookham, Mr Clandon,' began Dorothy hastily, 'and—and—Miss Clandon, Mrs Dunley (the archaeologist), Mrs Denbies (the violinist), George, Bugle——'

'What *have* you been doing?' asked Bob. He scowled at her dangerously. 'Don't you dare to try pulling my leg!'

'I've been walking, I tell you, and having a birthday dinner with George and Lady Catherine and——'

'Cut it out! Did you meet Hoskyn?'

'Yes, of course I did. He was quite easy to recognize from your description, darling, and——'

'Did you explain about my confounded ankle?'

'Yes. How is it, by the way? You didn't tell me.'

'Rotten. What did Hoskyn do when he heard?

Went off in a huff, I suppose. I knew he would.
He can't bear to have things upset when he's got
them planned. Did he say where he was going?'

'He came with me; or, rather, I suppose I went
with him. We got lost, and then we came to this
house and they made us have dinner, because it
was George's birthday, and then the chauffeur drove
us to the station, and we began coming home. But
they made us go back because they couldn't get
up from table. Then Claudia Denbies played to us
all, and we came home in Mrs Bradley's car. Bob,
it's all been most peculiar and exciting. You might
take an interest, you pig!'

'Where's Hoskyn?'

'In the dining-room, downstairs. I told him to
help himself to whisky.'

'What!'

'Oh, do you mind? I thought there was plenty
in the decanter. I'd better go down and stop him.
I told him I'd only be a minute. Can he sleep in
here if I fix him up a camp bed?'

'No, he can't! And I didn't mean the whisky!
You knew that perfectly well. I meant about your
bringing him home. And, anyway, if he's going to
stay the night, what's the matter with the spare
room?'

'I'm not sure if the sheets are aired, and I think
mother sent the eiderdown to be cleaned. He won't
want sheets and things on a camp bed, will he,
if you let him have your sleeping bag and one of
your blankets?'

'I *want* all my blankets, damn it!'

'Oh, Bob, don't be selfish! How many have you got?'

'Five, and I want 'em all. You brought him home, so you jolly well go and forage for him. Although what the devil it's all about I can't imagine.'

'Oh, Bob! We must give him a bed!'

'Dump him in the parents' bedroom, then. What's the matter with that?'

'I don't know whether Ellen has changed the sheets yet.'

'Good Lord, he won't look at sheets! Go and get him, and bung him in here to talk to me while you have a look to see that everything's ship-shape. And then you get into bed, You look as though you'd had enough for one day.'

'Yes, I think I have,' said Dorothy, suddenly realizing that she was very tired. 'And I don't think I liked it after all. Good night, then. We shan't be long.'

'You mind you're not! I'll give you twenty minutes.'

Dorothy went to the door. Bob called her back.

'Er—what do you *think* of Hoskyn, by the way? And what does he think of *you?* I'll bet he's thinking long, long thoughts of both of us now we've gone and spoiled his holiday.'

Dorothy did not answer. She returned to the bedside and kissed the end of her brother's firm and pugnacious nose. Bob caught her and pulled her down, wincing as she landed on the bed, but holding her tight.

'Answer the questions,' he said, 'you little fiend.'

'I can't. And he'll be wondering where I am.'

Bob rumpled her hair and kissed her.

Chapter Four

'My hounds are bred out of the Spartan kind,
So flew'd, so sanded, and their heads are hung
With ears that sweep away the morning dew.'
SHAKESPEARE, *A Midsummer Night's Dream*

BREAKFAST NEXT morning was taken by the three of them together, for Bob had swung himself downstairs. He sat by the fire, with his injured foot on a cushion placed on top of a small stool, whilst the others sat at the table.

'What are you going to do now?' he asked, when, the meal over, both men had lighted their pipes and were occupying armchairs, and Dorothy, seated in the window, was watching the maid clear the table.

'Oh, I don't know,' said Roger. 'Have you a dog that wants taking out for a run?'

'No. Only a sister,' said Bob, with a lordly grin. 'But what about your holiday? You can't spend it here with us.'

'Can't I? I'd rather hoped I could. After all, it's

your fault we aren't walking together, you old mudhead.'

'Well, damn it,' said Bob. 'I can't help it!'

'I'll tell you what,' said Roger, suddenly addressing Dorothy. 'Let's hire a car and take this surly invalid to Whiteledge.'

'Whiteledge? I've never heard of it.'

'You've been there, though. We needn't stay to dinner this time, of course, but I do want to go there again.'

'Oh, it's the name of that house!'

'It is. I found the County History in your bookcase, and I've already had a look at it. The house is quite famous, it seems. Sort of three star Baedeker and all that. I'd rather like Bob to see it.'

'I could manage all right in a car,' said Bob cheerfully. 'I call it a brain-wave, old man. Dorothy can ring up the garage. Will yon drive, or shall she get them to send a man? The parents have taken our car.'

'What make of car will it be?'

'A Morris, most likely.'

'Can do. And I'd much rather be on our own.'

'Good. So would I. All set? Buzz along, young D. and get contact. Tell them we want it for the day.'

'Dash it! I can 'phone a garage!' protested Roger.

Dorothy, who realized (without altogether being aware of the fact) that Bob and Roger were, for the moment, antagonistic, and that she was the bone of contention, went at once to the telephone. She did not, in the ordinary course of events, readily accept orders from her brother, but on this particular occasion she took a perverse, particular pleasure in obeying him, for Roger met this obedience with a scowl.

The response from the garage was favourable. A car was forthcoming within twenty minutes. The three climbed into it in a holiday spirit which was particularly noticeable in Bob, who had not expected any kind of a holiday, and who, aided by Roger and Roger's ashplant, 'made the grade,' as he put it, without disaster, and settled comfortably on the back scat.

The main road ran through fairly open country, but there was a prettier drive by way of secondary roads and a water-splash. Guided by Dorothy, who sat beside him, Roger drove carefully, as became one who did not know the road and who had (as Bob insisted) an invalid on the back seat, past fields and beside a golf course, and then on a right-of-way through a large and handsome park.

The road turned sharply then towards the east, and gave a view of the race-course. About two miles further on, it crossed the water-splash and then began to mount, although not steeply.

At the top of the rise the secondary road dropped southward, to merge with the main road somewhere nearer the coast, but the eastward course was continued by a lane just wide enough to take the car. This lane was part of an old Roman road, and some distance along it they saw the old mill and met the boy George.

The mill, with its enormous, slatted sails, stood up behind a small, dilapidated farmhouse. Roger had to pull up on rough grass by a crazy fence to let a farm-cart go by, and it was whilst they were waiting here that they saw George swinging on a gate. The gate gave on to a field on the slope of a hill. It was a ploughed field, dark with its level furrows and crowned at the top by a wood. The lane led onwards through the gate on which George was swinging, climbed the hill, and was lost among the trees.

The farm-cart turned into the farmyard, Roger let in his clutch, and the car crawled forward. George slid down from the gate and politely held it open. Roger stopped the car in the gateway, leaned out and said:

'Hullo!'

'Oh, good morning,' said George, who, in shorts and a sweater, looked even more handsome than in polo-collar and riding breeches or in his evening clothes. 'I say, I don't think you'll get much farther along this track. It ends in the wood up there, and then you're stuck.'

'Yes, I thought that myself,' said Roger, 'but there doesn't seem room to turn here.'

'Back into the farmyard. I'll open the gate,' said the boy. 'The farmer's gone to market, but his wife won't mind a bit, so long as you give her a shilling. She collects quite a lot of money in the summer. She buys her boy's boots out of motorists. She told me so just now. She saw you coming, so she's ready for you.'

'Does she get a shilling from everyone?' Dorothy asked.

'Mostly. She's got a bull, you see, and as people have to get out of their cars to open the gate if she isn't doing it for them, they mostly pay up, and let her do it.'

'You're a long way from home,' said Roger, having digested and approved of the farmer's wife's thrift and sagacity.

'Yes. I've been turned out,' said George. 'Mr Lingfield hasn't come back, and they've sent to the police about him. I'm not supposed to know, but, of course, I do. I think I've been got out of the way.'

'Mr Lingfield? Not——'

'Yes, the man who was missing from the table. He's a sort of uncle of mine. He owns the house. Aunt Mary and Great-aunt Catherine and I just live there. Anyway, he hasn't turned up. I expect he's gone off to Central Africa. He does that when people annoy him. I think Mrs Denbies annoyed him yesterday. I say, I was awfully glad you came along last night. Great-aunt Catherine wanted to ask Miss Pigdon or Mr Bookham to have dinner alone, but I couldn't agree to that, as I like them better than anyone else in the house, and, after all, it *was* my party. So we were stuck, until you two came. I do thank you very much. I didn't have a chance to speak before you went.'

'We had a jolly good time,' said Roger. 'The thanks are all on our side. I suppose we can't give you a lift?'

'You'd better not, thanks. I shall hang about here for a bit, and the farmer's wife will give me my dinner. Then, at three o'clock, I'll go home.'

'But surely it's more than ten miles?'

'Not by the way I shall go. Back her, if you're ready. I'll shut this gate, and then the farmer's wife will open the other one as soon as you've given her the shilling.'

'You seem jolly keen on this shilling business,' said Roger. 'Do you and the farmer's wife divvy up, by any chance?'

The boy laughed, and then asked suddenly:

'Did Sim pick you up last night? We forgot we'd be thirteen if Mr Lingfield came in. I wanted to be first up to see what would happen, but Great-aunt Catherine wouldn't let me. I think superstitions are silly. Besides, it's awkward when she will insist that there are the wrong number present. I don't like it. After all he *didn't* come in.'

'Oh, yes, he found us,' said Roger. 'I wished at first he'd missed us, but it was worth a lot to hear Mrs Denbies play. How is her back this morning?'

'Oh, just the same, I think,' replied the boy. 'She's worried about Mr Lingfield. I think they all are. Rather silly, really. I'm sure he's simply gone off exploring again.'

'I suppose he didn't go by train?' asked Roger. The boy looked at him intently for the moment, and then said he did not know. Roger was tempted to follow up this question and ask whether the boy had been a witness to a quarrel between Lingfield and Mrs Denbies, but he knew that it was not his business, and regretfully abandoned the idea. 'By the way,' he added, 'what did he do with his horse?'

'His horse? Oh, he sent it back to the house, I suppose. He had Strawberry, and Strawberry is certainly in his stable this morning, because I saw him there myself.'

'Oh, I see,' said Roger. 'Well, so long! Oh, I didn't get a chance yesterday to wish you Many Happy Returns.'

Dorothy echoed this wish, and George, acknowledging their congratulations, observed:

'I've come of age, you know. We do, in our family, at thirteen. That's why Great-aunt Catherine wanted me to have a decent party. And it wouldn't have been a decent party without Mr Bookham and Piggie, so I really am glad you turned up.'

'Talking of turning, I think the farmer's wife is waiting for us,' said Bob, who, for some reason not understood by himself, felt irritated by this conversation.

'I think she is,' George agreed. 'I say, I think I'll come back to lunch after all. I suppose you couldn't give me a lift?'

'Hop in,' said Bob, making room.

By using the farmyard gate, the motorists found the turn a simple matter, if rather muddy, and, having gained the end of the Roman road, Roger drove southward until a side-turning, half a mile long, brought the car to the station approach.

It was not very far to the house. Dorothy realized, as soon as she saw it, that she had never expected

to find it; yet here it was. The archery butts had
been removed, but, apart from this, and the severe
purity of the architecture of the house itself, nothing
seemed exceptional. Nevertheless, she and Roger
gazed at the house in silence, and even Bob sat
without a word. George opened the door and got
out.

'Won't you come in?' he enquired. But Dorothy
had packed up some food, and now proposed that
the party should drive on to the common and
picnic there. Bob was in favour of this, and Roger,
who would have liked to accept the invitation to
re-enter Whiteledge, said nothing and so was held
to be in agreement.

He backed the car away from the house, and, as
he did so, an easily-recognized figure passed George
and, descending the steps from the portico, began
to walk towards the gate.

'Oh, do stop!' said Dorothy. 'Look! It's Mrs
Bradley, and I think she's waving to us.' Mrs Bradley
soon came up to them. She was wearing a tweed
costume in which a remarkably lordly purple was
the predominant hue, and had on a woollen jumper
in another shade of purple. A bright yellow hat,
which made her sallow complexion look muddy and
tired, and a pair of wash-leather gloves completed
her attire. Her black eyes were as brilliant as ever,
and she held on the end of a lead a young Alsatian
dog of exuberant disposition and inquisitive habits
with which she seemed unable to cope.

Dorothy lowered the window and wished Mrs
Bradley good morning.

'Oh, it's you,' said Mrs Bradley. 'I thought it might be.'

'What made you think that?'

'When I was your age, dear child, wild horses would not have kept me away from a house into which I had been kidnapped; which I had left in a hasty and surreptitious manner following some (probably fatherly) advice given me by the butler; and to which I had been persuaded, or, shall we say, compelled to return.'

Dorothy, who had seen most of the previous night's proceedings in exactly this light, smiled appreciatively.

'Ah,' said Mrs Bradley, 'but it's serious.'

'I know,' said Dorothy. 'We met George, and brought him back with us, as you saw.'

'I thought you would. I posted him there to meet you and ask (I hope he did it tactfully) for a lift.'

'But he wasn't on any road that we ought to have come by! How could you think we might meet him? And does that mean—?' She paused. It seemed pertinent but slightly impudent to ask whether Mrs Bradley had wanted to see them again.

'Sim,' Mrs Bradley explained, 'had heard you ask for your tickets. I had a word with Sim when he had brought you back to the house. Then I drove you home. I did not imagine that you would repeat your long walk of yesterday to get to the house, and therefore it seemed feasible to suppose that you might come by car. I had gathered enough of Mr Hoskyn's mentality and reactions . . .'

she grinned at the tall young man—'to deduce
that he would not come along main roads if he
could avoid them, and I trusted to luck that our
Roman road might appeal to him, and that neither
you nor he would know that it petered out in a
wood.'

'Well, I'm dashed!' said Roger. 'Oh, by the way,
Mrs Bradley, this is Bob.'

'My brother,' Dorothy explained. 'He's sprained
his ankle.'

'So I heard at dinner last night. Down, Fido!' she
added, addressing, apologetically, the dog.

'Is his name Fido? Isn't he a darling?' said
Dorothy.

'His name is not Fido, and he is not a darling,'
Mrs Bradley responded. 'He is good-looking and
a villain. I hope, however, that he may be useful
to the police. Or, if not to the police, perhaps to
me.'

'George mentioned the police,' said Roger. 'I say,
I do hope there's nothing seriously wrong.'

'We don't know what to think. Mr Lingfield left
Mrs Denbies at about five o'clock last evening,
and since then nothing has been seen or heard of
him. Mary Leith thinks he may have met with an
accident, as his riderless horse galloped back to its
stable at six. I have decided to go out on to the
moor with the dog, and see whether he can pick up
a trail. He is young and undisciplined—he belongs
to Miss Clandon—but he may do something. He
was always petted by Mr Lingfield, and would try
to go everywhere with him.'

'Do let us give you a lift,' said Roger at once. Mrs Bradley accepted the offer. The dog, which apparently had followed the conversation, got into the car as soon as Bob opened the door. Having been prevented from lying down on his feet, it then jumped up beside him, buried its nose in his coat and lay perfectly still.

'Bob's good with dogs,' said Dorothy, turning her head. Roger, who was not good with dogs, accelerated rather viciously. The drive to the burnt-out car took twenty minutes.

'This is where we got lost, I should say,' he observed, as he brought the car to a standstill. 'At least, I felt yesterday that we were on the right track until we reached this car. After that, I didn't quite know. We walked on, and trusted to luck, and certainly were glad to see your house.'

'We were glad to see *you*,' said Mrs Bradley. 'And, speaking for myself, more glad to see you upon your second appearance. The fun of sitting at table long after the meal is over can wear thin.'

'I can imagine it,' said Roger. 'By the way, what made Lady Catherine appeal to the police quite so promptly? I understood from George that Mr Lingfield has a habit of popping off to Central Africa when things don't please him here.'

Mrs Bradley caught his eye in the inside driving mirror, for she was sitting in the back with Bob and the dog.

'What makes you ask that about the police?' she enquired. 'As you've stopped the car, let's get out, and then we can talk.'

'Well,' said Roger, when, except for Bob, they were all standing out on the common, 'on the way home we had a strange experience. The first time we went, I mean. It seemed that the driver had some sort of seizure or hallucination or something, and swore he'd seen a headless corpse on the line. The guard and the fireman got down and searched, using lanterns, and then came along the train to ask for a doctor. There wasn't a doctor on the train, as it happened, so, as I know a fair amount about accidents—I'm a prep. schoolmaster and take some jerks and games—I offered to give any help I could, and went along.

'Well, of course, there wasn't any corpse, and no sign of anything—blood, I mean, or anything like that—so we soothed the driver, and the train went on again, and that was all about it. It was rather a curious experience, all the same.'

'Curious, indeed!' said Mrs Bradley. 'What was the engine driver's name?'

'MacIver.'

'Ah! Of course, that might account for lots of things. May I ask what the time was when this happened?'

'I don't know exactly. Somewhere about a quarter past ten, I should think.'

'Ah, yes. Too bad, of course.'

'The driver wasn't tight, if that's what you mean,' said Roger. 'I said so to Dorothy at the time.'

'Are you a judge of tightness, child?'

'Well, near enough. I mean, I've been tight myself, and I've seen other blokes tight, and I'd take my oath the driver hadn't had a drop. I even went so far as to smell his breath—at his own request, that was—and there's no doubt about it.'

'Interesting,' said Mrs Bradley. 'Let us follow the nose of this hound, who appears to be remarkably restive, and see where his instinct leads us.'

'To the nearest rabbit-hole, I expect,' said Roger grinning. 'I say! This does look a bit of a blasted heath!'

He led Mrs Bradley and Dorothy towards the burnt-out car which they had examined the day before.

The dog, calming down, cocked his tail and hung out his tongue. He sniffed round the car for a bit, found it boring, and set off very soon in pursuit of rabbits.

'Bother the dog,' said Mrs Bradley. 'It looks as though we shall need to do our own exploring. Let's go as far as the church.' But before they moved on Mrs Bradley glanced inside the car. Roger followed her example.

'I've a better idea,' said Roger. At this moment he caught sight of a policeman who was patiently and rather painfully searching among the gorse. 'I'd like to have a word with that bobby. Excuse me a moment, would you?'

He shouted, and the constable looked up, and then came slowly towards him.

'This car,' said Roger. 'What about it?'

The policeman looked at the car, and then at Roger. He looked puzzled and not very pleased.

'I don't know what you mean, sir,' he said.

'Well, only this,' said Roger, beginning to wonder whether he had spoken too soon. 'When I passed this car yesterday I could have sworn it had been burnt out. But this car hasn't been burnt at all. It's been wrecked. Not very badly, either.'

'I'll make a note of what you say, sir,' said the policeman, 'and report it to the superintendent. I don't think there is anything in it. The missing gentleman didn't travel by car, and, if he did, and this was his car, we should have found the body, but we haven't.'

'All right I expect I'm wrong, and this is the same car,' agreed Roger. 'Just thought I ought to mention it, that's all.'

'No harm done, sir,' said the constable, recognizing Mrs Bradley and saluting her. 'Good morning, mam. *You've* no other news, I suppose?'

'Mr Lingfield's riderless horse galloped home. It came back last night, it appears,' said Mrs Bradley.

'We knew about that, mam, thank you.'

'In any case, he was the kind of man who, without a thought, would take himself off, I understand,' Mrs Bradley went on. 'The return of the horse would indicate no sinister circumstance.' The constable agreed, and walked off to continue his search.

Mrs Bradley cackled.

'What were you going to suggest, Mr Hoskyn,' she enquired, 'before the wrecked car distracted your attention?'

'I was going to suggest that we started from where Dorothy and I first caught sight of the three riders.

Then we could try to find out what Lingfield did, and where he went.'

'That seems a reasonable suggestion. Let us by all means adopt it.'

They covered the distance in their own car, and soon reached the spot where Roger and Dorothy had rested. Roger caught Dorothy's eye and smiled, remembering how he had kissed her. Mrs Bradley intercepted the smile, drew her conclusions and nodded benignly at him as though in benison. Roger grinned, and returned to the subject in hand.

'This is the way they went,' he said. 'Not very easy to see hoof-marks, though, on this turf. Look, Dorothy, you go back and sit down again, and yell very loudly as soon as we're out of sight. That might give some idea, don't you think?'

Mrs Bradley agreed. Dorothy returned to her seat on the grassy mound, and almost immediately called out. Then she got up and joined them.

'No use,' said Roger, speaking gloomily. 'Looks as though they rode straight into gorse, and they couldn't have done that, you know. The horses wouldn't have faced those spiny prickles. They must have gone over in that direction, I think. But there's really nothing to show.' He pointed south.

The dog, which at first had found most entrancing entertainment on the heath, but was tired of its own society, now came up to them and, without being asked to do so, went to heel, and followed meekly and soberly for more than a mile and a half.

Suddenly it put its nose to the ground, sniffed,

took a short cast to the right, came back to the trail, looked up and barked short and sharply. Mrs Bradley, who was carrying the lead, said:

'Catch him!'

Roger grabbed the dog, which whined and shivered, and Mrs Bradley affixed the lead to its collar. Suddenly it started off away to the right again, checked, came back, went off, and then, like a bullet, tore towards a copse which was bordered by a light wooden fence.

Here the dog scrabbled, whined and tugged. At a nod from Mrs Bradley, Roger, who felt certain that the copse held the man they were looking for, released the dog from the lead. The dog, with a beautiful bounding leap, surmounted the fence and disappeared among the undergrowth. Roger vaulted the fence and, to his great surprise, Dorothy also vaulted it (far more neatly and precisely) and immediately joined him. They were followed by Mrs Bradley, who climbed over in a manner suited (she imagined) to her years, and the three hastened in Indian file after the dog.

Roger suddenly halted, and then turned round, holding out an arm as a policeman will hold up traffic.

'Stay where you are!' he said. 'I think there's—I think there's something rather rummy here.'

Dorothy obediently held back: not so much because an order had been issued as because the voice in which it was given seemed to hint at facts which she felt instinctively it would be kinder to Roger that she should not face. Mrs Bradley, it seemed, was of the same opinion, for she clutched the girl with a grip there was no gainsaying, and observed:

'Go back, child, to the other side of the fence, and keep an eye lifting for gamekeepers. Don't come back unless we call.'

Dorothy retired to the fence, climbed it in sober fashion, glanced back, and saw Mrs Bradley and Roger step delicately into the underwood of the coppice which immediately hid them from view.

Suddenly she heard an unpleasant belching noise, and her cavalier, green as the grass, came staggering back, his handkerchief pressed to his mouth.

Conquering a feeling of sympathetic but otherwise unwarrantable nausea, she got down from the fence on his side of it, and ran towards him. Roger, with a deep groan, bent over and was horribly and spectacularly sick.

'Oh, dear!' said Dorothy, recoiling. He half-turned and waved her away, but she advanced resolutely, took his limp arm and dragged him towards the fence. Shaken and almost crying, he climbed over, and dropped full length on his face when he gained ground on the opposite side.

Dorothy sat beside him and stroked his hair, pulling little tufts of it gently between her fingers. This treatment for shock proved effective. He sat up, his face very flushed, took her hand in both his, and said:

'Thanks. Oh, my God! Where's Mrs Bradley? I say, she ought to come out of there! Oh, Lord!'

'What happened? Is it——? Did you find him? Is he——?'

'Yes. I'm sorry to tell you, but I must. It's frightful. It's simply unspeakable. I'm a swine to tell you, but I must! He—his head—he—that chap on the line—'

'Are you quite sure it's him?'

'Why the devil can't you say "he"?'

'I'm sorry. He, then.' But she was far too much worried about Roger's reactions to care anything at all for his manners.

'I'm sorry, too,' he said at once, gripping more tightly her hand. 'You're so nice and sane. And that isn't sane—that in there. And I *don't* know it's Lingfield. It's a big man and he's naked. I suppose it must be Lingfield, but really there's nothing to show. Oh, I *wish* I hadn't seen it. I'll never forget it!'

'The war was much worse,' said Dorothy. 'Put your head in my lap. Don't think about him any more. You needn't if you don't want to.'

Roger tried to pull himself together, but it was easier and pleasanter to hide his face in her skirt and feel her hard knees pressing into his cheek. At last he raised his head.

'I'd better go back,' he said. 'Can't leave her alone to cope. It's true she's a doctor, but, all the same—I suppose I had better go.'

'I'd better come with you,' said Dorothy.

'Please don't! I couldn't bear that!' said Roger at once. He pulled her up but kept firm hold of her hands. 'Please don't come! I'll soon be back. Stay

just where you are! Please promise! I—I couldn't
bear it if you saw him. He—you see—oh, damn
it! He hasn't got a head!'

He let go of Dorothy and thrust the hair from
his forehead. He took away a hand that was wet
with perspiration. He wiped it and then wiped his
brow, put the handkerchief back in his pocket, ran
to the fence and vaulted over it. As he reached the
soft leaf-mould soil on the other side, Mrs Bradley
emerged from the coppice and blew three long
blasts on a whistle. Then she held up her hand
and waylaid him.

'No, child. Stay where you are. The police will
be here in a minute. They are not far away, as we
already know. There is nothing we can do except
wait and show them the place. Let's go back to
the other child, please.'

Not by word, look or inflection did she give the
faintest indication that she was at all perturbed
by the horrid sight they had seen, or that she
remembered anything whatever of Roger's unmanly
conduct. The two of them returned very soberly
to Dorothy's side, and then all three sat down
on Roger's mackintosh to await the arrival of the
police.

'Where's the dog?' asked Roger suddenly. He
whistled. The young dog came crawling out of the
little wood, squeezed through the lower bars of
the fence and crept towards them, his tail between
his legs. Roger took him between his knees. The
puppy whined and shivered, looked up in Roger's
face and absent-mindedly licked him.

'Curiosity killed the cat,' said Mrs Bradley, regarding the shivering animal unconcernedly. 'At what time, I wonder, did your engine-driver see the body on the line?'

Chapter Five

'The bubble's cut, the look's forgot;
The shuttle's flung, the writing's blot;
The thought is past, the dream is gone,
The water glides; man's life is done.'
SIMON WASTELL (or Henry King),
Man's Mortality

'IT'S A good thing you were all three more or less together,' said Bob, when he had heard as much as the other two could tell him. Mrs Bradley had driven off with the police, and the three holiday-makers, at her request, were returning to White-ledge to await her arrival. 'If any one of you had been alone when you found a dead body you might have found yourself in queer street, I believe.'

'I don't see that,' objected Dorothy. 'No one would think that any of us had——' She looked anxiously at Roger.

'It's all right. You can say it,' said Roger, looking sheepish. 'I've got over all that. I know what you mean,' he added, turning to Bob, 'but I also know what Dorothy means. No one in their senses would think that Dorothy or I had cut off a fellow's head, and I can't imagine Mrs Bradley——'

'Can't you? Oh, I can,' said Bob. 'If the spirit moved her, that is. I wonder how it did happen, though? How far is the railway from here?'

'Ah, that's the point,' said Roger. 'You've put your finger on the spot. That chap's head was most probably cut off by a train. But when we admit that, we come up against a snag immediately. A very nasty one, too. I *know* that engine-driver fellow wasn't tight. Obviously he saw what he said he saw, and that was a body on the line. But, according to Mrs Bradley—and she's a doctor, she ought to know—the fellow—the corpse, you know—couldn't have been dead as soon as that. It's the devil of a complication.'

'The real question is,' said Dorothy, 'how did the body get from the railway to that copse? It's rather a long way away.'

'Somebody moved it,' said Roger. 'What's more, they moved it in that wrecked car. I wonder what they did with the burnt-out car? We ought to look for that. Meanwhile, I suppose we must make for Whiteledge, if that's where the inquisition will be held.'

'The police were nice,' said Dorothy. 'I don't think they'll keep us very long. We shan't go into the house, I suppose, until Mrs Bradley comes back? We can wait in the drive in the car.'

'I don't see why we shouldn't go in,' said Roger.

'It isn't as if we don't know the Whiteledge people. And it looks as though we're going to know them even better in the near future. After all, the chances are that one of them murdered the bloke.'

'But you can't say that! We don't know who the dead man is,' said Bob. 'You're simply taking it for granted it's this chap Lingfield, but, after all, it may not be. You'd have to find the head to be able to prove who it is.'

'It *must* be Lingfield,' said Roger. 'And, what's more, Mrs Bradley knows it. That dog knew it, too. Took us straight to him, you know, as soon as he got on the trail.'

'There might be another explanation of that,' said Dorothy.

They reached Whiteledge an hour before Mrs Bradley arrived in the police car with an inspector and a sergeant of the County Constabulary. She seemed surprised to find them outside the gates of the house, and accepted with an eldritch but non-committal screech of laughter Dorothy's reason for their having remained in the drive.

She left the police conferring in their car, took Dorothy and Roger up to the door with her, and knocked. The impeccable Bugle opened to them, and Mrs Bradley, hustling them past him in a way which seemed crudely unceremonious, thrust her two young people in at the first round-headed doorway.

There was nobody in the room but the spinsterish young-old woman who had been seated on Dorothy's left at the dinner party.

'Look after these children, please, Mary, my dear,' said Mrs Bradley, 'and tell me where I can find your mother.'

Before Mary Leith could reply there came an official-sounding knock at the front door, and Bugle, after a suitable interval, appeared in the doorway of the room.

'The police, Miss Mary, Mrs Bradley. Inspector Oats, accompanied,' he announced.

At this, Mary Leith looked anxiously at Mrs Bradley.

'Are they—have you . . .?' she enquired.

'They are, and we have,' Mrs Bradley replied composedly. 'So you see how necessary it is for you to find your mother at once.'

'Indeed, yes,' said the pale woman. She left them. Bugle hovered in the doorway.

'Show the inspector in here, Bugle,' said Mrs Bradley, 'and bring along some sandwiches and drinks. We are going to be here a long time.'

'Very good, madam.'

The inspector and the sergeant entered, and everybody sat down until Lady Catherine and her daughter came in, followed by Captain Ranmore. The inspector, the sergeant and Roger got up at Lady Catherine's entrance, and then there followed a slight reshuffle of seats which brought Roger and Dorothy together on a settee. They sat and surreptitiously held hands, both needing support and sympathy. Lady Catherine glanced at them once, and then addressed the police.

'So you found him!' she said. 'I did not think you would. Poor Humphrey!—I mean, poor Harry! His was a tragic life and a tragic death. How did he do it?—A shot—"So quick, so clean an ending"—and I doubt it. It does not seem like him. Besides, shooting was too good for him, anyway. Now do tell me all about it!' She settled herself cosily to await the revelations.

At this the inspector coughed.

'I think, Lady Catherine,' he said, 'the inquiry had better be conducted in an official manner, if you take me. An unfortunate gentleman's body was discovered in circumstances which lead us to believe we have a very serious affair on our hands, although, of course, the inquest will have to come before we can move very far, because of the difficulty of identification. So, if you wouldn't mind answering a few questions, that is all we shall need for today.'

The sergeant took out a notebook. Lady Catherine looked haughty but was really—she confessed afterwards—mad with curiosity, and only too determined to tell every detail she knew. 'It's not as though I *liked* poor Harry,' she said later.

'Very well, inspector,' she observed. The inspector thereupon gave another slight cough and said:

'I understand a gentleman is missing from this house.'

'Yes. The owner, Mr Lingfield, did not return to dinner last evening, Inspector, and we have heard no more of him. As you know, we rang up the police this morning, as soon as I realized that Mr

Lingfield was still missing. I was not, myself, in favour of this course, as, of course, I dislike the uniforms, although I see you don't wear yours, but, as I was over-ruled, we called you in.'

'Yes, Lady Catherine. You did. Did you formulate any opinion as to where the missing gentleman might have got to?'

'No. He was temperamental, and was apt to be inconsiderate. I did not trouble myself to wonder where he was, but I *did* feel a certain amount of exasperation at having my table put out because he had chosen to pick a quar——'

'Please, Lady Catherine,' said the inspector, raising a formidably large hand with a curiously pale palm. 'I don't want you to volunteer any information at the moment unless I specifically ask for it.'

'Oh?' said Lady Catherine, taken aback. 'Very well.' She waited for the next question.

'If the gentleman was odd in his habits, as you suggest, Lady Catherine——'

'But I *don't!*' said Lady Catherine vigorously. 'You are not to put that in your notes!' she observed, turning towards the sergeant. 'I said nothing of the kind! Odd in his habits indeed! Anyone would suppose poor Harry was a Mormon elder! . . . Although I'm not sure that that is totally unreasonable, either,' she suddenly added.

'You said Mr Lingfield was eccentric and temperamental, Lady Catherine,' pursued the inspector.

'Yes, I did. I agree. That *is* what I said. I did *not* say that he was odd in his habits. The idea! I certainly should not enter the house (of my own volition) of anyone who was odd in his habits!'

She stared severely at the sergeant, who had discovered a microscopic portion of yolk of egg on his tunic and was methodically removing it with the nail of his right forefinger. He blushed, and applied himself to his notebook.

'No, Lady Catherine?' said the inspector in a tone which he meant to be encouraging. 'Certainly not. But, if you don't mind telling me——'

'I will tell you everything,' said Lady Catherine, in tragic and dramatic tones. The inspector coughed again, and caught Mrs Bradley's eye.

'Very good, Lady Catherine,' he agreed. 'Now, first, was there any reason for you to suspect that anybody wished Mr Lingfield any harm?'

'Good gracious! Of course!' said Lady Catherine. 'But you mustn't take any notice of what I say.'

The inspector ignored this.

'Now, Lady Catherine,' he said, 'at what time did Mr Lingfield leave this house the last time he went out of it?'

'I don't know exactly. It would have been at half-past three, no doubt. I was told he would go out then, so I suppose he did.'

'Then you cannot be sure he went out at half-past three?'

'Well, no, but Mrs Denbies and my grand-nephew—George, you know—went out with him. They all went riding on the Common. Ridiculous, actually. Quite the wrong time of the day. The morning would have been far better.'

'Mrs Claudia Denbies and Master George Merrow,' said the inspector, dictating these names to the sergeant.

'Very good, sir,' said the sergeant, writing them down.

'Very good, Lady Catherine,' said the inspector. He turned towards Roger, who bestowed on him no very friendly gaze.

'You are taking it for granted, Inspector,' said Mrs Bradley, 'that the corpse is that of Mr Lingfield?'

'Well, no, madam, certainly not. The inquest will settle all that, or so we hope. But the fact remains that a gentleman is missing from this house, and a male corpse has been discovered in the vicinity.'

'Of course, there's such a thing as coincidence,' said Roger. The inspector turned on him immediately.

'How came you, sir,' he asked, 'to come upon the corpse in the coppice?'

'I was looking for it,' said Roger. 'That is to say, I was looking for Mr Lingfield. That is to say, I was helping to look for him, you know.'

'You knew Mr Lingfield, then?'

'No, but the dog did. At least, we hoped it did.'

'The dog, sir?'

'We were tracking Mr Lingfield with the help of an Alsatian puppy.'

'Why on the Common, sir? I mean, Lady Catherine says he went riding on the Common, but how did *you* know that?'

'First, Inspector, I dined yesterday at this house.

Secondly, it was where we had seen him last. At least, we look it to be Mr Lingfield, but, of course, it may not have been. I couldn't be sure, as I've never met him in my life.'

'You had better explain all that, sir. You understand that the sergeant is taking down all that you say?'

'Oh, Lord, yes, of course. I only hope he can spell.'

'And that you may be required to sign your statement?'

'Well, dash it, I've no reason to tell lies!'

'Nothing would be gained by it, sir, if you had. We know what we know. I am here to make enquiries as part of my duty. Now, sir, perhaps I had better have your statement apart from those of the other witnesses to the finding of the body.'

'Oh, yes, yes, yes. Carry on,' said Roger, slightly panic-stricken because the inspector refused to lose his temper.

'Very well, sir.' The inspector looked at Dorothy and then at Lady Catherine.

'Ring the bell, Mary,' said Lady Catherine, 'and when Bugle comes tell him to let the police have the small ante-room. Although I shan't allow them to have the girl in there without a chaperone, mind. It wouldn't be suitable. What do *you* say, Mrs Bradley?'

'I think it would be quite suitable, in the circumstances,' Mrs Bradley replied, 'but I will go with the child when her turn comes, if you prefer it.'

'I don't see why we can't both be together,' said Roger.

'I prefer to obtain your two stories quite separately, sir,' said the inspector.

'We're not in collusion, dash it!'

'No, sir, of course not. And, if you will accept my advice, that is not the word I should use if I were you. But the young lady might find it embarrassing, did she not quite agree with your statements, to contradict what you said, or even give a different account of the matter, in front of you.'

'Of course I shouldn't,' said Dorothy. 'I shouldn't find it at all embarrassing to contradict him. And, after all, I know what *he* saw, and I know what *I* saw. It was exactly the same thing, and we *couldn't* give different accounts.'

'Nevertheless, miss,' said the inspector, 'I think you will find it more agreeable to bear with my ways just for once.'

Bugle appeared, and took Roger, the inspector and the sergeant to the small ante-room. It contained exactly three chairs. The inspector now looked at Roger rather as though he were an overdone steak when the inspector had particularly requested that his steak should be underdone, and fired away with his questions.

'Where were you, sir, when you saw, as you allege, Mr Lingfield riding by across the common?'

'I don't *allege!* I don't know who it was I saw. It happened that I was out for a walk with Miss Woodcote, and we saw three people on horseback. Two of them, as I now know, happen to be staying at this house, and the third I have not seen since; therefore I conclude that the third may have been Mr Lingfield, as he is missing from the house party, and as he is said to have been riding on the Common on the day in question and with the two people I mentioned.'

'I see, sir. Got that down, sergeant?'

The sergeant, unemotionally, and with word for word correctness, read out what Roger had said.

'Now, as to your little jaunt, sir. May I ask if you were expecting to come to this house to spend the evening?'

'No, of course I wasn't! We got lost, and we'd walked a long way, and I came to the house to ask to be directed to the railway station. That's all there was to it. But Lady Catherine had us stay to dinner because she didn't want to sit down thirteen, although, as a matter of fact——'

'And it was after you were received at the house, then, sir, that you knew that Mr Lingfield was missing.'

'Of course it was!'

'Very good, sir. Now if you wouldn't mind just giving me a simple account of all that occurred . . . .'

Roger gave a grudging but unexaggerated account of all that had occurred, including the remarkable statement made by the driver of the train, and then, in response to another question, detailed how he and Dorothy and Bob had met Mrs Bradley that morning.

'But what made you think of returning to this house this morning, sir, in the first place?' enquired the inspector.

'Oh, I don't know. The whole episode was rather peculiar, and——'

'The episode was peculiar?' said the inspector. 'What do you mean by that, sir?'

'Oh, I don't know. The whole thing seemed a bit odd.'

'You mean the business of the corpse on the line, sir?'

'That, and all the rest of it. Our being rushed in to make up the dinner numbers, particularly, and then being brought back after we'd set out for home.'

'Yes, I see, sir. Can I take it that you had no previous knowledge of any of the people living in this house?'

'Well, it depends on what you mean by previous knowledge. I'd never *met* any of them before, but at least four of them were known to me by repute.'

'And those, sir?'

'Well, Mrs Bradley, of course, Mrs Denbies the violinist, John Hackhurst the poet, and this chap who's missing, Lingfield.'

'I understand, sir. But, apart from their reputations, you knew nothing about them?'

'Nothing at all.'

'That seems clear enough, sir. Now I'd better have your name and address, and then I can interview the young lady.'

Dorothy's version of their arrival at Whiteledge and the reason for it corresponded with what Roger had said, and the next witness to the finding of the body was Mrs Bradley herself.

It was the dog, it appeared, which fascinated the inspector.

'Just what led you to take him, mam?' he enquired.

'Oh, I don't know. We both needed exercise,' Mrs Bradley replied. The sergeant solemnly wrote this statement down.

'I see, mam,' said the inspector. 'But you were not surprised when the dog located the body?'

'I was neither surprised nor the reverse, Inspector. It was one of the things that happen.'

'Did you—were you well acquainted with the missing gentleman?'

'No, I was not. I am almost newly arrived at this house.'

'Is it your opinion that the body is that of Mr Lingfield, mam?'

'My acquaintance with Mr Lingfield, as I have stated, is slight, Inspector. In any case I should be obliged to deny a knowledge of so much or so little of him as I saw of the corpse this morning.'

The inspector coughed.

'Yes, of course, mam. (Don't put that question and answer down, Sergeant.) I should have said, mam——'

'Of course you should, Inspector. And I should have replied that I have no opinion to offer.'

'Had Mr Lingfield enemies, mam?'

'I'm afraid I can't tell you. I hope not. Lady Catherine might know. He was, after all, her nephew.'

'Then I will enquire of Lady Catherine, mam. I suppose'——he cocked a wary eye at the doorway—'I suppose Lady Catherine is a reliable witness, mam? Her response at present seems—well, mam, flippant is the word that presents itself.'

'Do you think so?' asked Mrs Bradley. 'I am only fairly well acquainted with Lady Catherine, Inspector. I am, as you know, a mental specialist by profession, and I was called here on Wednesday to give a professional opinion upon the condition of someone who seemed to need the services of a psychiatrist.'

'May I ask, mam——?'

'No, you may not!' said Mrs Bradley vigorously. 'When you have identified the corpse you may ask me that question if it still seems to be part of your enquiry, and I shall feel compelled to answer it. But, until then, professional etiquette suggests to me that I do not disclose to you the name of my patient. It cannot possibly help you at present,' she added, much more kindly.

'Perhaps I'm the best judge of that, mam,' suggested the inspector with kindling eye.

Mrs Bradley cackled.

'I wonder whether you are a judge of cars?' she retorted. 'It took young Mr Hoskyn to point out that the abandoned car on the common was not the car which has been there for some months, but quite another car which certainly was not there yesterday afternoon.'

'We have examined the car in question, mam,' said the inspector amiably, 'and there is nothing whatever to suggest that it ever carried a headless corpse, I assure you.'

Chapter Six

*'Once in my ear did dangling hang
A little turtle-dove.
Once, in a word, I was a fool—
And then I was in love.'*

ANONYMOUS (16th century)

'THAT'S THE point,' said Lady Catherine, upon being appealed to on the question of whether Lingfield were married. 'He was. Far too much married, poor man. Bigamy. Didn't you hear? The scandal of two continents; three, if you count India as Asia.'

'I remember his wife,' said Mrs Bradley. The inspector looked bewildered.

'Bigamy, Lady Catherine?' he said. 'I never heard of a Mr Lingfield——'

'Oh, it didn't come into court, of *course!*' said Lady Catherine, amused. 'But there was no doubt whatever about it. One in Buenos Aires and another in Paris. Before the war, naturally. We were less democratic then, and bigamy was not allowed in the Foreign Office.'

'But was Mr Lingfield a member of the Foreign Office?' asked the inspector, now thoroughly puzzled.

'Of course he wasn't. But he was a bigamist, say what you like. Apart from poor Claudia, I mean!'

If the inspector did say what he liked, it was under his breath, for it was Mrs Bradley who spoke next.

'I think the inspector's point is that he must try to find someone to identify the body,' she said. The inspector looked at her gratefully.

'Well, that shouldn't be difficult,' said Lady Catherine. 'Anybody here could do it.'

It was explained to her, carefully and gently, why this statement was a little too wide to be acceptable.

'Oh, well, that makes a difference,' she remarked; and then, as though the full purport of the information had suddenly dawned on her, she added, 'Good gracious! But how perfectly dreadful! Where did he leave his clothes?'

'It's his head we are as much concerned about,' said Mrs Bradley kindly.

'Oh, yes, of course,' said Lady Catherine. 'But what can have happened to the poor man?'

'Accident, suicide or murder,' replied the inspector, who was becoming fatigued.

'Accident? On the railway, I suppose?'

'Yes, Lady Catherine, very likely.'

'Then how did he get to the Common?'

'Presumably somebody carried him there.'

'But why?'

'That is just one of those things I have to find out, Lady Catherine.'

'How dreadful! Because, of course, nobody would have done that unless they were concerned in the accident, would they?'

'That is an inference, Lady Catherine, by which I hope to be guided.'

'Quite right. One should always be guided by inferences. I remember quite well inferring, when I heard of his second marriage, that it must be bigamous, you know, because I knew for a fact that at the time poor Lilian was living in Kent with her old nurse. And I did know, too, that there hadn't been any divorce.'

'Ah, yes,' said the inspector, brought back to the point upon which he had previously touched. 'His wife. I suppose you don't know where we can find her? Would she still be in Kent, do you suppose?'

'I see no reason why she should not be, and I see no reason why she should be. I will give you the last address I have.'

She went out of the room and returned in about five minutes (during which the inspector stared out of the window and the sergeant, rather more woodenly, at the mantel piece and its carvings) carrying a large piece of writing paper.

'Ah, thank you very much, Lady Catherine. That should be of material help,' said the inspector. 'Well, I don't think we need trouble you further, unless you can tell me whether Mr Lingfield had enemies.'

'Who hasn't?' replied Lady Catherine. 'But our enemies, for the most part, lack the courage of their convictions. Now, if I did not lack the courage of mine, Inspector——'

'Yes, no doubt,' said the inspector hastily. 'Mr Lingfield, then, had no particular enemies that you could name?'

'I could name dozens,' said Lady Catherine, looking prepared to do so. 'Who could not?'

'Then it comes to the same thing, madam. I will keep you in touch with the march of events, and you shall know what transpires when we get this unfortunate gentleman identified.'

'Very well,' said Lady Catherine, baulked not too tactfully of the monologue she had prepared. 'I suppose we must not take up your time, even with matters which may assist you.'

'Oh, there *is* one more thing,' said the inspector, as though upon inspiration. 'It has come to my knowledge that somebody in this house is under treatment for—for——'

'Amnesia,' said Lady Catherine. 'Yes, quite true. What of it?'

'Amnesia, Lady Catherine? But I understood——'

'Amnesia I said, and amnesia I meant. If you want any more information upon *that* subject, Inspector, you will have to ask Mrs Bradley. She is the visiting specialist. I suppose,' she added, with a shrewdness which her questioner had certainly not expected, 'that you have already asked her and have failed to obtain a satisfactory reply. I don't call that a nice way to go on. I thought you were more intelligent than that.'

So saying, she left him, taking Mrs Bradley with her. The inspector, looking worried and slightly dazed, gazed at the doorway through which she had passed, and then discovered that the sergeant's eye was on him.

'Peculiar, these old families, sir,' said the sergeant sympathetically.

'I don't know about that,' said the inspector. 'Got their heads screwed on the right way. Or if it's the wrong way, they're still screwed on pretty tight. Well, we'll have to see the rest of them, I suppose, because if that dead man's not Harry Lingfield, then I'm a Dutchman, which, incidentally, I partly am, on my mother's side. Touch the bell, my lad, and ask for Mrs Denbies.'

Claudia Denbies kept the inspector waiting. Then she appeared dressed in a Chinese robe of great beauty. Its patterns had a background of jade green against which her Titian hair looked, as she intended, splendid, untidy and bizarre. She was wearing no make-up except some orange lipstick, and her extremely white face looked somewhat heavy and old in the hard, clear light of the morning.

She took an armchair and crossed her feet, which were bare except for their jade-green sandals. She gave the impression of an exotic and heavily-flowering plant, healthy enough to have made strong growth in an alien soil, but, nevertheless, out of place, and living in a climate really much too cold for it.

The inspector and the sergeant, a couple of bare and thorny shrubs of native stock, gazed rather helplessly at Claudia; then the inspector, scraping his chair and giving the usual slight cough which introduced such of his remarks as he suspected might be going to give offence, demanded, in tones louder than he intended:

'And to what do you attribute the absence of this missing gentleman, madam?'

'To his quarrel with me, of course,' replied the lady, studying the tips of her fingers and then flexing and unflexing her hands. 'You don't mind if I fidget, do you? I am giving a recital tomorrow, and I have to keep my hands ready.'

The sergeant, who had often been instructed by his superior that, if you want to know when people are giving themselves away, lying, or withholding information, you watch their hands rather than their faces, snorted with sudden amusement at seeing this theory overthrown. The inspector took no notice of him.

'So you admit that you quarrelled with Mr Lingfield, madam?'

'Of course. We were always quarrelling.'

'But——'

'And he always left me. He would shut himself away and do his sculpture. He *could* have been a quite respectable pianist, but that would have made things rather difficult.' She raised her eyes candidly and met those of the inspector. 'I thought everyone knew all that,' she added. 'Poor Harry is temperamental. I disagreed with Lady Catherine that there was any need to put the police on his track. He'll return in due course. He always does.'

'He *has* returned, madam,' said the inspector, with dramatic emphasis. 'At least, we should be obliged if it could be known that it is he.'

'Known?' Her eyes widened, but it was, the inspector thought, a histrionic and not an involuntary reaction. 'What do you mean—known? He isn't—dead?'

'The gentleman we have been shown is most certainly dead, madam. We should be very glad to be told whether it is Mr Lingfield or not.'

'Well, I could tell you, of course.' She looked down at her hands again. 'Poor Harry! I always told him that one day he would be thrown and break his neck. I knew he would. Riding off like that in such a passion, and threatening my life, as usual.'

'Break his neck?' said the inspector, interested.

'Oh, he was no horseman,' said Claudia Denbies tensely. 'I always told him so. In fact, that was the cause of our last quarrel. Where is he now? In this house?' She sounded nervous, the inspector noticed.

'No, madam. In the mortuary at Guildford. He—the fact is, madam——' He met her eyes again as she looked up.

'Disfigured?' She spoke as offhandedly as before, but it was still with the effect of unbearable nervous tension. 'Pity. He was a handsome brute, in his way.'

'Worse than that. He—you must take a bit of a hold on yourself, madam—he is without his head. We think a train——'

Claudia Denbies threw back her own head and laughed herself into hysteria. Much taken aback at this reaction to what he himself had considered a tactful breaking of the news, the inspector rushed to the bell, rang it violently, opened the door and shouted for assistance.

It was Mrs Bradley who appeared, closely followed by Bugle, Lady Catherine, Roger and the pallid Mary Leith.

'I'm sorry. I'm afraid I was precipitate, madam,' said the inspector, addressing Mrs Bradley. She took no notice of him, but went over to the patient and addressed her sternly and in a peremptory tone.

'Be quiet, Mrs Denbies. Stop your nonsense. Tell the inspector all he wants to know.'

To the astonishment of everybody present, Claudia Denbies lifted her head, gazed at the inspector as though she were hoping that he would make the next move, and then said:

'Yes, of course.'

'Well, madam,' said the inspector, embracing this unexpectedly lucid interval with self-congratulatory warmth, 'I may want your story later—I can't tell as to that—but at present it's only this: we cannot have the least idea whether we are still looking for Mr Lingfield until we get this body cleared away. If we could get it identified, beyond question, as *not* being Mr Lingfield, we should know far better where we were. And if it *is* Mr Lingfield——'

'Then that would be just too bad for me!' said Claudia, with a flippancy which was even more upsetting to the inspector than her hysteria had been. He looked beseechingly again at Mrs Bradley, and Lady Catherine, interpreting his gaze, spoke lucidly and kindly enough, and in a manner which contrasted agreeably with her previous utterances.

'We must get this over. It's very bad,' she said to Mrs Bradley in a whisper which Roger, who was near the door, heard as clearly as though she had spoken it into his ear. 'The question is,' she continued, 'whether it would be better for Claudia to get it over before or after her recital. I am inclined to think——'

'Yes, so am I,' said the inspector suddenly. 'I am inclined to think, with you, Lady Catherine, that the sooner it's over, the better it will be for all of us.'

'But I wasn't going to say that!' exclaimed Lady Catherine, very much annoyed at having words taken out of her mouth. 'I was going to tell you——'

Greatly to Mrs Bradley's admiration, the inspector held up one of his large, pale palms, and, taken aback by this demonstration, Lady Catherine amended her remarks to the meek and feeble formula:

'Do as you like. I wash my hands of it.'

To prove that she meant what she said, she walked out of the room, ushering in front of her Claudia Denbies, who was closely followed by Roger. The inspector went out after them, leaving Dorothy, who had followed the others in response to the shouting of the inspector, unexpectedly in Mrs Bradley's company.

'I suppose,' said Dorothy, gazing, in not too friendly a fashion, at Roger's back, 'I suppose he'll be back at some time?'

'And meanwhile,' said Mrs Bradley, 'our course is clear. Will you assist me? The female child, I find, is apt to be more dependable than the male.'

'I'd love to help,' Dorothy replied. 'What would you like me to do?'

'I'd like you to keep your eyes open whilst you are in this house, and to allow your young man to minister for a time to Mrs Denbies. What about it?'

'He isn't my young man,' said Dorothy, detaching from these suggestions the one which seemed to her important.

'I am glad to hear it,' Mrs Bradley replied, 'although I think it more than possible that you will change your mind about that. Now, first, about keeping your eyes open. I want you to observe, particularly, the dog.'

'The dog? But——'

'I know. The dog found the body, and, one would suppose, can now pass out of the picture. But there are two ways of looking at the dog and its exemplary behaviour.'

'How do you mean?'

'Well, child, the dog certainly found the body——'

'Yes?'

'And that indicates that the body may be that of Mr Lingfield. On the other hand, we must not lose sight of the equally important argument that it may be the body of a stranger.'

'Yes, I know. I thought of that myself.'

'You thought of what, child?'

'Why, that the dog may have followed the scent of the person who carried the body to the bushes, and not Mr Lingfield's scent. It's more likely, really, isn't it? I mean, the fact that the body was being carried——'

Mrs Bradley gazed at her admiringly.

'You're an intelligent child,' she said. 'So intelligent that I want to give you a hint. If what is indicated is true, and Mr Lingfield is dead, the murderer (for *somebody*, as you rightly observe, must have carried the body to that copse) may be living in this house.'

'You don't think Mrs Denbies did it, do you? I could never believe it.'

'Never mind what I think, There is one thing I should rather like to know, but perhaps it will come out as time goes on. But whatever I think, there can be no doubt that the sooner this business is cleared up the better it will be for everybody, particularly for Mrs Denbies. An interpretive artist is quite the worst subject for all this kind of muddle.'

'I can't quite see,' said Dorothy, 'why anybody took the trouble and ran the risk of moving the body from the railway line when the train had cut off the head, Surely it would have been very much better to leave the man there to make it look like suicide? And why have taken the clothes?'

'The idea seems to have been to remove all marks of identity, child. And yet——'

'Everyone here would guess it might be Mr Lingfield,' Dorothy put in.

'One might think so,' said Mrs Bradley. She spoke absently. Dorothy glanced at her. Mrs Bradley's black eyes were gazing at the doorway, as though she were expecting the murderer to walk in. But the only person to enter was the correct and fatherly Bugle.

'Is it your wish, madam,' he said, addressing Mrs Bradley, 'to accompany the party to the mortuary?'

'No, no,' Mrs Bradley replied. 'Mrs Denbies will manage very well. Mr Hoskyn'—she glanced at Dorothy—'will support her. I wonder how long they will be?'

'About a couple of hours, madam, the inspector informed me when I asked him. They should be back in time for tea.'

'And that reminds me,' said Mrs Bradley suddenly, 'that you and I, child, have not lunched. And that your unfortunate and patient brother is still outside in your car. Let us all three drive into Dorking, shall we, taking George if he is still in the house, and lunch together. I took the precaution to telephone for a table.'

'That would be nice,' said Dorothy, who was by now extremely hungry. At this moment George came in.

'I say, Great-Aunt Bradley!' he exclaimed. 'Immense excitement! Mr Lingfield has been discovered in a quarry, and someone has cut off both his feet!'

'You are misinformed, George,' said Mrs Bradley. 'A person unknown (so far) has been found in Baker's Spinney, and something—we suspect the down train—has cut off his head.'

'Oh,' said George, dashed, 'that's nothing. It happened to a chap's sister's fiancé at school, It could happen to you or to me. But, feet— that's rather different. I rather wish it were feet.'

'It is easier to identify a person without feet than without a head, my dear George,' said Mrs Bradley. George nodded, and looked solemn. After a considerable pause, he observed:

'Of course, *I* could identify Mr Lingfield, head or no head. Very easily, too, I should rather imagine.'

'You could?' said Mrs Bradley.

'Oh, yes. But it doesn't make any difference. I'd never be allowed to go within a mile of a mortuary. No such luck,' George responded.

'But how do you mean—you could identify him—head or no head?' Mrs Bradley demanded.

'Bathing, you know,' said George. 'He had an old crocodile bite.'

'Where?' Mrs Bradley demanded. George grinned and then blushed.

'Do you want me to draw the marks?' he asked. 'They were here.' He indicated on his body the position of the bites. 'They were shaped like this, you know.'

He helped himself to a large sheet of writing paper out of the drawer of a desk, took a pencil from his pocket, gazed in abstraction for a moment, and then, with a wide sweep, indicated the outline of a buttock and on it made two marks the shape of what, on a pair of trousers, would be called hedge-tears.

'The scale of the bim—or semi-bim,' said George, 'is about one to three, and Mr Lingfield was fairly fat. The scale of the crocodile bites is life-size. That is why they look rather large. So you can multiply the bim by three or divide the size of each bite by three—one or the other—and you get the right proportion. Do you see what I mean, Great-Aunt Bradley?'

Mrs Bradley said that she did. She looked appreciatively at the drawing, which had the merits of artistry and scientific accuracy combined, folded it very carefully so that the creases in the paper did not come across the tooth-marks, put it into her capacious pocket and said to George:

'You shall see the body at the mortuary. What you have told me is most valuable.'

George looked taken aback by this unexpected promise.

'I'm—I—well, thank you very much,' he stammered. 'But, perhaps—I mean——'

'But after all, it won't really be necessary,' Mrs Bradley interpolated, bestowing on him her unnerving grin. 'Mrs Denbies has gone.' George looked relieved at this statement.

'After all, I don't suppose my evidence would be accepted,' he observed. 'I'm of age for this family, but I suppose, by law, I'm still a minor. I'm glad you like the drawing.'

'I certainly do,' said Mrs Bradley. With less satisfaction she looked at the sheet which Lady Catherine had handed to the inspector. It was inscribed only with the words: *Tomorrow's Fool.*

Whilst Mrs Bradley was taking the other young people to lunch, Roger, who had fallen suddenly, violently, passionately, abruptly (and he supposed eternally) in love with Mrs Denbies, escorted her to the mortuary.

'I say,' he said shyly, when he was seated beside her in the police car which was driving them to Guildford, 'it was a great treat to me yesterday to hear you play. Not that I know a great deal about music, I'm afraid——'

'You are a poet,' said Claudia Denbies. 'Therefore you must know, in one sense, a very great deal about music.'

'Oh. I say! I didn't know you knew——'

'Mrs Bradley has a copy of your volume of poems called *Marigoldana*. Who was she? Do tell me about her.'

'About——'

'Marigold, of course. Aren't all the sonnets to her?'

'Oh, well, she's pretty mythical, of course, actually. I mean, I never thought about her objectively until—well, as a matter of fact, until today.'

'Really?'

'May I,' said Roger desperately, 'may I, if ever I get a second impression printed, dedicate it to you?'

She laid a hand on his knee.

'That's really lovely of you, Roger. I may call you Roger, mayn't I?—I should be most honoured. But what will the original Marigold say?'

'There isn't, honestly, any original Marigold. I mean, there was, of course, but only—I swear it—in my imagination.' He crushed down an obtrusive recollection that on the previous day he had been tempted to call Dorothy Woodcote Marigold.

'You're wonderfully gifted!' breathed Claudia.

'I say,' said Roger, completely overcome by this tribute, although it was, in crystallized form, his own opinion of himself, 'I say, you shouldn't say that! I mean, anything decent in those sonnets was simply, don't you see, anticipatory, as it were. I *knew* you'd come along some day, and—and—well, here you are!'

'And old enough to be your mother,' said Claudia Denbies, nipping in the bud this delicate flowering of compliments.

'Oh, don't talk rot!' said Roger, in an anxious shout. 'You can't be a day more than——'

'Shush! You may put your foot in it.'

'No, but dash it, I mean to say, what has actual age to do with it?'

'And a boy's best *friend* is his mother,' continued Claudia Denbies, with deadly emphasis. 'All the same, it's very sweet of you to want to be in love with me. I——'

'I don't *want* to be,' said Roger. 'I am!'

'And what about that very charming and lovely girl you brought along with you last evening and then this morning again?'

Roger had to admit to himself that if Dorothy had not witnessed his unlucky vomiting that morning at sight of the corpse he might have been in love with her still. He crushed down this realization, however, and said:

'She's a child! I couldn't possibly think of her like—*this*! It wouldn't be right. I think of her as a young sister, I swear that's all.'

'Oh, dear!' said Claudia Denbies. 'Very well. But, darling, don't grip my hand like that. I've got to play on Saturday, if this wretched back of mine will let me.'

'Isn't it any better? Good Lord, to think that you should suffer!'

'Neuritis, I think. I'm not getting any younger.' She tried to look pathetic, but Roger was furious.

'Oh, *don't* begin that ghastly tripe over again! Oh, I'm so sorry! Of course, I didn't mean——'

'Neuritis, rheumatism, sciatica, gout—I shall get them all now, I suppose. It is what one has to look forward to, I believe,' said Claudia, thoroughly enjoying this jeremiad.

She lay back, her ripe mouth, even more heavily coloured than usual, smiling tenderly, and her lively amber eyes amused and wistful. Roger tried to kiss her, but was pushed off.

'I don't look forward in the least to old age,' she said, 'and to the gradual surrender of looks and vitality and love. And even if it were suitable to love you (which it isn't), you see, darling Roger, you're not rich. If I could retire, and only play when I want to; if I'd ever saved any money; if I'd been in the kind of job that ended in a nice lump sum and a good fat pension———'

'Oh, damn! Be quiet!' shouted Roger. 'I can't stand any more of it. I love you! I love you, I tell you! Why won't you take my love for granted? What do you want? I'm young, healthy, not bad-looking; in fact———'

The car drew up.

'The mortuary, sir,' said the sergeant.

Chapter Seven

'To William all give audience,
And pay you for his noddle;
For all the Fairies' evidence
Were lost if it were addle.'

RICHARD CORBET,
A Proper New Ballad, etc.

CLAUDIA DENBIES failed to identify the body, except negatively. The police and the mortuary authorities made her task as easy as such a dread ordeal could be by making certain that the fact that the trunk was headless should be kept discreetly veiled.

The proceedings were tactfully conducted, and were soon over. Nevertheless, she fainted at the conclusion of them and was carried into the open air by Roger, who, although he was staggering under her not inconsiderable weight, would not permit a single policeman to touch her.

His feelings, when, having summoned every ounce of muscle and sheer endurance he possessed, he at last got her outside the mortuary and on to the chair which a kindly young constable immediately slid in position beneath her drooping thighs, were kaleidoscopic. So many-coloured were his emotions, and so rapidly did these colours swim before him, that he could only express himself by kneeling on the concrete surface of the yard. Then, taking Claudia's head upon his breast, he adjured her in hoarse parenthesis to speak to him.

She complied with a whispered, 'Darling!' Roger, who had been prepared in any case to die for her, now felt that he could face burning for her sake. He clasped her closely.

His embraces appeared to revive her. She pushed him away and got up.

'But it wasn't—it isn't—Harry,' she reiterated, as, with the solicitous young constable—he who had brought the chair—in close attendance, Roger took her tenderly to the gate and out to the car. 'I'm so certain it wasn't Harry!'

The inspector, who was also there, coughed aggressively.

'I'm glad of that,' said Roger, uttering this dreadful lie without a blush. Why the hell couldn't it have been Harry, he wondered. And yet—if it lessened her distress—no, even if she loved the brute—it was better, far better as it was. His love was as much in the knight-errant stage as present-day custom and usage will permit. ' 'Tis better to have loved and lost,' he murmured to himself in the car going back to Whiteledge, quoting a poet whom normally he despised but now found spuriously comforting, 'than never to have loved at all. But all the same—he occupied his anguished soul with visions of what might have been, and peopled an island with Claudia, himself and a household of Nubian slaves, whilst Claudia, in the crook of his arm, cried dismally on his shoulder.

By the time they reached Whiteledge Mrs Denbies, however, had recovered. She had made up her face in the car towards the end of the journey whilst Roger, to his tender and tremulous delight, carried out her orders to hold her steady. Her artistry and his devotion were so far attended by success that she was able to present to Lady Catherine a bright smile and the presumably joyful tidings of a still unidentified corpse when the chatelaine met them on the doorstep.

'Well, it's rather inconsiderate,' said Lady Catherine, when she heard what Claudia had to tell. 'I do think Harry might have saved us all this trouble. I had the ante-room carpet cleaned for Christmas, and now here we are, still only in March, and policemen's boots all over it! I do think that if people are going away in a huff, and all over nothing at that, they might at least send a message to say that they haven't tumbled down on the railway line and had their heads cut off. It really is most vexing! Who *is* the wretched man, then?'

Mrs Bradley, returning from lunch with Bob, Dorothy and young George Merrow, heard the tidings from a gloomy inspector who, for reasons best known to himself, was still haunting the house.

'And my view is she's lying, mam,' he observed. Mrs Bradley sought Claudia in her room.

Claudia's blinds were drawn and the room was almost in darkness. Mrs Bradley, having knocked, went in upon the knock and found Claudia lying fully dressed, except for her shoes, upon the bed, and discovered, by hearing the sounds, that she was crying.

'So you've got your unpleasant job over, and I hear it was not Mr Lingfield,' said Mrs Bradley, who had the brusque, brisk, female attitude to tears. Claudia sat up, and the bed creaked heavily.

'No,' she replied. 'I'll draw the blinds if you want to talk to me.' She rose and went over to the window. As soon as she could see clearly enough to find a chair, Mrs Bradley sat down.

Claudia went to the door and turned the key.

'I'm not crying about Harry,' she said. She put eau-de-Cologne on a handkerchief and dabbed her forehead with it. 'I'm crying because I'm in love.'

'Good heavens!' said Mrs Bradley with robust, incredulous warmth. 'Not with that tall thin child who came to dinner last night!'

'Not exactly, and yet—I don't know. He's so very young, and so very sweet——'

'Now, look here,' said Mrs Bradley, in admonishing tones but with a cackle, 'you let him alone, do you hear? A love-sick expression will not suit that Hamlet countenance of his, and neither,' she added coarsely, eyeing Claudia long and steadily, 'will the fatuous grin of a corn-fed, high-stepping gelding.

Whatever way you treat him, it will be wrong. You leave the child to his betters, and none of your nonsense! And it won't do your playing any good, let me tell you that.'

'But that's just what it will,' protested Claudia, betraying not the faintest distaste for Mrs Bradley's observations. 'Well, I thought perhaps it would,' she added, suddenly smiling in her turn. 'Lately, I don't know why, I've been going off, I think. I need a stimulant.'

'Try gin,' said Mrs, Bradley, speaking firmly. 'But I did not come to talk about your troubles. They are, after all, your own business. I want to know all about the body.'

'It isn't Harry, and that's as much as I can tell you.'

'I thought you would say that. Go on.'

'What about? It isn't Harry, that's all.'

'How can you be certain, without seeing the face, I wonder?'

'By the—there are certain marks.'

'Well, the body I saw was slightly scarred across the middle of the left buttock. The man was naked when we found him. How long had Mr Lingfield had his scars?'

'They weren't scars, and they were on the chest.'

'How long have you known Mr Lingfield?'

'Since 1917, I think. He was only nineteen.'

'Good gracious!'

'Oh, yes. I knew him before Babbie went into the mental home, and when he was so lonely we saw a good deal of one another. Of course, I was younger then. Then he gave up everything, left Lady Catherine to look after this house and all his things, and went off exploring and big-game hunting for years.'

'Why?'

'Well, to keep his mind off his troubles.'

'And what were his troubles?'

'Well, Babbie, I suppose.'

'Do you really think so?'

'No,' answered Claudia Denbies, looking away. 'No, I don't really think it was that. I don't know what they were. He wanted me to live with him, and I did, and then I had that long concert engagement in America (although, poor boy, he begged me not to leave him), and when I came back in 1935 he had gone. He—I did not see him again until three years later. We quarrelled very soon after that, and off he went. During the war years I saw him now and again—fairly often, as a matter of fact—as often as he could arrange. We spent all his leaves together, but we couldn't really agree. Last year we parted for good—at least, that was mentioned, I remember—and the next thing was that Lady Catherine invited me here and—I found him. He seemed very glad to see me. The rest I suppose you can guess.'

'You agreed to try to agree, but you quarrelled yesterday morning,'

'And tried to make it up in the afternoon. That's why we went out riding. We planned to go out alone, but George wanted to join us——'

'And what was the quarrel about? The police may want to know that.'

'They won't believe me when I tell them. You will, but then—you understand how people's minds work. We quarrelled about Palestrina. That was in the morning.'

'About Palestrina?'

'Yes. It began with Palestrina and then went on to Brahms.'

'You astonish me.'

'Yes, but you believe it. I'm afraid the inspector won't. Still, as the dead man isn't Harry, that doesn't matter at all.'

'I'm not so sure of that,' said Mrs Bradley. 'I wonder whether you would object to outlining the quarrel to me?'

Claudia Denbies sighed.

'It shouldn't have been Palestrina. He is not a subject for quarrel,' she observed. 'But, you see, it began when I happened to remark that Byrd's songs were intended to be accompanied by four viols.'

'I think Mr Eric Blom mentions it in his *Music in England*,' Mrs Bradley remarked. 'What has it to do with——'

'Palestrina? Well, Harry said that Byrd was a mere song-thrush compared with Palestrina, and that if Palestrina had had a language as fit as English for setting to the music of the time, Byrd would never have been heard of. And then he said that the Protestants made Byrd famous. Ridiculous, because, of course, Byrd composed as much for the Roman church as for the reformed church, and, in any case, it is quite absurd to compare Byrd's secular songs with Palestrina's plainsong——'

'I can see how the argument went,' said Mrs Bradley, realizing, from Claudia's flushed cheek and curling mouth that, if she did not interrupt it, it would be re-stated all over again. 'But how did Brahms come into it?'

'Because he was poor, and disliked England and refused a degree at Cambridge.'

'Poor?'

'Not a poor musician. A poor man.'

'But I can't see——'

'Neither could I. All I said was that Brahms performed his own music, and at that—the remark developed quite naturally from what had been said about viols and which had followed on from some talk (quite amicable) about lutes—Harry began to quarrel, saying that I was ignorant and unread, and that musicians had regularly played their own compositions up to and including the seventeenth century—a thing I had never denied—and that to say that a man was a beggar simply because he played what he composed—Oh, it's no use going over it again. He did—does—know quite a bit about music, but there's no doubt he was determined to quarrel. There was no other way of looking at it. Then he went on to polyphonic melody, and he became rather horrid. He was obviously determined to upset me.'

'But why?' Mrs Bradley enquired.

'I don't know. It was all completely unnecessary

and utterly silly, and it made me very unhappy.
After all, I don't care whether Brahms accepted
a musical degree at Cambridge or not, and as for
Palestrina's polyphony——'

'Interesting,' said Mrs Bradley.

'Then he proposed this afternoon ride. I didn't
want to go, but when George came and said that
Harry had told him we were going and that he
should like to go with us—well, one likes to please
George——'

Mrs Bradley agreed.

'But the reconciliation did not take place?' she
asked.

'Of course it didn't. We had to send George
away home. Harry kept referring, in an oblique
sort of way, to the quarrel, so I told George he'd
better ride home or he might be late for the party.
He didn't know we were on the verge of another
quarrel—at least, I don't think he knew—but he
rode away at once. When he'd gone I let Harry have
it.'

'Oh, you did?'

'Oh, yes. It was obvious that Harry had no
intention whatsoever of making it up. He wanted
to feel ill-used, and, when a person wants that, there
is nothing for it but to let him have a thundering
row or else go away and let him think he has
won.'

'And you weren't prepared to let him win?'

'I did go away in the end. He meant I should.
But it wouldn't have been much good to tell the
police I did if the body had happened to be Harry's.

I know they wouldn't believe it. They always think quarrels lead to murder.

'It won't be much good telling it them now,' said Mrs Bradley.

'I'm afraid we shall have to make up our minds to that, unless somebody saw him alive after you had returned to the house.'

'Well, I don't suppose anybody did,' said Claudia carelessly. 'The moor is lonely. It would be the merest accident if anybody had seen him.'

Mrs Bradley went away thoughtfully, and almost bumped into Roger on the threshold of Claudia's room.

'She will require some notice before you go in,' she said. He looked apprehensive and worried.

'Is she worse?'

'Worse than what?'

'Worse than she was this morning at the mortuary.'

'Why, was she ill at the mortuary?'

'She fainted. Those brutes! I think the police ought to be——'

'Hush! Let me tell you something. She probably fainted from relief. The body, she declares, was not that of Harry Lingfield.'

'You mean——?' He grew pale—a lover's pallor. 'You mean she's still in love with Lingfield?'

Mrs Bradley wagged her head.

'Take courage, child,' she said. But Roger would not be comforted.

'And what do you mean by that?' he demanded angrily.

'That life begins at forty,' said the reptile, grinning into his flushed face and furious eyes. She passed on and descended the stairs. Roger tapped at Claudia's door, and waited. He tapped again. The door did not open, and next moment he had joined Mrs Bradley in the hall.

'She won't let me in,' he said, like a sulky child. 'I had things to say, but she doesn't want to listen to a word. She told me not to be a nuisance!'

'I warned you,' said Mrs Bradley with a cackle. 'She's been lying down. Middle-aged women don't arise from bed looking like Venus Anadyomene, you know. If you wish to see the dawn in your lady's face you must look at young Dorothy Woodcote.

> *Of pansy, pink and primrose leaves,*
> *Most curiously laid on in threaves:*
> *And, all embroidery to supply,*
> *Powdered with flowers of rosemary,'*

she continued, regarding him kindly.

Roger snorted in passionate remonstrance.

'At least,' he said, 'Claudia can't give evidence at that hellish inquest. Will you get her out of it? Surely you could if you tried?'

'But I myself am most anxious to hear what she has to say at the inquest,' protested Mrs Bradley.

Roger bestowed on her a look of loathing. She cackled, prodded him in the ribs, to his great and evident annoyance, and remarked that, in any case, the inquest would have to be postponed at the end of the merely formal proceedings, she suspected.

'To give the police time to frame a case against someone, I suppose,' said Roger unjustifiably.

'It's as well for you that you have an alibi for the time of death,' said Mrs Bradley. Roger flushed with bitter fury at this gibe, and left her. In a minute, however, he was back.

'The only thing is, what *was* the time of death?' he demanded.

'Oh, after midnight,' said Mrs Bradley. Roger's long jaw dropped.

'But—but——' he stammered. Then he pulled himself together. 'All right, don't tell me,' he said with dignity.

'But I *am* telling you,' said Mrs Bradley. 'You are going to mention the engine driver, who saw the headless body well before midnight, aren't you?'

'Yes, of course. He couldn't have seen it if it wasn't there!'

'His name is MacIver, I think,' said Mrs Bradley. 'Have you never heard talk of the gift?'

'Of course, but I don't believe in it.'

'Very likely not, Horatio, but, all the same, the possession of second sight is not a matter of faith but one of fact. Hector MacIver will be called at the inquest. You should make a point of being there.'

'I'm being called in any case,' said Roger. 'Well, I suppose our party might as well start for Bob's place. We'd better get back before dark.'

'Oh, I don't think there's any need to hurry,' said Mrs Bradley. 'Mrs Denbies will probably admit you in a few minutes. I'll go and see how she feels. You had better wait here until I come.'

It was Lady Catherine who next appeared upon the scene.

'Sh!' she said, approaching Roger, her finger to her lips. 'Whoever it is is still practising, I shouldn't let them know that you have seen them.'

'Now, Aunt Catherine,' said Captain Ranmore, entering just behind her in company with Mary Leith, the chauffeur Sim, young George Merrow, Bugle the butler and Eunice Pigdon, 'what about tea? I think everyone would be better for it.'

'It dawns on me,' said Mrs Bradley, returning with a transformed and radiant Claudia, and looking with great commiseration at Roger, 'that that poor child hasn't had his lunch. No wonder he wants to go home!'

'It's getting dark, too,' said Captain Ranmore. 'Do you think you will find your way?' be asked, turning to Roger.

'Oh, I shall go with them,' said Mrs Bradley, at once. 'Bugle, what have you done with Mr Bob?'

'He and his sister are in the small drawing-room, madam,' said Bugle, 'and that is where her ladyship ordered tea.'

'Come on, then,' said Captain Ranmore, leading the way.

'You sent for me, sir,' said Sim.

'Oh, yes, to go into Dorking.' Ranmore left the others and went out with the chauffeur to give him his instructions.

'And that wretched policeman,' said Lady Catherine suddenly. 'Find him, Bugle. I knew I wanted you for something, and as I can't think of anything else, I expect that's what it is. Go and fetch him at once.'

'He is looking at the archery butts, madam.'

'Of course he is. That's how Harry Lingfield was killed, but there's no need for policemen to know that. Send him into the small drawing-room at once.'

Chapter Eight

'The streams still glide and constant are:
Only thy mind
Untrue I find,
Which carelessly
Neglects to be
Like stream or shadow, hand or star.'
WILLIAM CARTWRIGHT, *Falsehood*

'So YOU were not satisfied with Mrs Denbies' identification of our corpse?' said Mrs Bradley, meeting the inspector on the Common two days later.

'Her non-identification, mam, it was,' replied the inspector, straightening up from peering into a gorse-bush. 'We were not at all satisfied, mam. I suppose you knew that Mrs Denbies was out in her little car on the night before you found the body thrown in here?'

He indicated the small copse whose environs he was surveying.

'Oh, you've found that out, have you?' said Mrs

Bradley, regarding him thoughtfully. 'Yes, you were bound to, I suppose.'

'So you knew it, mam?'

'Certainly.'

'You didn't tell us.'

'I assumed that if you had considered it important you would have questioned Mrs Denbies herself.'

'May I ask how you came to be aware, mam, that Mrs Denbies had been out of the house that night?'

'Mrs Denbies told me.'

'How did that come about, mam?'

'She had asked my advice about a private affair of her own, disregarded it, and came to tell me that she proposed to run contrary to it that very night.'

'And was going to be out of the house, mam?'

'And was going to be out of the house.'

'You didn't actually see her go, I take it?'

'No, but I had no doubt that she went. Her bed, you see, was not slept in. Lady Catherine was rather annoyed about that. She called it "goings on," and I dare say she was right.'

'I'd better see Lady Catherine, mam. You ladies,' said the inspector, wagging an admonitory head, 'are not altogether co-operative, mam, if you don't object to my saying so.'

'It depends upon what you mean when you say so,' Mrs Bradley replied with a startling little cackle. 'I should say that over Mrs Denbies you and I have been quite remarkably co-operative. If

you are asking me to tell you about Mrs Denbies'
private affairs, however, I must decline to do so
without her permission.'

'Ethically, mam, your attitude may have much to
recommend it,' said the inspector, motioning to the
sergeant, who had just crawled out from a bush,
to come and join the party, 'but as for socially,
well, there I am inclined to think it subversive
and isolationist.'

Mrs Bradley bowed gravely at this rebuke. The
sergeant scratched a piece of mud off the thigh of
his left trouser, and then looked in an embarrassed
manner at his officer.

'And when is the adjourned inquest?' Mrs Bradley
enquired. The inspector sighed deeply.

'Trouble is, you see, mam,' he observed, 'that
the adjourned inquest is fixed for tomorrow
fortnight, and we don't feel we've got satisfactory
evidence yet of the identity of the corpse. Mrs
Denbies has only confused the issue. We, and,
between ourselves, mam, the coroner, too, all
think the lady is mistaken, and that the corpse
is Mr Lingfield, whatever she may choose to say.
To take the most obvious point of identification,
now. No lady is going to own in court she knew
that a man had scratches on his—um—er, now is
she?'

'I see your point,' Mrs Bradley gravely admitted.
'Can't you find somebody who valeted him? That
should dispose of that point if Mrs Denbies is
inclined to be squeamish. The court would accept
the views of a valet, I presume?'

'But where, mam, can I lay hands on such an individual?'

'I should ask Bugle,' Mrs Bradley replied. 'Meanwhile, how go your researches in other directions?'

'They don't, mam. There is nothing to show how the body came to be placed in this copse. There's not a single footprint that's of any use to us.'

'Curious. One would have thought that, at this time of year, the ground might be soft enough to take impressions. The corpse would have been a heavy one, I imagine?'

'Pretty heavy, yes, mam. About twelve stone ten, with the head and the full suit of clothes. Whoever carried it——'

'Was not a woman,' said Mrs Bradley firmly, 'and that disposes of Mrs Denbies, I think.'

The inspector put on a wooden expression and answered:

'There is that, mam, of course. But you can't rule out an accomplice. A good many people have been in.'

'I wonder where the clothes are?' Mrs Bradley remarked.

'We haven't found them, mam, and that's another mystery.'

'But you've looked all over the moor?'

'Combed it from end to end, mam, right over from the other side of the railway and all along the line and the embankments and cuttings, in the tunnels—everywhere. There's nothing to be found within a radius of ten miles of the house. Of that we're certain. We've had over fifty men on the job from the various police stations in this part of the country. Those clothes are either further off than we've searched, or else (as I'm more inclined to think), they're in somebody's house.'

'I see.'

'But this identification—we'll need to get that done with certainty. Can't have the corpse queried. That wouldn't suit our book at all. Does it strike you as rather peculiar, mam, that Mrs Denbies should be so unwilling to identify the body as that of Mr Lingfield?'

'No, it does not strike me as peculiar in the least, Inspector. As a matter of fact, the alternative theory is that somebody took care that the corpse should have some marks of identification similar to those of Mr Lingfield.'

'What makes you say that, mam? I know you wouldn't lead us up the garden, and you've got the medical knowledge, *and* you found the body. I'd be glad to have your views in full, if I might. I don't want to make a mistake over this, as you can well imagine.'

'Well, Inspector, I cannot help you much, except to tell you that the little boy, George Merrow, has seen scars, similar to those of the corpse, on Mr Lingfield's body, but, it seems, on the other buttock.'

'How and when, mam? This is news to me!'

'It seems that George Merrow occasionally went swimming with Mr Lingfield. He saw the scars then.'

She produced George Merrow's drawing and showed it to the inspector.

'Not much doubt about that, mam. 'We can take it, then, that Mrs Denbies' negative evidence washes out, and that the body is that of Mr Lingfield. I don't think there's any need to take any notice which side of his bottom the boy drew the marks. Of course, in spite of Mrs Denbies, we'd concluded the corpse *was* Mr Lingfield, but it's helpful to have it confirmed. I'm much obliged, mam. Mind you, our Doctor Shoesmith also believed it was Mr Lingfield he examined. Size, height, weight, length of arm—all corresponded to what he knew of Mr Lingfield, although——'

'He had never attended Mr Lingfield professionally, I imagine?'

'That's just what I was going to remark, mam. Dr Shoesmith is our police surgeon, and doctor to a couple of football clubs—more that sort of thing. And as good a vet. as he is a doctor, I believe. He's often told me—joking, mam, of course—that he could have made his fortune if he'd gone in for horse-coping, and—serious, this was—that old Lord Amplewood had once offered him about five times what he makes in his profession if he would act as vet. to his racing stables.'

'And you think that, being such a very fine judge of horseflesh and such an able minister to its ills, he would have——'

'Known that the body was Mr Lingfield's, mam? Well, it seems crude, put like that, but I think perhaps it's true. He didn't know, of course, about the scars.'

'Still, it's not evidence of identification,' said Mrs Bradley, 'and we certainly don't want to bring little George Merrow into a coroner's court.'

'And that's the trouble, mam, to return to what we were saying. But you think the butler could help me?'

'I think he might know of a valet, as I said. The coroner would accept, no doubt, the evidence of a valet?'

'No doubt at all, mam. Come on, sergeant. Let's go. Oh, by the way, mam, the young gentleman, Mr Hoskyn, was right to query the wrecked car. It is not the one that has lain here since the war. Some Good Friday holiday-makers found the pieces of that in the bushes and holes and so forth. We broadcast an appeal as soon as the gentleman queried the car, and weren't long in getting a result. Holiday-makers, nuisances though they can be, aren't a total loss.'

'You seem to have put in an enormous amount of work,' said Mrs Bradley. 'Congratulations.'

'Well, you see, mam, this is the second case of murder I've handled, and I had a bit of luck here and there over the first one—old Thomas Crooks, that was, on the other side of the county—and I got my promotion on the strength of it. So, naturally, I'm out to have a similar go at this one, especially as it's considered a more important case, Mr Lingfield being a noted man and that.'

'Well, you get hold of Bugle,' said Mrs Bradley. 'He's the man to find your valet for you.'

'Many thanks, mam. Well, we'll be off. Could we give you a lift to the house?'

'No, thank you. I am going to London after lunch. I am not staying at Whiteledge now. Well, good luck, Inspector. Don't be too hard on Mrs Denbies. Remember, she gives her recital this afternoon, and I'm afraid she is in a nervous state already.'

'Are you going to attend the recital, mam, may I ask?'

'I am, and I want to enjoy it.'

'Mrs Denbies is neither here nor there, so far as we're concerned, until we get the body identified beyond question. I shan't be worrying her again yet. There's nothing more I can ask her until her story is proved or disproved, and that must be done at the resumed inquest. Some funny things will come out in that, I shouldn't wonder.'

'Have you questioned her, then, about her midnight drive?'

'Oh, yes. She says she was disturbed in mind, and drove out into the night to be alone with her thoughts.'

'And you find that incredible, do you?'

'By no means, mam. I know the feeling well. But it's awkward, from our point of view, that she had the urge on that particular night. There's witnesses, but they don't help her. She stopped for petrol at a garage near Junction Station. Being rather a striking-looking lady, and her picture in the *Radio Times* and what-not, the garage hands remember her clearly. It's not too good on the face of it, mam. It's too near where the engine-driver swears he saw the body on the line.'

'Oh, dear! Yes, that *is* awkward.'

'Taken in conjunction with the fact that the body was brought—presumably by car——'

'To this copse, and therein tossed——'

'And that Mrs Denbies refuses to identify the body as that of Mr Lingfield——'

'But admits she quarrelled with him on the day of his death . . . yes,' said Mrs Bradley, as one who adds up a list of money to be paid to various creditors and finds the amount rather startling. 'Yes, I see your point, of course. She might almost be the victim of a conspiracy, mightn't she? Had you thought of that?'

The inspector glanced at her sharply, but her brilliant black eyes told him nothing, and neither did her beaky little mouth, pursed now in calculation of the odds against Claudia Denbies.

'All it wants,' said the inspector, now laying his cards on the table, 'is for this valet, when I find him, to identify the body as that of Mr Lingfield, in contradiction of Mrs Denbies and in support of what you've just mentioned about the young gentleman. If that happens, mam, I should say we've got the case sewn up in a parcel. Motive—the quarrel, which she owns to; opportunity— that midnight drive she took; means—it all fits in.'

'There were no bloodstains in her car, were there? And do you *really* think a woman of Mrs Denbies'

age and physique could have tossed the corpse into
this spinney? I thought we agreed——'

'She strained her back doing it, mam.'

'You have an answer for everything, Inspector. Do
you also believe she had two cars? Her own—the
one she had when she came to Whiteledge—is still
in the garage there, intact and not bloodstained.
Where did she get the means to transport the corpse
from the railway line to the station? Where did
she garage the wrecked car, if that was the vehicle
used? Further to that particular question, how is Mr
Lingfield believed to have been murdered? There
are no wounds on the body, and you will not get
me to believe that Mrs Denbies tied him up and
deposited him alive on the rails so that the train
could kill him.'

'I've an answer even to that, mam. What would
you say to a revolver wound through the throat? All
these people can shoot. I had that from Bugle, the
butler. No, mam. I tell you it's what the Americans
call an open-and-shut case, I'm afraid. I'm as sorry
about it as you are, speaking in my private capacity,
mam, as a music-lover and an admirer of the sex,
but, take it from me, it's as plain as the nose
on my face that Mrs Denbies is pretty squarely
implicated, and I don't really think she'll wriggle
free. Of course, this is all off the record, but I'm
telling you because you've helped me over my
biggest fence, identification, mam.'

'You really think that a quarrel of that sort—the
kind of quarrel, which, on her own admission and
on the evidence of numbers of other people who

must have known both of them well, she had
had with Mr Lingfield a dozen times before—was
sufficient inducement to Mrs Denbies to murder
Mr Lingfield?'

'Not in itself, perhaps, mam. But I've seen Mr
Lingfield's solicitors, and, without giving away
anything which won't very soon be public property,
I can tell you that he made a new will a fortnight
ago, and left more than half his property to Mrs
Denbies unconditionally. She isn't well off, mam,
you know. We've been going into things a bit. The
quarrel by itself might not have been sufficient,
but with that will to back it up——!'

'Dear, dear! It only needed that!' observed Mrs
Bradley. 'You *have* built a case against her, Inspector!
And even before the identity of the body was
proved,' she added reminiscently. The inspector
flushed, and the sergeant grinned, at this thrust.

'There's not much doubt you've given us the clue
to the identity all right, mam,' the latter respectfully
observed. 'I knew Mr Lingfield pretty well, and
I certainly concluded it was him we'd got in the
mortuary.'

'Yes, yes, of course,' said Mrs Bradley. 'Well,
it is all very confusing and interesting, and Mrs
Denbies will feel better when her recital is over,
that's one thing.'

'Oh, we shan't disturb her any more, mam, until
the resumed inquest,' said the inspector. 'Not until
we pinch her for it,' he added in low tones as
he walked towards his car. The sergeant looked
slightly troubled.

'I don't like the old lady's attitude, sir,' he complained, as he followed the inspector across the heath.

'What old lady? Mrs B.? No one could be more helpful! Don't you go getting ideas in your head about *her!* Why, she's as keen to get the body identified as that of Mr Lingfield as ever we are ourselves.'

'Is she?' said the sergeant, not very hopefully. 'Ask me, sir, she's got something up her sleeve. You can see it in her eye, I reckon.'

'Nonsense, my lad! Respectable old parties like her, with plenty of money and an interesting, poke-nose job of work, can't afford to have anything up their sleeves! Not where the police are concerned.'

'Well, I wouldn't say that,' said the sergeant. 'I had a great aunt. . . . Nobody couldn't cope. Artful as a cartload of monkeys . . .' He continued to brood, and started up the car in silence. 'Besides,' he added, about three miles further on along the road, 'ask me, the whole thing's too easy. There's not been a single snag. I don't trust life when it's too easy.'

The inspector laughed.

'And how long have you known life?' he demanded. 'And what's biting you, anyway? Lost your Easter holiday? Well, that can't be helped, for once. You'd have been on duty some of the time in any case.'

'I don't like holidays,' said the sergeant. 'I just say it's all too easy. Murder doesn't come open and shut like that.'

'It does, with women. Women can't cover their tracks. They haven't the brains, lad. Especially passionate women, Here . . .' he went on, struck by a sudden thought. 'You haven't gone and fallen for Mrs Denbies, like that other young idiot, have you?'

'I don't know who you mean,' said the sergeant, sounding his horn with some violence at a rather rash chicken as it skipped across the road in front of his wheels.

'Why, him that offered to punch me on the jaw if I upset Mrs Denbies any further. Him that saw what *you* didn't see . . . that the wrecked car up here was a new one.'

'Oh, *him!*' said the sergeant. 'No. Though I know his sort. He'd sock you . . . or, as it might be, me . . . as soon as look at you if he felt like it. He's a ruddy poet, too,' he added, glowering.

'Now, look here, Ambrose Bierce,' observed the inspector, 'he may be a ruddy poet, but you're a ruddy police officer, and if you're going to work with me . . .'

'All right, sir,' answered the sergeant, calming down. 'But I still say that this Mrs Bradley can bear a lot of watching. Scalp the very hair off your head, and then argue you into thinking you'd look better, anyway, in a wig, she would,' he concluded, 'if it suited her book to do it. I don't trust brains in ladies. I wouldn't actually put it past her to do a murder herself if she felt it was needed.'

The inspector stared at the sergeant's youthful

neck, bull-like, brick-red, and did not continue his homily. His opinion was, however, that the sergeant could also bear watching.

'Needed!' he said. 'What the devil do you mean—*needed?'*

'Oh, nothing,' said the sergeant, keeping his eyes on the road.

Mrs Bradley arrived at the concert hall a quarter of an hour before Claudia's recital was timed to begin. She was not at all surprised to see Roger Hoskyn and Dorothy Woodcote there, but she was far more interested (although equally prepared) to encounter the Clandons, brother and sister, and Mary Leith.

She took her seat and studied the programme of music. Claudia was sharing the concert with a young Welsh tenor named ap Gwilym who was due to appear first.

He sang well. After his second song there was an expectant hush when the applause was over, then Claudia came on with her pianist. She played two Czech dances and a Kreisler lullaby.

The audience, made up for the most part, Mrs Bradley suspected, of Claudia's admiring but largely non-critical following, applauded with that almost hysterical generosity bestowed only at concerts, operas and performances of the ballet. Mrs Bradley joined in politely, admired the Welsh tenor's next songs, and awaited with great interest Claudia's second appearance.

She played flawlessly, but without enthusiasm, Busoni's *Elégie*, and followed this by the Bach *Partita in E Minor*. It was like hearing a *dhombie* perform, and it gave Mrs Bradley a feeling of horror, as though she were present at a dance of death in which mummies writhed free of their wrappings and skeletons provided the rhythm. During the applause she left her seat and went to the back of the stage.

She heard the beginning of the new burst of clapping which greeted young Mr ap Gwilym, and then the close-fitting door closed softly behind her, and she found herself unexpectedly in the presence of the inspector and his sergeant.

'Good heavens, Inspector! she exclaimed. 'You haven't made up your mind already?'

'No, mam,' the inspector replied, treating this enquiry as a thirst for information and not an attempt to tease and annoy him. 'The inquest is still adjourned as arranged. I am here to ask Mrs Denbies a question or two, failing the answers to which we can hardly proceed to give her the benefit of the doubt that her evidence of identification was genuinely mistaken.'

'Indeed?' said Mrs Bradley. 'You've found your valet, then? Does Mrs Denbies know that you are here?'

'I trust not, mam, for I have no wish to interfere with her recital, that being contrary to my conception of the treatment due to an artist and a gentlewoman. We have held up the enquiry until now——'

At this moment, a man in evening dress, whom Mrs Bradley took to be the lessee of the concert hall, came by and asked whether he could be of any assistance.

'I particularly want to see Mrs Denbies,' replied Mrs Bradley at once, before the inspector could speak. 'I am afraid she is not feeling well.'

'Are you a doctor, by any chance?'

'Yes, I am. I also know her quite well.'

'I am most relieved. Mrs Denbies is anything but well. She complains of her back, and says she does not think she can go on again this afternoon. Perhaps you would come this way. You say she knows you?'

'I think I said I know her. It is not, perhaps, quite the same thing. My name is Lestrange Bradley.'

Claudia was half-sitting and half-lying on a divan bed. She put her feet to the ground when Mrs Bradley was announced.

'Don't move,' said Mrs Bradley. 'Where is the pain?'

'Here, at the back of my neck and shoulder, and down my right arm. I hardly know how to hold my bow,' replied the sufferer. 'I've told Montague that I don't think I can play any more this afternoon. I'm afraid the audience won't like it, but what can I do? If I can't play with this shoulder, well, I can't.'

'I thought it was your back,' said Mrs Bradley. 'I thought you said you had strained it.'

'It *is* my back,' said Claudia wildly. 'But surely you see that I can't admit that now!'

'Why ever not?'

'Because there is too much against me already. That inspector is here! I saw him just before I went on to the platform, although he tried to keep out of sight. He's only waiting for my concert to be over to arrest me! He thinks I did it, and nothing I can say will help me! I was a fool to tell him the truth! I see that now. I shan't tell the truth any more! If I'd never confessed we'd quarrelled I'd never have been suspected! I see that now! It's too bad I wasn't warned not to speak! Somebody should have told me! I know nothing at all about the law!'

The man in evening dress put his head round the door.

'What about it, Claudia?' he said. 'Or shall I go in front and explain?'

'Yes, you'd better,' said Mrs Bradley. 'Mrs Denbies isn't fit to go on. She has very severe—you'd better call it neuralgia. Everybody understands that, and it ought to shut the critics' mouths. Refer to her heroism in consenting to appear at all this afternoon. And then, if you want a stop-gap—and you *will* want one, I suppose—go and have a word with a tall thin youth in Row C. He's sitting with a very pretty girl dressed in cornflower blue. There are three other young people, a girl in dusty pink, a young woman in tweeds, and a boy in a dark suit, all seated in the same row. The tall boy is wearing a grey suit. He's the one you want.'

'What can he do?'

'Recite his own poetry. It ought to go well with this audience.'

'Thank you. Er—is he known?'

'Of course he's known!' said Claudia Denbies vigorously. 'He's Roger Hoskyn, you ignorant lump!'

'Oh, really? I'll go and get him, then. Roger Hoskyn.' He scribbled it on his cuff. 'He won't refuse, I imagine?'

'Of course not. Tell him Mrs Denbies sends him an S.O.S. to take over for her,' said Mrs Bradley, with a cackle. 'Meanwhile,' she added, 'although in no sense a virtuoso, I can, at a pinch, render *Ave Maria* on the 'cello. Lend me yours, Claudia, and I'll go and relieve the tension which must already be gathering in front.'

She was right about the tension. Mr ap Gwilym had been off the stage for some minutes, and even the polite, non-critical audience was becoming slightly restless. Mrs Bradley, followed by the pianist carrying the 'cello, went to the front of the platform, and observed, in her beautiful voice:

'Interlude. *Ave Maria.*'

This seemingly impious observation passed unremarked except by Roger, who suddenly guffawed. The rest of the audience dutifully applauded, and Mrs Bradley, seating herself, took the 'cello, shot the startled pianist a leer which made him choke, gave the impression that she was feeling the pulse of the instrument and then drew her bow experimentally across the strings.

It was not the worst interpretation ever suffered

by Schubert's little sugar-plum, and the audience was pleased with it. Mrs Bradley, smirking like a satisfied boa-constrictor, applied herself again to her instrument and rendered a Spanish dance. Then, with a bow to the accompanist and a leer at the audience, she resigned the 'cello to the pianist, who carried it off the stage as though it were a large, unwieldy but infinitely impressive bouquet, and retired back-stage and so to the auditorium.

The audience then greeted Roger, who was introduced briefly and with a certain degree of not disagreeable effrontery by the lessee as 'our youngest and most reputable poet, whose major work is known to you all.'

Roger, whose mouth felt full of sand, and whose knees were knocking together, stumbled against the edge of the piano, and, in the agony of so doing, suddenly retrieved his nerve, and was able, at least, to speak.

'It is good of you to welcome me,' he said, in a voice rather loud and high-pitched, but otherwise under control. 'We are all most disappointed about the concert, and perhaps you would like it best if I first gave you my new sonnet, which is, as a matter of fact, to Claudia Denbies herself, whose courage, in appearing at all when she felt so ill is—well, you all understand and appreciate it, I'm quite sure.'

When the polite round of clapping had ceased he drew a deep breath, felt slightly faint, and then began.

'Sonnet Sixteen: to Claudia,' he stated roundly. It was really to the fugitive Marigold, but it had been altered during the past three days. He recited, for a poet, rather well. Even Dorothy, who had been applying to him some of those round adjectives and sturdy nouns kept by modern girls for the description of flighty suitors, began to feel rather proud of him.

The inspector, on the other hand, was neither pleased nor proud.

'The point is, mam,' he said in aggrieved tones, waylaying Mrs Bradley before she could leave the auditorium, 'I'm not here to put up with any jiggery-pokery. What I do say is that we shall get nowhere if we don't put our cards on the table and let each other see the moves.'

'A statement open to challenge,' returned Mrs Bradley briskly. 'But pray continue.'

'Mrs Denbies, mam. She's gone. And it looks like a put-up job.'

'Gone? I am not surprised. I thought it might take her that way. She thinks you came here to arrest her.'

'Did you tell her so, mam?'

'Why should I?'

'Well,' said the inspector, aggrieved (chiefly, Mrs Bradley rather suspected, at being made to look a fool in front of the sergeant), 'it's a kind of a funny thing that when you come in at the door my suspect flies out of the window.'

'Does she really?' asked Mrs Bradley, interested. 'I should hardly have thought it possible.' She transferred a benign, enquiring gaze from the inspector's brick-red face to the very small and closely-barred aperture opposite them. 'Of course, I do see that it is wide open.'

'In a manner of speaking, in a manner of speaking, of course, mam,' said the inspector, closing it irritably. 'What I mean is, she's vamoosed.'

'But didn't you have the other entrances watched?'

'Why should I? She wasn't supposed to know I was anywhere on the premises.'

'Well, she did know. She told me she saw you. I agree it's very silly of her to have run away like this, but, of course, as I said just now, I can understand it. You had better leave her to me. I'll undertake to find her for you, and produce her when she's wanted. You must be satisfied if she turns up all right at the inquest. Have there been any developments since I saw you on the common this morning?'

'I'll say, mam. As you guessed, I've got the valet's evidence. I got on to Bugle, the butler, and he gave me Sim the chauffeur, who acted as valet to Mr Lingfield while his own man was down with influenza, being as how he'd been his batman and driver in the war.'

'Oh, they've known one another some time, then? When was the influenza? Recently, I imagine?'

'I don't see why you should imagine it, mam, but you happen to be correct. It was in the middle of February. To be absolutely exact, it was between February tenth and twenty-third.'

'There was a good deal of influenza about just then,' said Mrs Bradley. The inspector shot a suspicious and the sergeant an interested glance at her. She seemed to both of them rather more pleased with the result of her apparently unimportant guess than there was reason for.

'Influenza, yes, mam,' the inspector repeated. 'Well, I got on to Sim. to come and identify the body. We drove him to the mortuary—the sergeant here did the driving—and the poor fellow—you know these corn-fed chauffeurs, mam, when they're driven in a car they don't know by a driver they don't trust—well, I've never seen a bloke in such a sweat.' He laughed appreciatively. 'You might have thought we were taking him along to charge him. If he'd been driven by the corpse itself he couldn't have been in more of a stew.'

'Proper case of nervous prostration,' interpolated the sergeant, with a grin.

'Anyway,' continued the inspector, 'he identified the body all right, although he was still green about the gills when he came out.'

'He identified the corpse, did he?' said Mrs Bradley. 'As Mr Lingfield?'

The inspector, who had proposed giving this as a startling and significant piece of information, and in a far more dramatic form, swallowed angrily, but answered, like a gentleman:

'That's it, mam. Mr Lingfield to a dot, he said it was.'

'To a rope, you mean,' retorted Mrs Bradley. She fixed him with an eye as bright and implacable as that of a robin. 'You're barking up the wrong tree, Inspector. Claudia Denbies did not kill Harry Lingfield. Of that I am absolutely certain.'

'There's some pretty conclusive evidence she did,' observed the inspector.

'There's some *pretty* evidence,' Mrs Bradley retorted. 'None of it is conclusive. What you need is a major operation, Inspector.'

'Eh, mam?'

'You want your fixed idea removed, and a bump of impartial judgment grafted on.'

With this rebuke, for her a remarkably severe one, she parted from him and made her way by cab to her Kensington house.

'Is Mrs Denbies here?' she asked her maid as soon as she arrived.

'But no, madame! Zere is nobody 'ere *sauf une jeune fille*, Miss Woodcote, whom I place in ze drawing-room, as she is not, I sink, one of ze patients of madame.'

'Quite right. She isn't.'

'And, dinner, madame?'

'Oh, yes, dinner. Anything Henri can manage.'

''E manage oysters, a *bouillon*, turbot——'

'Not a bit of good. Tell him he must manage smoked salmon, Scotch broth and a roast chicken. A young girl will never touch oysters, and all well-brought-up children loathe turbot.'

'It is Easter Saturday, madame.'

'All right. Send out for some jellied eels or something.'

'*Bien, madame,*' said Célestine, looking bitter. 'It will be your Scotch broth and roast chicken, without doubt.'

'I thought perhaps it would be,' said Mrs Bradley, grinning. She went into the drawing-room to greet Dorothy, but scarcely had they seated themselves, after Dorothy had helped Mrs Bradley off with her coat and the hostess had taken off her hat and pushed her black hair into place, when there was a knock at the front door, and Célestine, all smiles this time, was announcing Mr Roger Hoskyn.

Upon Roger's entry into the drawing-room the atmosphere became so tense and strained, not to say atmospheric and electric, that Mrs Bradley, pleading the necessity of seeing about dinner, left the two youngsters together.

Roger, who had not expected (as was obvious from his manner) to find Dorothy in Kensington—they had parted, Mrs Bradley learned later, on the steps of the concert hall—at first had nothing to say. Dorothy felt a similar constraint. She sat in a big armchair by the cheerful fire while Roger walked over to the window and stared gloomily and Byronically out on to the blameless, respectable square in which Mrs Bradley lived when she was in town.

Dorothy, who believed in the feminine strategy of making the enemy fire first and so expose himself, sat for ten minutes without so much as a movement except for (but Roger did not see this, and would

not have been enlightened if he had) the fidgeting
of her small brown fingers with the clasp of her
handbag.

The constraint and the silence were soon more
than Roger could bear.

'I suppose you think I'm a swine,' he suddenly
said. This surprising statement caused Dorothy to
sit up a little straighter, but she did not even turn
her head.

'No, of course not,' she said. 'Why should I think
you're a swine?'

'Oh, I don't know,' said Roger, baffled. 'I
mean—oh, I don't know. I say—that awful woman's
at my digs.'

'What awful woman?'

'Claudia Denbies, dash it! I don't know how to
bung her out.'

'Oh!' said Dorothy, in a colourless, uninterested
tone.

'I say—don't you mind?' asked Roger
anxiously.

'Why should I? It's nothing to do with me if you
take women into your digs. I should think it's for
your landlady to object if she doesn't like them.'

'What do you mean—*them?* I *don't* take women
into my digs!' said Roger, in an anguished howl. 'You
know that as well as I do! I mean—well, you may
not know it, but old Bob knows it. Ask *him!*'

'Why should I? It's of no interest to me,' said
Dorothy. 'If you don't want Mrs Denbies, and can't
get rid of her, I suppose you can sleep at your
club?'

'I haven't *got* a club, dash it, except P.P.'

'P.P.?'

'Poets' Pub. We've a couple of fairly lousy rooms in Drupe Street. I couldn't sleep *there!'*

'Well, I can't think of anything else. I can't ask you back to our house because my people are home, and, anyway, you wouldn't want to come.'

'She says,' said Roger, coming up to the fire and standing with his long legs wide apart as he warmed his hands, 'that the police are on her track for murdering Lingfield, and that the last place they'll think of looking for her is with me. But that's the very *first* place they'll think of, once they discover she isn't at her own flat or at Whiteledge. Besides, as you pointed out, I've got my landlady to consider. You know, Claudia's marvellous in her way, of course, but she's apt to be exotic, and—well, you know—caviare to the general where landladies are concerned. And I can't shift her, dash it! She cried all over me. You've no idea what a woman of that age looks like, with furrows all down her make-up!'

'I thought your sonnet went awfully well,' said Dorothy, with deadly innocence.

'As a sonnet,' said Roger, turning his back on the fire and pausing to kick the rug, 'as a *sonnet*, mind you, it wasn't bad at all. Not bad at all. In point of fact, rather good. But I don't want to think of it again. And if I knew of any decent rhymes to "Dorothy"——'

'I didn't, personally, think "Claudia" rhymed too well with "disorder," ' observed the armchair critic dispassionately. 'Besides, I thought you didn't go in for rhyme. Isn't it a new departure? Did it rhyme when it was supposed to be to Marigold?'

'Oh, damn and blast!' shouted Roger, exploding suddenly.

'Why don't you sit down?' enquired Dorothy. 'It might be a good idea.' She sniffed the air very delicately, as might a fawn when it lifts its head at evening from drinking by the ferny water-brooks. 'I think you're scorching your trousers.'

Chapter Nine

'I bring ye love: What will love do?
Love will fulfil ye.
I bring ye Love: What will love do?
Kiss ye to kill ye.'

ROBERT HERRICK,
Upon Love, by Way of Question and Answer

IT WAS Mrs Bradley who ousted Claudia from her hiding place and took her to the Kensington house.

'It makes a bad impression,' she insisted, 'to seem to be running away. They want to ask you more questions, and one very serious obstacle has cropped up. You must be brave enough to face the fact that the chauffeur, Sim, has identified the body as that of Harry Lingfield.'

'But it *isn't* Harry! It couldn't be!'

'Nevertheless, this man Sim says it is.'

'But how could he know? . . . Oh dear! He used to valet Harry while Misset was down with influenza. They might believe *what* he says!'

'Exactly. His evidence is at least as good as yours—for legal purposes possibly even better. That is the fact you have to face.'

'But, in that case, they'll arrest me! I knew that inspector had it in his eye! They'll believe him, and that means they'll think I'm lying. If he swears that the dead man is Harry, they'll say I killed him! It stands to reason! Don't you see?'

'So clearly,' said Mrs Bradley, 'that I have come here to advise you that you hide from the police at your peril—possibly even at peril of your life. You have everything to lose by running away from trouble, and nothing at all to gain, because they will find you so easily. How long is it going to take this woman here, Mr Hoskyn's landlady, to hand you over as soon as she reads your description in the papers or hears it over the wireless later on? Nothing looks worse than trying to skulk in corners! You're a brave woman, and you must know that!'

'They wouldn't broadcast for me as though I were a common criminal?'

'Why not? The very fact that your name is known to everyone, and your appearance, too, is an added reason for using the radio to find you. Don't be silly.'

'Very well,' said Claudia, resignedly. 'I'll come. Where? To the nearest police station?'

'No. To my house,' said Mrs Bradley. 'I will telephone to the inspector and you can be interviewed in comfort.'

'You will stand by me, won't you?'

'Yes, I will. This case, although simple in essence, has what Sherlock Holmes would call some unique features. Tell me,' she added, when they were in a taxi on their way to her house, 'what were you doing when you went out late in your car on the night of the crime? You told me, when you asked my advice, that you were going to meet your husband, but, although I did not say so to the inspector, I have never believed that was true.'

'I went to meet Harry, but I can't tell that to the police. I should be in worse case than before.'

'I don't think you would, eventually, if that could be proved to be the truth.'

'It couldn't. Nobody knew.'

'Nobody?'

'I'm positive nobody knew. If I'd been going to tell anybody I'd have told you.'

'But I thought you had quarrelled on the ride with Mr Lingfield?'

'Yes, we had. And I knew that Harry wasn't coming back to dinner as soon as I got his note. He said he should never return to England, but wanted to see me once more before he left. I went—I was always a fool!—but I was scared, too. That's why I let you know I was going out that night. I felt I wanted someone to know.'

'Did you think he would turn quarrelsome again?'

'I suppose so. I don't quite know. I was always half afraid of him. He was never violent—at least, not in his actions—but his intensity used to frighten me. I'm rather intense myself, as a matter of fact, and that's how I know what he was like. He was like a flare of magnesium to a candle compared with me.'

'I don't think you do yourself justice,' said Mrs Bradley. 'But if you were really afraid of him, why were you tempted to go?'

'Curiosity. I can't conquer it. I can't bear not knowing. I never could.'

'No,' thought Mrs Bradley, glancing at her companion's Titian hair, delicious nose and wide, disarming mouth, 'I can understand that, of course.'

There was nothing secret there, in the *gamine* face, the candid eyes, the good, strong bones of the head. There was nothing secret, either, about the splendid body, the milky skin, the muscular arms, the beautiful, sensitive hands. Mrs Bradley, from the first, had felt a good deal of sympathy for Roger, irresistibly attracted, if only for a while, by all this splendour. This woman would be like flame to his sun-starved youth, and not a candle-flame, either, unless one compared him to a moth.

'What do you think I ought to tell the inspector?' asked Claudia, when they reached Mrs Bradley's house.

'The truth, the whole truth, and nothing but the truth,' Mrs Bradley replied, 'but, at present, only so far as will serve to answer his questions. It is the inquest we have to think of, not the inspector.'

'But it wouldn't be the truth to say that the body I saw was Harry Lingfield's. I know it wasn't, and nothing will make me alter my opinion.'

'There is no need to alter it, my dear Claudia. The only thing is—don't embroider. Far more people have found themselves in trouble through over-elaboration than for telling a bald and improbable tale.'

'The inspector won't believe me.'

'So much the worse for him.'

'For me, surely?'

'No, child, not in the long run. For one thing, even if the inspector doesn't believe you, there are plenty of people who do, and I am one. As a matter of fact, I know most of the truth already.'

'You do?'

'Oh, yes, child.'

'Well, for my sake, can't you prove something? Can't you put the inspector off the track?'

'No, I hardly think I can—particularly as he is not on it at present. My advice is this: You must try not to worry. And don't prepare conversations in your mind before the inspector questions you. It is most improbable that you will need your careful sentences, and it will confuse you, you'll find, when the conversation takes a different turn.'

'I suppose he won't come until the morning? I shall pass a wretched night,' said Claudia, groaning. The first part of this prophecy proved true; the second, thanks to Mrs Bradley's witch-brewed sleeping draught (administered to the patient in a glass of egg-flip at bed-time), entirely false. Claudia slept well and came down to breakfast at nine.

'At what time do you think the inspector will

come?' she asked nervously. Mrs Bradley leaned forward and poked the fire.

'I haven't telephoned him yet,' she replied. 'There's something I ought to ask you to be prepared to tell me before he arrives.'

'I—I don't think there's anything at all that I haven't told you.'

'Except the real cause of your refusal to identify the body as that of Mr Lingfield.'

'But I—but you said you believed me!'

'Yes, I know I did, and so I do. But it would have made things so much easier, after all, if you'd said what everyone expected you to say. I just wondered—'

'You really want me to—come clean?'

'I think it might be better if you did, child.'

'You're very clever,' said Claudia Denbies, plucking at one of her ear-rings and taking it off. 'So clever that you make me nervous.'

'How so, child?'

'Well, you believed me when I told you our quarrel was about music.'

'Yes, I did believe you, but I think it led to something else.'

'Well, yes, we did talk about something else, but—anyway, it wasn't anything that mattered.'

'Are you sure of that?'

'Of course I'm sure,' said Claudia, dropping the ear-ring on the floor and groping to pick it up.

'You told me you had known him since 1917.'

'Harry Lingfield? Yes.'

'What happened in 1929, child?'

'Yes,' said Claudia, going to the mirror and replacing the ear-ring with great care but trembling fingers.

'What do you mean—yes?'

'We had a child.'

'Ah!'

'It died. Harry said I poisoned it.'

'Did you?'

'No.'

'What name was it buried under?'

'My married name is Vesper.'

'Where was it buried?'

'In Paris. We—it was born there, you see.'

'Did he really believe you had poisoned it?'

'No, I don't think so. I thought *he* had.'

'Did you? Why?'

'I don't know. I mean, I don't know what I had to go on. I felt quite certain at the time. I've been afraid of him ever since. I shan't tell the inspector all this. I needn't, need I?'

'It depends how the conversation goes, child. You left Whiteledge fairly late at night. . . .'

'At half-past twelve.'

'Went to the *rendezvous* in your own car. . . .'

'Yes, I hadn't put it back in the garage. I got Sim to leave it in the woods. I told him my sister was very ill and that I was expecting a telephone call, and would not want to rouse the house with the sound of my car if I were suddenly called away.'

'Yes, yes, I see. Was Sim surprised?'

'He didn't show it. Lady Catherine's servants

never do. He offered to drive me, but I said it
wasn't necessary.'

'Where were you to meet Mr Lingfield?'

'At the station.'

'And what happened?'

'He wasn't there.'

'You were surprised at that?'

'Oh, no. I thought he had changed his mind. I was
furiously angry, but not surprised in the least.'

'Isn't there anything else you'd like to tell
me?'

'No—no, there isn't!' said Claudia pleadingly. 'I
didn't mean to tell you all this. I don't know why
I did. You won't tell the inspector, will you? He's
such a—such an unsympathetic man.'

'I'll say nothing which will implicate you. I
promise you that.'

'There's one thing you haven't asked me,' said
Claudia, with a sudden cat-like smile.

'I know,' said Mrs Bradley. 'But I know the
answer to that. You did not attempt to put your
car away. There is, however, one more question I
would like to put, if I may.'

She grinned at Claudia's terrified expression.

'What else?—I don't see what else you can
possibly ask me if you don't ask me. . . .'

'Whether the dead man, if he is not Mr Lingfield,
is known to you?' Mrs Bradley enquired. 'Well, I
can guess the answer, and will not press you. No,
it is simply this: what was the real relationship
between Mr Lingfield and yourself? . . . Don't tell
me if you would rather not, but I am a psychiatrist,

as you know, and am accustomed to the recital of dark secrets.'

Claudia laughed in so relieved a fashion that Mrs Bradley looked at her in surprise as she answered lightly:

'Oh, I've no objection in the least to telling you all about that. We were, in spite of all our quarrels and my fears, always completely in love.'

'Ah!' said Mrs Bradley. 'I am glad you are honest about that. And at the present moment?'

'If he came into this room at this moment I think I should die,' said Claudia with tragic emphasis.

'But you say you don't believe he is dead?'

Claudia glanced at her in the fearful fascination of sheer terror.

'You mustn't ask me that!' she said huskily.

'Right,' said Mrs Bradley briskly. 'Then I shall telephone the inspector—'

'No! You can't do that!'

'—and tell him that I will be responsible for your appearing at the inquest, and that he must save all his questions until after it is over, because you're in no state to answer them now. It's perfectly true. You're not. Now let's invite those two children out to lunch. It will do you good to have to pass policemen without blenching.'

Chapter Ten

'Now let us sport us while we may . . .
Let us roll all our strength and all
Our sweetness up into one ball,
And tear our pleasures with rough strife
Through the iron gates of life.
Thus, though we cannot make our sun
Stand still, yet we will make him run.'
ANDREW MARVELL, *To His Coy Mistress*

'YOU WON'T forget your promise?' said Roger.

'No, I won't forget. I'd love to see you play. What are the Seven-a-Sides? I've never been.'

'Oh, what it says, actually. I mean, seven of us play instead of the usual fifteen; the pitch is the same, more or less—well, actually rather less—and the time is shorter, that's all. It's all run on the knock-out system. We've drawn a pretty hot lot for the first round, so I rather doubt whether we'll survive.'

'Oh, you're sure to. I'm looking forward to it, awfully.'

'Wish I could say the same. Actually, I've got cold feet. I'm playing wing three-quarter, and I don't think I'm fast enough, really. Still, we've got a good man in the centre. I shall just have to sell the dummy if I can't get rid of the pill, and hope for the best.'

'And we get off at Richmond Station?'

'Well, I think you'd better. Then you only have to push on to that bus that I told you of, and you're practically on the spot. You can see the ground from the corner. Anyway, old Bob knows it, so he'll see that you don't get lost. I'm glad his ankle's all right.'

Roger had returned to his lodgings. His landlady, he discovered, far from being upset by the unexpected appearance of Claudia Denbies in that haven of refuge and abode of peace, had been greatly flattered by the invasion because she had heard Claudia play 'over the wireless.'

'She could have stayed and welcome, Mr Hoskyn. There's always the spare room, isn't there?' she said in hopeful tones.

Roger, who had several times tried in vain to book the spare room at week-ends for hearty and noisy male friends, could do nothing but gawp at her, speechless. He would never understand women, he decided. He had met Dorothy twice since Easter Saturday, once with Bob and once (at lunch in town) by herself. She had been very charming to him, but Roger was sensitive enough to realize that he was being kept at arm's length, and honest enough to believe that he deserved it.

He was due to return to his post on the
Wednesday following the Seven-a-Side Finals on
Saturday, but had contrived to push this knowledge
to the back of his mind. He did not want to think
about that Wednesday because to do so involved
thinking about the inquest on the previous day.
He was to be called as a witness, and intensely
disliked the idea.

Saturday came, however, with the threat
of Tuesday to follow, and Roger went down to
Twickenham to play in the sevens. In his Rugger
shorts and close-fitting blue and white hooped jersey
he looked taller and thinner than usual. He trotted
modestly on to the field and then proceeded, in a
manner that Dorothy found thrilling and surprising,
to prove himself the fastest and most enterprising
player in the game.

Until almost half-time he had no opportunity to
score, but five minutes before the whistle sounded
the ball flew loose from a pulled kick and he fled
to it, took it in its flight, steadied himself, and
kicked for touch. After the line-out he gathered a
difficult pass and tore all out for the line.

It was a breath-taking, magnificent run. He
concluded it by selling the dummy to the opposing
back, and then, running round in almost a complete
quarter-circle, he planted the ball between the
posts.

There was a hush, as of death, whilst the full back
came up to take the kick. The crowd watched the
almost unpredictable flight of the ball. It soared, and
then seemed to be dropping slightly short; then it

suddenly flew at the cross-bar and fell over it like a high-jumper clearing six feet two or three.

The game improved about half-time, and the opposition had somewhat, but not much, the better of it. They scored a try rather far out which they did not convert, and then another chance came to Roger. He gathered a pass which was meant for one of the opposing forwards and galloped towards the goal-line with the ball held awkwardly. He saw the full back, a good deal more wary this time, cantering across to obstruct him, ducked under an outstretched arm, swerved, ran in, and then, to circumvent the full back, almost doubled on his tracks before going full-out for the line. A welter of the opposition fell on him, but he got the try, far out on the left of the goal posts. He got up, dizzy with the weight of three men who had flung themselves on him just as he went over the line, and then, as he got to his feet, he tripped and fell. He was aware of a sharp, thin pain which seared his right ankle like a hot iron run through the bone. He fell forward, and, at the moment he touched the ground, somebody kicked the back of his head, and he was down and out as the whistle went for time.

He came to in the dressing-room to find the captain of his seven sitting anxiously beside him.

'Oh, Lord!' said Roger. He put a hand to his head.

'I wouldn't touch it,' said the captain. 'You take it easy, old man.'

'When's the next round? I suppose we won?'

'We won all right, but there's no next round for you. We'll have to play Bates, and hope for the best, that's all. I shall shove him in with the forwards, and bring Ralledge out of the pack to outside three-quarter, and leave Serry there in the centre. It *may* work out all right.'

'When's the next round? Don't be foxy.' Roger sat up, winced at the pain in his head, put his feet to the ground, and then remembered his ankle. Cautiously he stood up. His head swam and he felt sick. 'I want some fresh air,' he said, 'whether I play or not. My ankle's all right. That's what really worried me. I thought it might be broken. I suppose I just gave it a twist.'

At this point one of their late opponents came in.

'Hey, you!' he said, noting Roger. 'What's the idea?'

'Air,' said Roger, clinging to the captain's shoulder. 'Nice, clean, rain-washed air.'

'What happened, exactly? It wasn't our fellows, was it?' asked the enemy. 'Lean on me as well, old man. This is foul luck, after those two tries.'

'Some damn fool of a spectator,' said the captain, 'sitting just inside the wooden barrier. Grabbed up the ball, took a drop kick, missed the ball, and landed on Hoskyn.'

'I thought I picked up the ball myself,' said Roger. 'But I hardly remember what happened. After I got the try two or three of them got up off me, and that was all right, but then I felt my ankle go, and as I went down someone kicked me. Did we win, does anybody know?'

'I've told you once that we did. You know, you ought not to be walking about. You're concussed.'

'I should think the fellow who kicked you got pretty well lynched by the crowd at that end of the ground,' said the enemy. 'One thing, you needn't worry. You've got a sitter next round.'

'Who?' Roger looked at his captain.

'An Old Boys' team from somewhere off the map. We ought to eat 'em, so don't you worry. Anyway, I shan't play you. I refuse to have an inquest on my hands.'

'Oh, Lord!' said Roger with a groan. The other two looked at him anxiously. 'How's the time?' he added.

'Oh, we've got tons of time, I'm glad to say. There are four more first rounds to be worked off yet before we play our second,' replied the captain.

'Let's go and see how they shape.'

'I should think you'd better take it easy.'

'Oh, no. I'd rather get some air. Come on. Support the weak.'

He walked on gingerly, supported by his two stalwarts, until they were encountered by another player who was just coming into the dressing-room.

'Bad luck, Hoskyn,' said this man. 'I say, I don't want to sound hysterical, but it looked to me as though that kick at your head was done a-purpose. Who have you been annoying of? Why should you get yourself disliked? Caggers and I made a bee-line for the fellow, but the crowd was a bit annoyed, too, and he was off before we could get near him.'

I don't see why anyone should lay for me,' said Roger. 'I haven't a quarrel with anyone, so far as I know. But it felt like a boot all right. I can tell you that. My skull feels horrid like jelly.'

'Well, I'd like to have got the bloke by the neck,' said the captain. 'I'd have screwed it round for him, and that I do know.'

As soon as they came out by the side of the grandstand Dorothy came up and stood before them.

'How is it?' she asked. Roger grinned. Two players got up from a bench, the captain and the opponent melted away, and Roger and Dorothy sat down. 'I suppose you won't play any more?'

'Oh, I think I shall be all right,' he responded, putting a hand to the bandage. 'And the ankle's fine, so long as I don't get a kick on it.'

'Roger,' said Dorothy, after a pause, 'you don't know a square, dark man with an astrakan coat-collar and a long, rather ragged moustache?'

'Sounds like a moneylender. If it is, I'm not guilty. Don't owe a sou to a soul.'

'I'm serious. He's the man who kicked you on the head.'

'Oh, well, these things happen.'

'Yes, but he did it deliberately, and as soon as he'd done it, and people began to surge round, he dived through the crowd and went off. We left our seats and ran round to the gate, but couldn't see any sign of him. Bob would have killed him, I think, if we could have caught him.'

'Bob's always been an admirer of my beauty. No, honestly, I'm glad you didn't find him. I know Bob in moods like that. But it couldn't have been deliberate. No one would kick a bloke's head in because he happened—more by luck than by judgment—to score a try. And if it wasn't for scoring a fairly fluky try . . .'

'It was a very good try. You needn't be modest about it.'

'I'm not. That remark was conceit.'

'I thought it might be. Well, next time, you see that somebody else scores the try if he's going to get his head kicked in for it.'

Roger laughed. Then he said soberly:

'Tell you what, though. Ever since Mrs Denbies' recital I've had an idea that someone has followed me about. Furthermore, I've a hunch I know who.'

'How horrid. Who is it? Anybody I know?'

'Sim, that chauffeur. Remember?'

'Whatever makes you think that?'

'Well, he keeps popping up. I found him near me in a pub one night in Guildford.'

'Guildford isn't so very many miles from Whiteledge.'

'Then at the Dogs . . .'

'Everybody goes to the Dogs.'

'Again in Regent Street.'

'Regent Street?'

'Yes. By the way . . .' He felt in his pockets. 'Oh, damn! Of course, I'm in shorts. I've got something to show you. Remind me.'

'Of course I shall. What?—Another poem?'

'No,' said Roger, blushing. 'And you shut up!'

'I'd better get back to Bob and Mrs Bradley.'

'Good heavens! Is Mrs Bradley here?'

'Oh, yes. I think she's taken rather a fancy to Bob. They discuss the murder——'

'And the inquest, I suppose. Have you fully realized that you and I may have to make a public appearance?'

'You will. I shan't. Do you think they suspect Mrs Denbies? The inspector and the sergeant, I mean.'

'Well, of course they suspect her! As far as is known, she was the last person to see the fellow Lingfield alive.'

'Yes, *as far as is known*. I'll never believe she had anything to do with it, though. She couldn't have! She isn't that kind of person.'

I agree, but why our certainty? Red-haired people are notorious for preferring to hand out the swift slosh rather than the word of admonition and remonstrance.'

'Yes, but—his head!'

'She was out on the night it was done—and in her car. She admits that to everybody now.'

Yes, but the car that was found abandoned and wrecked wasn't hers.'

'That was the only thing that saved her, I believe, from being arrested after the first inquest.'

'Oh, well, that inquest was only formal, wasn't it? I wonder whether she'll stick to her story that the dead person wasn't Mr Lingfield? Rather silly, I thought, to have said that at all.'

'Oh, I don't know. If she killed him, you see, it would work out best for her if she could throw doubt on the idea that he was dead. It was rather intelligent really.'

'I don't agree at all. And even if that's true, it would only have been intelligent if she really had killed him, and I thought we were agreed that she didn't do it. *You* don't think she did it, do you?'

'No, of course I don't think she did it. . . . Only, you see, there's no alibi, and . . . well . . . she did admit they quarrelled.'

'A fine friend *you* are! I hope *I* never get mixed up in murder or crime!'

'Murder *or* crime?'

'Yes. They are not the same thing; not always, anyhow.'

'It depends on the motive, doesn't it?'

'I thought it went badly against Mrs Denbies that Mr Lingfield appears to have left her a good deal of property.'

'Oh, did he? I didn't know that. Any money?'

'I understand there wasn't much money. Hadn't he drawn most of it out?'

'I don't know, I tell you. How do you come to be so well-informed about all this?'

'I don't know. We were in Mrs Bradley's drawing-room feeling rather aimless, and she came out with one or two things.'

'The devil and all she did!' said Roger, staring. 'And when are the rest of us going to hear any news?'

'I should think it would come out at the inquest.'

'Will it? Perhaps I shan't be listening. What did he leave her, then?'

'Oh, I don't know. Shares in things, and some houses. . . .'

'Mostly mortgaged, I expect.'

'You don't like what you know of Mr Lingfield, do you? I thought men always backed up other men.'

'They do, when they know them. I didn't know Lingfield, and that lets me out, you see. As I see him, he was a swine, and what he got serves him right.'

'Does it? I suppose that's all right then. By the way, if Mrs Denbies—I mean, suppose that they thought she *did* murder Mr Lingfield, she couldn't—I mean, could she inherit anything?'

'No, of course she couldn't. You can't, under English law, gain anything by murdering your benefactor. I'm perfectly sure of that.'

'Something ought to hang on that, somehow, but, in this case, I can't see what.'

'Some*one*, you probably mean, but—take it as read. I say, I feel a lot better. I think I'll go and smoke a cigarette. One should always break training (into which, incidentally, I never really go) before the final round.'

'But this won't be the final round.'

'I expect it will for us,' said Roger with great philosophy.

'So you lost in the final round?' said Mrs Bradley. 'There is something Greek about that.'

'Of all things, not to be born into the world is best,' said Roger, grinning. He looked fagged but cheerful, and his scalp wound had been found to be superficial. The aggressor had either missed his kick or not kicked hard enough. Nevertheless, the victim, having played three games since the accident, was feeling that he had had enough for one day. He said as much.

'Never mind. You played a splendid game. My hearty congratulations,' said Mrs Bradley. She patted his muscular shoulder. 'And did you enjoy the matches?'

'Not so that you'd notice,' said Roger, touching his bandaged head. 'One of the spectators seemed to think this was the ball.'

'I know. Too bad. May I look?'

'Oh, I think it's all right. I didn't have any concussion.'

'That *can* come later. Let me look.'

'No, really, it's quite all right.'

'You weren't thinking of going on the spree tonight by way of celebration, by any chance?'

'Well, we did think we'd go up to town.'

'Not you, child. Alcohol won't help this head of yours.'

'Oh, but really . . .'

Mrs Bradley made an almost imperceptible sign to Dorothy.

'Please come with me, Roger,' said the girl.

'Come where?' He looked surprised.

'To Mrs Bradley's country place at Wandles. We're invited there for Sunday, and as long as we like to stay.'

'Are we?' He looked very pleased and, suddenly, very young. 'To tell you the truth, I'm not feeling much like a night on the roof with the lads. When and how do we go?'

'At once, if you like. Henri and Célestine went down this morning, and Mrs Ribbon is always there to keep the place aired,' said Mrs Bradley. 'My secretary also is there. I think you'll both like Laura. Bob also has promised to come, but he has to go back tomorrow evening.'

'I'll have to go back to my digs and pack a bag.'

'I'd better come with you,' said Dorothy.

'I'll pick you up at your lodgings,' said Mrs Bradley. 'I am sorry to say that Claudia cannot come.'

'Thank goodness for that,' muttered Roger. 'No, I'm going straight home,' he added to two members of his Seven who were just coming out of the gate. 'Sorry and all that. Some other time.'

'Are you really glad Mrs Denbies isn't coming?' Dorothy asked, as they took the road towards the station.

'You bet!' said Roger emphatically, tucking her arm in his. 'I say, it's cold! What's this place of Mrs Bradley's? I've never heard of it.'

'Just a nice old stone house, she says, with a garden and stables and a garage. And she's got a French cook and a French maid (husband and wife), and a Highland secretary. . . .'

'Who's Laura, then?'

'The   secretary.   Educated   partly   in England. . . .'

'You mean partly educated, don't you?'

'—and perfectly tame, although rather large and energetic. And we can do exactly as we like all the time. *Exactly* as we like.'

'As long as we like the same things,' said Roger grinning. 'Do you think there's any chance we might?'

There were various answers to this question, and there were those among them which Dorothy had half a mind to give. However, the kick on the head and his bandage had given him a pale and interesting appearance, and she found him, apart from this, not unattractive, so she compromised by smiling her secret smile and then observing:

'I wouldn't know. Would you?'

'I could make a guess,' said Roger. 'Do you think we could stay until Tuesday, and then go under her wing to this damned inquest?'

'You're scared of it. Why?' asked Dorothy.

'Oh, I don't know. Here's the trolley. I don't know where we have to change.'

'Don't you bother. I'll find out.'

She was rather concerned at his blackened eyes and the listless expression of his mouth. She did not ask whether his head hurt him, but, having

got him to his lodgings, she made him drink some
tea and then lie on the bed and direct the packing
of his suitcase. His landlady happened to be out,
so they had the place to themselves, and left her a
note when Mrs Bradley's chauffeur, a respectable,
kindly man, came up to the door and knocked
for them.

Chapter Eleven

'At length one chanced to find a nut,
In the end of which a hole was cut,
Which lay upon a hazel root,
There scattered by a squirrel
Which out the kernel gotten had;
When quoth this Fay, "Dear Queen, be glad;
Let Oberon be ne'er so mad,
I'll set you safe from peril." '

MICHAEL DRAYTON,
Nymphidia: The Court of Fairy

CLAUDIA'S PANIC-STRICKEN letter broke upon the household at Wandles Parva just after the newspapers were delivered on Monday morning. Claudia stated that she knew she was going to be arrested for the murder of Harry Lingfield, and would be cautioned ('in that loathsome way') that anything she might choose to say would be taken down in writing and might be used in evidence.

Claudia's response to this timely warning, she added wildly, would be—and the police could make

the most of it—'I didn't kill Harry, and you know
it! I didn't kill anybody, and anyhow, the dead
man isn't Harry, as I keep on telling you! In any
case, it's such nonsense to talk to me about his
silly will! I didn't want his money, and, even if I
did, he hadn't any!'

'Which last fact,' said Mrs Bradley, facing a
wrathful Roger, an interested and very thoughtful
Bob, and a non-committal Dorothy, 'is quite
true. I had it from the lawyers. There wasn't a
penny. Mr Lingfield had gradually drawn it all
out, realized his shares, mortgaged his house and
become increasingly in debt to his tailor and wine-
merchant.'

'Then she's right!' exclaimed Roger. 'It isn't
Lingfield who's dead!'

'I've always thought she was right about that,'
said Bob. 'Thing is now to produce him alive and
well. I suppose that would put the candle-snuffers
on the inspector.'

'I still don't see why they took Sim's word rather
than Mrs Denbies',' said Dorothy. 'In any case, I
don't see how you could be sure of identifying a
body without seeing the head.'

'Oh, yes, you can,' said Bob. 'Wasn't Mrs Crippen
identified by one bit of skin with an appendicitis
scar on it, or something?'

'Well, I think I must go and support poor Claudia,'
said Mrs Bradley, rising. 'You children, no doubt,
can find something to do whilst I'm gone.'

'I'd like to come with you,' said Bob. 'I'd have
to leave Wandles this afternoon, anyway, worse

luck, as I must be at the office tomorrow. This lazy
pair don't have to work——'

'Until Wednesday,' said Roger, luxuriously. 'All
right, Bob. Be good, and so will we.'

'Didn't *you* want to go?' enquired Dorothy, when
they were on their way back after having seen the
other two driven off by George the chauffeur in
Mrs Bradley's car.

'I couldn't do any good, you know,' said Roger,
scowling down at his shoes. 'Mrs Bradley will be
allowed to see her, I expect, if she's arrested, but they
wouldn't have me as prisoner's friend, or whatever
it is called, I'm afraid. Poor Claudia! It's all a damn'
shame! You don't think she *did* do it, do you?'

'I'm certain she didn't. I *was* certain, I *am* certain,
and I always shall *be* certain that Mrs Denbies
couldn't murder anyone. Besides, it was all too
difficult.'

'Too carefully planned, you mean? Yes, I think
that, too. Whoever did it must have had it in
mind for days; perhaps for months. The only snag
is . . .'

'Yes?'

'Well, you see, if the body *is* Lingfield, and,
although we don't think it is, there doesn't seem
any way of proving that it isn't—she had the motive;
two motives, in fact, if you believe she didn't know
he hadn't anything to leave her in his will. They
had certainly quarrelled——'

'Yes, I know, but so have you and I, and neither
of us is in the least danger of being murdered by
the other.'

'Speak on your own behalf, dash it! Besides—well, our relationship isn't exactly the same as theirs was, is it? I mean, they were as good as married. Had been for years, I imagine. Living together on and off, and that kind of thing, you know. I am wondering what will be said about that at the inquest.'

'Yes.' She was silent. Roger would have given a good deal to know her thoughts. He said, as they walked across the lawn:

'What shall we do now they've gone?'

'I wonder what Laura Menzies wants to do?'

'Dash Laura! She's got the dogs and a cat and things. She can't have us as well.'

'I thought she was head of the house in Mrs Bradley's absence. Still, if you think she wouldn't mind——'

'Of course she won't mind, chump! I loathe young Amazonian females, and this particular specimen makes me feel as though I'm ten years old and not more than a fly-weight at that.'

'I wish I could make you feel ten years old. What were you like at ten?'

'Do you mind not pressing that question? Ten is the average age of the fifteen little devils in my form, and I can't think why my parents didn't strangle me long before I was that age, if I was anything like those little blighters, and I've a horrible impression that I must have been.'

'Then you can't be feeling well,' said Dorothy.

Laura Menzies, Mrs Bradley's secretary, met them on the doorstep.

'Hullo,' she said. 'I say, you two won't want me, I trust? I've got stacks of work to do this morning, and I always go to bed on Monday afternoons to gather strength for the week. So do amuse yourselves, will you? I mean, I'm on tap if required, but if you don't particularly mind——?'

Roger assured her firmly that they did not mind in the least, and she whistled the dogs and walked off. At twenty paces she paused, turned her head and added carelessly:

'By the way, don't bother about getting back to lunch if you'd sooner take sandwiches or something, and go out for a good long walk. It's Monday, and I might as well give Henri the day off. There's nothing to cook.'

Roger grasped at this delicate hint.

'Sandwiches? Oh, rather. I say, thanks.'

'I'll tell Célestine, then, and you can rely on a really good dinner when you get back. The butcher will call at five. By the way, Mrs Croc. says I'm to warn you not to get lost. Have you got a map? I'll get you one out of the library. Oh, and Mrs Croc. also says you'd better each take an ashplant if you're going off the beaten track at all. There are half a dozen in the hall. Take your pick. Take two if you like.'

'I suppose Mrs Bradley thinks my ankle may go back on me,' said Roger, selecting a stick with care. 'I say, this might almost be my own old ashplant, don't you think? Remember our discussion on the bus that first day about superstitions and so forth?'

'It doesn't seem possible that it was such a short time ago,' said Dorothy. She glanced out at the pleasant spring sunshine and shivered as though she were cold. 'I *said* something horrid would happen that day, and it did! I only hope——'

'What?'

'That ashplants are not unlucky.'

'Well, the ash does have a bad name in witchcraft, I believe—almost as bad as the elm. Did you ever read a story by Montagu Rhodes James——?'

Discussion and mutual appreciation of *Ghost Stories of an Antiquary* lasted them for the first two miles of their walk. There was no doubt, thought Dorothy, that Roger, when not slavering around after women old enough to be his mother, was quite a companionable young man.

The country round Wandles Parva was pleasantly wooded. Roger and Dorothy strolled through the village along the main road which ran between Bossbury and London and went as far as Culminster Station before they struck off through the fields and woods, proposing to work round to the great park of the Manor House. In this park was the famous Druid Stone, sole survivor of what may have been a complete circle of trilithons or sarcen-stones. By the twentieth century, however, nothing remained save this one sinister, ugly, toad-like altar-stone, itself the sacrificial block in a local murder not more than twenty years old. A nineteenth-century owner of the manor house had planted a circle of pine trees around the Stone, and the place was reputed to be haunted. Roger and Dorothy, who had heard of the Stone from Mrs Bradley, were both very anxious to see it.

Once through the village they struck away from the highway and took to the common which adjoined it. The land here was open heath and birches, with occasional outcroppings of gravel and with little paths which seemed to have no particular beginning, purpose or destination, but which went running and winding up small rises and down long shallow depressions and then lost themselves among heather roots or in a gorse bush.

'Different from our last long walk,' said Roger. They kept the main road in sight and the woods round Wandles Parva at their backs, and came, at the end of an hour of easy walking, to Culminster, a little place where the railway branched to the south and west at a station which seemed disproportionate to the little grey stone town in which it stood.

They visited the Norman church and an ancient priory nearby, and then turned off to the north. This would bring them round in a circle to the Druid's Stone.

'It's a queer thing,' said Roger, after they had followed a little stream through a flat field into some woods, 'but I don't quite fancy these trees. Does it seem to you that there's somebody dodging and hiding?'

'Probably the village idiot,' said Dorothy, trying to speak lightly but aware of a most unpleasant sensation of fear. She, no less than Roger, had been aware of the uneasy atmosphere of the wood.

'You've noticed it, then?'

'I thought it was just my fancy.'

'That proves it isn't just mine. Look here, if it's that fellow Sim, I'm going to have it out with him once and for all. I'm sick of having that blighter trailing around.'

'But surely he wouldn't follow us down here? How could he know where we were?'

'That I don't know, but, if you don't mind being left alone for five minutes as soon as we come to a clearing, I'm going to make it my business to find out what he's up to.'

Dorothy disliked intensely the idea of being left alone, but she did not say so. Instead, as soon as they came to a clearing where woodmen had been at work and there were some fallen tree-trunks, she seated herself and said casually:

'Don't be long, and please don't get lost and not be able to find me again. I've never really liked the thought of being the Babes in the Wood.'

'Righto,' said Roger with equal casualness. 'I hope the blighter hasn't got a gun!'

He walked away into the smoke-green woods and left her alone with the tall pink willow-herbs, the wood anemones and her thoughts. He returned in a quarter of an hour.

'Mistaken,' he said briefly, seating himself beside her and filling his pipe. 'Nobody there. I've searched thoroughly. It's only a very small wood. We must be suffering from nerves.'

He was annoyed with himself, and they continued their walk in silence, both conscious, however, that the feeling they had of being shadowed was becoming, if anything, even more pronounced. Roger broke away twice to make a sudden raid into bushes, but came back moodily each time.

'I shan't be sorry to get back to the house,' said Dorothy.

'I agree,' he said. 'All right. Let's cut out the monolith, and get back to the main road, shall we?'

'I hate going back the same way.'

Both laughed, remembering the last time she had said the same thing, and then both grew sober.

'If we *had* gone back the same way, we wouldn't have got all mixed up with this headless body,' said Roger. 'But neither would we have had this week-end together. I tell you what—we'll toss. Fate shall decide for us.'

'It will, in any case,' said Dorothy, not without pessimism. 'Heads we go on, and tails we go back.'

'It's heads.'

'Oh! Oh, is it? Oh, well, I'm not really sorry. This is the prettier way.'

They tramped on, came out of the wood at last, and then followed a bridle-path in a long sweep north-westwards until they had encircled the Manor House. The last part of the walk had lain across open country, and, finding it perfectly empty, their spirits had revived and they were glad they had not given in to their nerves and imaginations.

Time and the war had wrought changes since
Mrs Bradley had first come to live in the Stone
House at Wandles Parva. For one thing, the Manor
House had ceased to be privately owned. It had
been purchased by the local council and later had
been commandeered by the Army. With the coming
of peace, the council had taken it over again, the
Druid's Stone had become a goal for sightseers,
and a right of way had been made between the
Manor park and the vicarage lane.

Roger opened the wicket-gate which led into
the grounds, and Dorothy led the way along the
narrow path to the circle of pines and the Stone.

Roger allowed her to go on, and then suddenly
he put down his ashplant and he himself dropped
flat on his face behind a rhododendron bush, and
cautiously peered round its edge.

He was not, after all, mistaken in supposing that
he and Dorothy had been followed. He waited
until the newcomer came opposite the bush, then
suddenly stretched out his long arms and grabbed
the man's feet away from under him.

There was an oath in a voice he thought he
recognized. Next instant he was astride his victim
and grinding his nose into the soft leaf-mould of
the park.

Dorothy turned in her tracks, and arrived at
Roger's side just as he stood up and yanked his
victim to a standing position.

'Now, then,' said Roger, who had hold of the
man by the front of his shirt, 'what do you think
you're doing, following me round?'

'I don't know you from Adam,' snarled the man. 'You let me alone, or——Why, I'm blowed if it isn't Mr Hoskyn! You must have mistaken me, sir. I——'

Roger clapped a long, hard palm over his mouth, and told him very roughly to shut up.

'You're coming to the police station,' he added. 'There's something damned fishy about you, Sim, and I'm going to find out what it is.'

'You'd better leave me alone!' said the man, immediately changing his tone. 'You've got nothing to charge me with, nothing! This path's a right of way. I've as good a right here as you have. Better, perhaps. I'm a Wandles man when I'm at home.'

'Look here,' said Roger, struck by a sudden idea, 'you were the fellow, I'll bet, who took a kick at me and did your best to settle my hash at Twickenham. Now you jolly well tell me why! And why did you sling me back my half-crown tip, dash it, at Whiteledge?'

'I haven't been in Twickenham. You've made a mistake. And you keep your hands off me, see, else I'll have the law on you,' returned Sim, more mildly but in the tone of what certainly seemed a good man's righteous indignation. 'I live in this village, I tell you. I've got a holiday from Whiteledge now Mr Lingfield's dead, and I'm stopping at home for a bit. Why should I do any harm? I can't help it if we run into each other, can I? It ain't no choice of mine!'

'Why did you swear the dead man was Mr Lingfield when you knew jolly well it wasn't?

Do you mean to swear Mrs Denbies' life away?'
demanded Roger wrathfully.

'I've got nothing again' Mrs Denbies, sir, and
you know it,' responded Sim. 'But I'll be on oath
at the inquest, won't I?'

They had to let him go. Dorothy watched him
out of sight, and then said:

'I'm positive it's the same man, although it's
hard to be certain without the moustache he was
wearing at the match.'

'It might be rather awkward if it weren't! You
weren't very close to him at Twickenham, and his
story seems reasonable enough.'

'I know, but—let's go back another way.'

'Chin up. We've scared him, I think. If he's up
to no good he knows we're wise to him. I don't
think we're likely to be bothered with him again,
and it's much too far round if we take any other
way now. Come on. Buck up. We'll hurry, and
keep him in sight.'

This, however, they were not able to do,
for, hurry as they would, they saw no more of
Sim.

The path led on through the woods direct to
the Stone, which squatted evilly in a clearing
surrounded by its ring of guardian pines.

Dorothy paused, and shuddered.

'I wish we hadn't come here,' she said. 'I—Roger,
I do wish we hadn't run into Sim like that down
here! And you said you were always finding him
at your elbow in pubs and places. Oh, Roger, you
don't think——?'

'What?'

'You don't think *he* murdered Mr Lingfield, do you?'

'No, I don't. I don't think that will wash at all. If Claudia is right, the body isn't Mr Lingfield, and until we know who it is we can't actually implicate Sim.'

'I suppose not. Let's get away. I feel thoroughly scared.'

'Do you? So do I. But I'd rather like to come here at night to get an authentic thrill.'

Dorothy shuddered. They walked along the path which skirted the pines and the Stone. 'By the way,' Dorothy began. Suddenly there was a sharp crack close at hand. Bomb-conscious, both dropped flat.

'Don't touch it! Fingerprints!' yelled Roger, getting to his feet. 'I felt it whistle past us. Did you?' He galloped up, pulled out his handkerchief, picked up a heavy spanner of the kind that are used in garages, and headed for the Vicarage lane.

'Come on,' he said. 'We've got him cold this time. We've only got to get this to the police.'

They arrived at the Stone House breathless. Laura Menzies came into the drawing-room to greet them.

'Hullo,' she said. 'I thought you were going to make a day of it. I suppose you were hungry. I knew you didn't take enough with you.'

Roger, prompted by Dorothy, recounted all their adventures, produced the spanner with his handkerchief still shielding it, and said they had eaten their sandwiches and were not in the least hungry.

'What were you going to say, Dorothy, when Sim chucked the spanner?' enquired Roger, when Laura had locked away the spanner in a cupboard.

'I forget. Oh, no, I don't! I was going to say that, if you work it out, it would have paid Sim to identify the body correctly if he were the murderer.'

'Why?'

'Well, he must have known that Mrs Denbies had said it wasn't Mr Lingfield, and, as she is the obvious suspect for the murder——'

'I get it. Rather too clever for Sim, though, I should have thought. He hasn't shown spectacular intelligence in his attempt to lay me out.'

'I suppose he does really mean to lay you out?' said Laura thoughtfully. 'I say, I expect you'd like some tea.' She rang the bell. 'I mean, take that kick on the head. You ought to have had a pretty severe injury from that, if he'd put a real jerk behind his boot. And, just now, in the woods, why not have used a gun if he really intended dirty work?——Or crept up behind you and coshed you over the head? I can't see any point in his goings-on.'

'But there *isn't* any point! I'm not dangerous to anybody. I don't know anybody's secrets. I can't make head or tail of it,' said Roger.

'Oh, well, we'd better leave all that to Mrs Croc. She'll be home first thing in the morning, I expect, if not tonight. I'm rather expecting her tonight. By the way, they've postponed the inquest for a day. You'd better ring up your boss.'

'I had notice. I have,' said Roger.

With this they did leave it, so far as conversation was concerned; but Roger was far from satisfied. It seemed to him that there was a mystery here which he (the most interested party, since his personal safety was involved) would do well to fathom. He decided to work out whether, unwittingly, he *was* in possession of somebody's dangerous secret.

To this end, he went up to his room at eleven o'clock, and, instead of going to bed, sat down with a notebook and took thought. He went over all the events which had taken place since he had met Dorothy on Maundy Thursday. He tried to discover any scrap of information which he might have obtained (and which he had not already given out to become public property either through police action or reports to the press) which might conceivably affect the safety of Sim or of anyone else at Whiteledge house.

Midnight approached and found him still unsatisfied. So far as he could tell, he had made no discovery except that the wrecked car was not the vehicle destroyed by the army exercises, and this fact he had immediately communicated to the police, who had been working on it for days. It was nothing to do with the car, then. Therefore there must be something further.

Midnight struck, and then twelve-thirty. He was not a whit nearer a solution. Action, he felt, was required, but the particular action which was applicable to his problem did not present itself. He was certainly not lacking in courage, but the thought of turning out into the night and searching for a will-o'-the-wisp antagonist who, for all he knew, might by that time have returned to his base in Surrey, seemed more than foolish.

He went to bed and put out the light. He did not fall asleep at once. His thoughts turned to Claudia Denbies. He wondered what she was thinking and feeling about her probable arrest and its consequences. He wondered what kind of woman she really was. The panic-stricken letter to Mrs Bradley indicated that she knew something more than she had admitted. He tried to visualize her appearance in court, and all the formality of a trial. He even began to fall in love with her again, but, before he could indulge this emotion far, he had dropped off to sleep.

He woke to the sound of a distinct (although he was inclined to think it not a very loud) noise. He sat up in bed and switched the light on.

'Put it out!' said a peremptory voice. Recognizing the voice as that of Mrs Bradley's secretary, Roger obeyed at once.

'Come and open the window,' said the voice. Roger leapt out of bed and as he got to the window he heard a curious scrabbling sound on the glass outside. 'Buck up,' said Laura, who seemed to be in the throes of gigantic effort. Roger thrust up the window and found himself confronted by a shock head which seemed to be moaning. 'Hike him inside—by the hair or something—I can't hold him any longer,' Laura continued, gasping. 'He's almost as strong as I am, and he's frightened to death.'

The captive, dumped by Roger on to the bedroom floor and threatened with disembowelling if he moved or uttered, was identified some two minutes later, for Laura drew the curtains, switched on the light, seated herself on the bed and then addressed the wretched object.

'So it's you, Smeary? I might have guessed it. Bumped your head for you, have I? Jolly good thing too. What do you mean by climbing up ladders at night? Do you want to be run in for robbery, you silly ass? Who do you think you are? Bally Romeo or something?'

The captive, permitted to sit up in order that he might reply to these enquiries, was an unkempt, daft-looking individual with a vacant, dull yet avaricious countenance. He began to whine and protest.

'I was to knock him on the yead,' he pleaded, nodding and grimacing. 'He's a German, he is. He's a German.'

'And you're an anti-cyclone!' retorted Laura. 'Of course he isn't a German! And, even if he were, it's none of your business to come here hitting people over the head. What d'you think Mrs Bradley would say?'

'I been with a fellow,' said Smeary, 'told me he was a German, and made Smeary promise to hit him over the yead.'

'What fellow? What did he look like?' demanded Roger.

'It's no good asking him,' said Laura. 'Listen, Smeary. Where's this fellow now?'

'By the Stone.'

'No, he isn't,' said Laura sharply. 'Where is he? Can you take us to him?'

Smeary looked cunning, and did not reply.

'Perhaps it's as well,' said Laura. 'He'd probably lead us up the garden. He's as cunning as a ferret.'

What did he give you?' asked Roger, going to work in the masculine way.

'Five shillin', and Smeary anna 'ad it,' mumbled the half-wit. 'Smeary anna 'ad it. But Smeary's goin' to 'ave it in the mornen.'

I'll come with you, and make sure he gives it you. Where are you going to find him?'

'He lodge along of blacksmith, so he do. He be black. Oh, ay, he be black as old Nickie.'

Roger glanced at Laura, and then hitched Smeary on to his feet. He patted him kindly on the head.

'Good man, Smeary,' he said. He gave him a shilling. 'Here you are. I'm not a German, you see. You find this black devil of yours, and tell him so. Miss Menzies, shall I boot him out now?'

'No. I'll give him a bite. He's probably hungry,' said Laura.

'Is he safe?'

Laura grinned.

'He won't be if he tries any tricks,' she said. 'And he knows it. Come on, Smeary, you old humbug. I've got a meat pie downstairs.'

She returned alone in half an hour.

'I saw him right off the premises and then unchained Lasher and Penn,' she said. 'We shan't have visitors with them let loose in the garden. I ought to have thought of it before. I wish I could understand this dead set at a lad like you. What have you been a-doing of? Any idea? Because, from what I got out of Smeary downstairs in the kitchen, *somebody* got at him to get at you.'

'I keep racking my brains, but nothing comes. I'm not in the least dangerous to anybody, if that's what you mean,' said Roger.

'Perfectly certain you're not? It was you discovered the body, wasn't it?'

'Yes, but Mrs Bradley was there, and Dorothy not far off, and the body gave nothing away. At any rate, not to me.'

'But you actually saw it first?'

'Yes, I did. That's correct. But, I tell you, that didn't mean a thing.' He remembered his own reactions and blushed with shame.

'You must have seen *something* you weren't intended to see.'

'I saw nothing except the body, and it was naked. There was nothing else at all. It looked perfectly beastly. I was sick,' he added, coming out with it.

'Yes, I'm glad it wasn't me. I've a horror of horrors. Well, that doesn't seem to get us anywhere. What other adventures have you had?'

'None.'

'Think clearly.'

'I *have* thought—until my head spins. There isn't a thing. I'm quite positive that I know nothing whatsoever that could harm a single living creature.'

'When the engine-driver had that remarkable turn on the night of the murder, I think you got out of the train?'

'I did, but I didn't see anything. I mean—not anything to do with the murder.'

'You wouldn't know, duck. You didn't know then that there'd *been* a murder, you see.'

'Well, I can't remember anything significant.'

'Pity you can't advertise those facts. What are you going to do now?'

'With your permission, I'm going to make my way to the blacksmith's at crack of dawn, lie in wait for this blighter, Sim, and mark him.'

'Mark him?'

'Literally. So that, whatever disguise he chooses to adopt, we're certain to know him again. I'm sick of being followed and waylaid.'

'Smeary keeps saying it was a black man. Oh, Lor!'

'What's up?'

'I suppose Smeary wasn't being used as a decoy duck?'

'Decoy——?' But Laura had gone. Roger followed, and saw her enter Dorothy's room. She switched on the light. The bed was empty.

Chapter Twelve

'Julia was careless, and withal,
She rather took, than got a fall:'
ROBERT HERRICK, *Julia's Fall*

'Whither, mad maiden, wilt thou roam?
Far safer 'twere to stay at home!'
ROBERT HERRICK, *To His Muse*

'NOW DON'T waste time swearing,' said Laura. 'Put on your clothes and come downstairs. How bright is this girl? The kind to go off with any handsome stranger?'

'No.'

'All right then. We add her brains to ours. Don't have a fit. Just be quick.'

Roger was quick. He pulled on trousers, a sweater and a sports jacket over his pyjamas and put on socks and shoes. Laura, who had been fully dressed, added a wind-jacket to her tweed costume.

'Get hold of a good thick stick,' she said. 'I've got a gun.'

'A gun?'

'Sure, bo. Mrs Croc. gets threatening letters sometimes. *She* never bats an eyelid, but *I* get nervous. Hence the gatling. Now for the plan of campaign. Remember that, so far as we know, it's you they want to get, not the wench. So watch out for yourself, and keep your eyes and ears open. I'll be right back as soon as there's anything to report.'

'Report be damned!' said Roger, resenting her cheerful tone. 'Let's go.'

'Spoken like a man, albeit a bone-headed one,' responded Laura. 'Come on, then. But you don't know the neighbourhood, and I do, so you takes your orders from me.'

'All right! All right! But for goodness' sake——'

'Get a move on? Right. This way.' She stepped to the French doors, opened them and walked out on to the lawn. Roger followed, pushing the doors to behind him and reflecting cynically that Mrs Bradley's French servants could probably take care of one another.

Laura, who apparently could see in the dark, gripped his sleeve, and, so joined, they walked across the lawn. By the hedge Laura stood still and listened. Then she pulled him down into cover, whispered, 'Keep still!' and searched the ground with a torch, after finding and leading off the dogs.

'Not this way,' she muttered at last. 'Come on.' They came round, still on grass, to the side-gate which led to the stables. They passed through the gate. The stable yard was paved, for the stables were used partly as a garage. Laura pushed Roger against the brick wall with a muttered caution to keep still, and studied the yard, illuminating it foot by foot until Roger could have leapt out and strangled her. He himself had no particular plan in his head for the rescue of Dorothy Woodcote, but Laura seemed to his overstrung nerves to be wasting precious time.

She herself did not think so.

'No car's been here,' she reported.

'Well, we'd have heard it,' said Roger.

'Possibly not. However, it means they can't have got far. We know what we're *not* looking for, and that's something. This is the shortest cut.'

'Where are we going? To the blacksmith's?'

'Vicarage. They've just been given a blood-hound.'

'The last dog I went out with——'

'I know. Don't worry. We shan't find a body this time.'

'Well, the brute will probably eat us.'

'Oh, no. He knows me.'

'By the way, I thought you said you'd unchained two brutes of your own?'

'I did. I've chained them up again now. They were prowling about. That's partly why I held you by the sleeve.'

'Thanks! As long as they didn't hold me by the seat of the trousers there's no harm done. Come along. Can't we walk a bit faster?'

The side road, or rather lane, along which they were walking was bounded by very high hedges, and was in consequence as dark as a pit. Roger did his best to step out, and, like most people who had experienced the black-out during the war, did fairly well. Very soon a tug on his arm brought him up short by the side of a long stone wall.

'Up with me,' murmured Laura, 'while I speak to the hound.' A whimper from somewhere beyond the wall lent point to this remark. 'There, then, Boss!' she added. 'His name's Boscastle. He was born there. Good boy! Come for a walk!'

She dropped down over the wall; there was the rattling of a chain, and then Laura's voice again. 'Stay just where you are, Roger Hoskyn. I'll have to come out of the door in the kitchen garden. There's a bolt on this side.'

She soon rejoined Roger. The dog, snuffing, laid his nose to what seemed a very hot scent, and they had much ado to keep up with him.

'Dorothy must have dressed, that's one thing,' remarked Laura. 'I've given the hound her pyjama jacket to smell. It was lying on the bed, so I brought it. He seems to have cottoned on. Of course the girl may just have gone out for a quiet country ramble. You never know.'

'If she has——' said Roger fiercely.

'Oh, hold your horses! You aren't married to her yet,' retorted Laura. 'If she has, we're no worse off. I think this is rather fun.'

'It might be, if it weren't so serious. My God! I hope we find her!'

'We'll find her, don't you worry.'

With the dog pulling hard, they came on to the

Culminster Road, but it was not until the dog struck off on to the common and commenced smelling its way along one of the rough little paths which began and ended without apparent reason, that Roger began to suspect that their errand was going to prove fruitless.

By the time the dog crossed the road—Laura, by this time, was keeping her torch on, and the progress they were able to make was rapid—Roger thought it was time to protest.

'I say,' he said, 'I know what's happening! This confounded brute is dragging us along by the way we went this afternoon! It's no manner of use at all! We're doing no good! And all this time——'

'Don't worry,' said Laura. 'I'm sure she's all right, but I think we ought to give the hound his head.'

Roger could have wept, but he could do nothing by himself, and he knew it. Miserable, frustrated and frightened, he strode anxiously after Laura and the dog.

The bloodhound faithfully followed the trail which led to the Stone in the Manor park. Twice more Roger tried to protest, but his objections were overruled by Laura, who suggested that, as they did not know where Dorothy had gone or been taken, it would be as reasonable to follow the dog's nose as to try to find out for themselves what had been done with the girl, or what she had done with herself.

The path through the Manor woods was inky dark. Roger summoned his courage. He was abnormally imaginative and strongly subject to impressions, and it seemed to him as though every dip and thick shadow concealed an enemy. He was thankful to come into the clearing ringed by the sombre pines, and to be able to say to Laura, as they shone the torch over the Stone:

'You see? A wild-goose chase, after all.'

This comfortable conclusion was ruined by the behaviour of the dog. It whined, tugged, attempted to bark, and then began to whimper, this last in accents which turned Roger's blood to water and even impressed the heroic Laura.

'Oh, lor!' she observed beneath her breath. 'I forgot that someone was murdered here. Dogs can see ghosts, so I've heard! Wonder what the brute *can* see?'

'You don't believe in ghosts, do you?' asked Roger, fearfully.

'I have Highland blood,' returned Laura, in a highly significant tone. The dog, which had been tugging, suddenly hung back; this with such force that Laura's wrist gave way and the dog, with his chain dangling, tore away, not in the direction of the Vicarage, but towards the Manor house.

'Now, what?' said Laura. 'Come on. We'd better get him back. The idiot must have gone crazy. Besides, he's A.W.O.L., so it certainly wouldn't do for us to lose him.'

A former owner of the Manor, during that oddly constituted period when port took the place of claret as a gentleman's wine, had built a watch-tower just outside his terrace boundaries. At the door to this tower the bloodhound sniffed and whined.

They could hear him from a considerable distance away, and it was Laura who, from her knowledge of the neighbourhood, was able to deduce where he was.

'You see?' she whispered triumphantly. 'I bet you didn't come *this* way this afternoon!' She tried the door. It opened. The dog began to scramble up the stairs. Laura, lighting the way with her torch, went after him. Roger, propping the door open with a large stone from the adjacent rockery over which, cursing in agony, he had tumbled, went bounding after her.

There was a door at the top of the stairs. Laura twisted at the handle, then transferred the torch to her left hand. She took the small revolver in her right, and kicked open the door whilst remaining in cover beside the wall.

There was no reaction from within. Roger came level with her, and bent to brush soil from his trousers.

'Keep behind my gun,' she said. 'Come on!'

Together they entered. The little room at the top of the tower was empty. Laura switched on the electric light. A door in the opposite wall led on to a balcony. She opened this door in the same manner as she had opened the first one. The light from the room streamed out and shone on the black, iron railings. At the foot of the railings was something pale-coloured and silken, upon which the dog threw itself in frenzy. Roger pushed the dog away and picked up some very pretty silk pyjama trousers.

'What on earth are these doing here?' he asked. 'Does this mean Dorothy, or doesn't it?'

'I suppose it's to your credit that you ask the question,' Laura replied with a grin.

She took the pyjama trousers from him, rolled them up and put them into the pocket of her waterproof.

'Come on,' she said abruptly. 'I think I see daylight now, but I'm still not absolutely sure. Anyway, don't worry any more. She hasn't been kidnapped, that's clear. We'll get back to the Stone House. She's probably there by now. I'll go down the stairs first. You switch off the light when I call. Here, take the torch. Got your stick ready clubbed? We may meet with trouble when we leave this place. I don't know. You've certainly been neatly got out of the way.' She whistled the dog, and went downstairs. She called up to Roger, and he switched off the light. In five seconds he was beside her, and they were heading by the shortest cut for Mrs Bradley's Stone House.

'For goodness' sake keep your eyes skinned,' muttered Laura as they made what haste they could over the turf of the park towards the wicket-gate which led to the vicarage lane. 'I don't want the thing to work out wrong. We've taken enough chances as it is.'

'You're telling me!' said Roger, between his teeth.

'I'm not worried very much about the wench, except in so far *as you're* concerned,' said Laura. 'Look out as we pass the bushes getting back to the house. There's a brain behind these manoeuvres and a pretty good one, though I say it. If you hear me say "Heel!" drop flat. I shan't really be speaking to the dog, although I hope that's what it will sound like to anybody listening in.'

'All right,' said Roger. 'Meanwhile I suppose we return him.' As Laura had left the vicarage garden door ajar, there was no difficulty in returning the bloodhound to his kennel. They chained him up, and then walked up the sandy lane and so regained the Stone House.

'Stand still a minute whilst I reconnoitre,' said Laura, as soon as they drew near Mrs Bradley's hedge.

'No,' replied Roger, with simple firmness. 'I'm not an egg that may get broken if I'm carelessly handled.' He continued to walk by her side. The wire which was stretched across the garden path of the Stone House from the trunk of a small laurel to a stone garden ornament weighing perhaps a ton and a half, shot them neatly on to their faces. Roger then thought that the house had fallen on him, but soon his Rugby football experiences aided his memory sufficiently for him to realize almost immediately that the weight on his shoulders was merely a very heavy man.

He lay flat, as though he had been completely knocked out by the assault. His assailant cautiously arose and began to turn him over, with the intention, Roger supposed, of smashing the back of his head on the gravel path. The man, he deduced, must be kneeling astride him, but he soon found that Roger's eleven stone six of dead weight was not as easy to turn as he had imagined. Roger lay like a log.

His assailant, confident that he was still unconscious, most unwisely got up from his strategic position astride Roger's body, and, stooping over him from the side, gave a last great heave and tumbled him on to his back. Roger flung out his right arm and turned his head to the left. His long legs then rose in a swift curve and shot over his head so that he made a complete back-somersault. His arm and hand turned with his body, and, as he completed the backward roll, he bent his right leg and brought it in close to his right arm. With his left leg he reached well back, and so came to his feet in a balanced position with his fingertips on the ground. As his unguarded opponent attempted to grip him, he got to his feet with a tremendous lunge and, throwing up his arms to get the distance, he jerked his head up under his stooping opponent's jaw.

As the man gave a cry and then crashed, Roger remembered Laura. He had lost her torch in the struggle, and now called out to her, hoping that she was not injured.

'I'm all right!' she replied. 'I lost touch with that blighter, Smeary, after the preliminary encounter. Where are you?'

'Here!' called Roger. 'I've lost the torch. I'd better try to locate it. By the way, my bloke wasn't Sim.'

'Never mind! Let's get back to the house. I've

lost the gun, too. We'll look for them both in the morning. It shot out of my hand when I took the toss over that wire.'

'I didn't hear it go off.'

'It wasn't loaded.'

'Wish I could have secured my bloke,' said Roger. 'Oh, Lord! My hands *are* in a mess from that gravel! How are yours?'

'In ribbons, I think. They feel like it. We'll have to wait until morning, and then put the police on the track.'

'But Dorothy?'

'Yes, I know. But it will be morning soon. I'll 'phone the police as soon as we get indoors.'

She could not keep this promise until she had bound up her cuts. By that time the dawn had come.

'I suppose,' said Roger, 'she's not come back while we've been gone? I've been thinking that if one of those fellows was Sim—I say, we really ought to have collared one of them, you know——'

'Let's go up and look,' suggested Laura. Dorothy was asleep. She woke when Laura went in and switched on the light.

'Hullo,' she said. 'I think I've been mixed up in the murder. I've had the most peculiar night. What have you done to your hands?'

Laura drew up the blinds, and the grey morning made the electric light look pale. Laura switched it off, and seated herself on the bed.

'We've had quite a peculiar night ourselves,' she said; she described their adventures. 'And it seems to me,' she added at the end, 'that whoever worked the scheme had a passable working knowledge of your boy-friend's psychological reactions. Mine, too, I regret to confess. They had even allowed for the bloodhound. Rather subtle of them, that. They saw to it that we were led a dance, and one that gave them nice time, I should think, to fasten that wire across the gateway. If we'd come in by the kitchen garden entrance, or the stables, it would have been just the same, I expect. I take it the entrances were all wired, and all they had to do was to pass the word to the others to tell them which way the little victims had selected. Very pretty for them, but rather annoying for us. And now, what happened to *you?*'

'I heard a noise, or so I thought, and got up. Then I heard you and Roger talking to someone— threatening him—so I dressed, and came along to share in the fun. But as I came out of this room somebody threw a thick cloth over my head and bundled me along towards the stairs. Then a man picked me up and muffled my head, still in this cloth, underneath his overcoat. I was not able to do a thing. He took me along to the garage, put me into a car, locked the car door and then took the cloth off my head. It was pitch dark. He said they wouldn't hurt me, and that I was not to worry. I was much too furious to worry. I didn't see his face. He had a scarf muffled nearly to his eyes, and a soft hat pulled right down. I suppose I was locked in the car for about an hour. It got so cold that I thought I should freeze. Then the

Frenchman—Henri—came out in his dressing-gown and unlocked the car, and brought me into the kitchen, and gave me some coffee and a hot-water bottle. Then he told me to go back to bed and not to worry. He put some brandy in the coffee. I didn't like it much, but it sent me to sleep, I think. I asked whether you two were all right, and he said you were.'

'Good old Henri,' said Laura. 'He's a sensible sort of old idiot. I must have a word or two with him. I suppose one of those men trailed the better half of your pyjamas to the observation tower, and left it there for us to find. Didn't you miss it, by the way?'

'Yes, but I kept my dressing-gown on when I came back to bed. I was frozen, and it seemed quite the best thing to do.'

'So it was. Look here, you'd better have breakfast in bed, and make sure you're not going to catch cold.'

'If I'm going to catch cold, I've caught it. I don't want to stay in bed. If there's going to be fun I want my share of it.'

'You'll do as you're told. It won't hurt you for once, I suppose?' said Laura, looking belligerent.

'No,' said Dorothy, meekly snuggling down. Laura regarded her intently, and then continued:

'Well, I should think they've shot their bolt. You didn't get any inkling as to the identity of the gentleman sportsman who put you in the car, I suppose? I know you said you couldn't see his face, but——'

'I'm almost certain I've heard his voice before, but I can't remember where. Except for that, and beyond the fact that he was pretty big—long-armed and broad—and was very gentle—most annoying! He behaved as though I were about two years old—I couldn't tell you another thing about him.'

'It wasn't the chauffeur, Sim?'

'Oh, no, not the chauffeur Sim!'

'Are you positive?'

'Absolutely. Sim is fairly broad, but I shouldn't think he's a quarter as strong as this man. No, it wasn't a bit like Sim. He was really rather nice, although it irritates me to admit it.'

'I see. Very odd. You don't feel all nerves? Or do you?'

'No, of course not.'

'Well, I don't know so much about that,' said Laura, getting up. 'For a delicately nurtured child who has been apprehended and gagged by thugs, and incarcerated in a garaged car at dead of night, you take things pretty coolly.'

'There's no other way to take them,' said Dorothy. Laura went downstairs and found Mrs Bradley at breakfast.

As soon as the sun was fairly up, Laura went out to investigate. She had been correct in her surmises. Wires had been fixed across the stable entrance and the side gate as well as the front gate by which she and Roger had entered. She had come out armed with a pair of wire-cutting pliers and soon removed the obstacles. Then she went round to the stables and had a look at the garage, but did not go in.

There was nothing much to be seen. Mrs Bradley had come back by car, so Laura called upon George, the chauffeur, who lived in a cottage adjacent to the house.

'Is the young lady any the worse, Miss?' enquired the chivalrous George.

'I expect so, but you wouldn't know it. That kid's got pluck,' replied Laura, regarding her own bandaged hands with pensive satisfaction. 'I got home on my bloke, George, and I shouldn't wonder if Mr Hoskyn's aggressor didn't pretty nearly chew his own tongue off. It's no joke being butted under the chin when you're not anticipating same, and the said Hoskyn is by no means such a string-bean as he looks.'

'Marked him, did you, miss?' said George, betraying sober and congratulatory interest in Laura's own exploits.

'Yes, I believe so. I haven't mentioned that to anyone else, so keep it under your hat. He didn't tackle me squarely, and I tore out a chunk of his hair. I've got it as a souvenir in a little tin box upstairs. Heaven send it's not lousy, that's all. By the way, you did a good job, George. Sober but hearty congratulations and all that. We could not have foreseen the wire. Now, mind! Not a breath to either of them! Glad you could help.'

Upon this secret and sinister note Mrs Bradley's henchmen parted. Laura returned to bed to make

up for the sleep she had lost, and all three young
people remained within doors all day. Mrs Bradley
showed herself in the afternoon, heard the whole
story and clicked her tongue, but made, to the
disappointment of her hearers, no particular
comment. In response to a question from Dorothy,
she reported that Claudia Denbies was as cheerful
as might be expected. She left it at that, and then
reverted to the events of the night.

'Deduced that you would use the bloodhound;
handled Dorothy as though she were a two-year-old
child (except that one wouldn't leave a two-year-old
child to freeze to death in a car), and selected a
young lady's pyjama trousers to lay a false trail. . . .
Ah, that paints a strange portrait,' she said, with
a sudden loud cackle.

'Further to that,' said Roger, who had been
keeping this news-item up his sleeve all day,
'somebody got into my room while we were gone
and has made a great dent across the pillow, leaving
a long, dirty mark.'

'Shows how necessary our plot was,' said
Laura.

Chapter Thirteen

'Go and catch a falling star,
Get with child a mandrake root,
Tell me where all past years are,
Or who cleft the devil's foot:
Teach me to hear mermaids singing,
Or to keep off envy's stinging,
And find
What wind
Serves to advance an honest mind.'

JOHN DONNE, *Song*

WEDNESDAY MORNING came and with it an outburst of early rising at the Stone House. Célestine had everybody up at half-past six, Henri had breakfast—that, to his mind, almost lascivious English cooked breakfast which, in over twenty years of service, he had not been able to train Mrs Bradley to cease from offering her guests—on the table by a quarter past seven, and George, the chauffeur, had the car on the gravel at eight.

The inquest was called for ten o'clock, and

was held in the dining-room at Whiteledge. A nervous Roger, an interested but slightly anxious Dorothy, an urbane but unusually silent Captain Ranmore, a peevish but recognizably uninhibited Lady Catherine, an incredibly beautiful Claudia, a smart, silent Sim with an incongruous bit of sticking-plaster on his head, a dignified Bugle and an alert and birdlike Mrs Bradley were provided with seats, and the coroner sat without a jury.

'This is not,' said the coroner, a precise but apparently non-committal man, a local solicitor, 'a court of justice but a court of enquiry. We are here to ask how a man came by his death. If any of the interested parties wishes to be legally represented, that can be permitted, but please to give your names distinctly so that I may write them in my notes.'

Roger's eyes travelled to a tall, dark, beautifully tailored man who rose at once and said:

'I represent Mrs Claudia Vesper, who is usually known as Claudia Denbies.'

'Your name?' enquired the coroner.

'Alastair Charles MacAdam.' Whilst the tall man was declaring himself, Roger noticed the inspector and the sergeant, who had seated themselves very unobtrusively at the end of his row. Whilst he was looking in their direction, another man got up and said that he was Algernon Bliss Simonds, and that he represented the railway company.

At this point the door of the courtroom opened, and three men were shown in. The coroner looked up sharply and asked:

'Who are these people?'

'The engine-driver, fireman and guard you called, sir,' answered the policeman who had let the men in. The coroner looked at them severely, and motioned them to a bench.

'Now perhaps we can proceed,' he said. 'Call Inspector Lucas.'

'Waste of time,' observed Lady Catherine. 'We had all this before.'

The inspector gave evidence of having been called to see the body. The doctor who followed gave evidence that the man would seem to have been dead for between eight and twelve hours when he saw him, which was approximately at twelve noon on Good Friday morning.

'Did you come to any conclusion as to the cause of death?' enquired the coroner.

'No, sir,' replied the doctor, who was a stolid man with a humorous mouth, 'I did not.'

'But I understood the corpse to be—to have been decapitated. You do not know whether decapitation causes death?'

'It can do so,' replied the witness, with austere enjoyment, 'but in this case I do not think it was necessarily the decapitation which caused death.'

'You mean you think that the man was already dead when he was decapitated?'

'That is my opinion.'

'What grounds have you for that opinion?'

'The complete absence of bruises, no sign of the man having been tied up, and no physical evidence that he had been drugged. The body presented no evidence of any recent injury at all, except that the head was missing.'

'Then, if so, I do not think I follow your reasoning. If the corpse showed no other sign of injury, why should you assume that decapitation was not the cause of death?'

The doctor employed a variety of learned terms unintelligible to anybody in court but Mrs Bradley, who happened to be a doctor herself, in describing the reactions of tissue injured before and after death, and then added, 'But the absence of other injury would be, in itself, in my opinion, sufficient proof. It is not consistent with the rest of the evidence to suppose that the man committed suicide, because of the missing head, and I am also not prepared to believe that he lay across the railway line merely at another person's orders.'

The next witness was Roger. He found that he was no longer nervous, for the court was so quietly formal, in spite of the fantastic evidence which had to be given, that he felt calm and entirely clear-headed.

'Now, Mr Hoskyn,' said the coroner, 'you are the person who discovered the body. I think you had better tell the court exactly what occurred.'

'I was walking on the common not far from Whiteledge on the morning of Good Friday last when I entered a small copse and saw the body.'

'One moment, Mr Hoskyn. Were you alone when this occurred?'

'Oh, no. I was with Mrs Bradley and Miss Woodcote.'

'Are they in court?'

'Yes.'

'Had you any particular reason for entering the copse?'

'Yes. I followed the dog which we had taken out for a run.'

'Could you not have called him?'

'No. He was not my dog and wouldn't have come, I imagine.'

'But you did not even try calling him?'

'No.'

'To whom did the dog belong?'

'To Miss Clandon, I believe, but at any rate, not to any of us who were with him.'

'Is it, in your opinion, right or reasonable to take out a dog over which you have no control?'

'Well, you see . . .'

'I think you had some special reason for taking a dog out that morning. Will you please tell me clearly what it was?'

'We thought the dog might track Mr Lingfield, who, of course, had been missing all night.'

'With your permission,' said Mrs Bradley rising, 'I should point out, perhaps, that the dog was taken out by me, and not by Mr Hoskyn. When the dog ran into the copse Mr Hoskyn gallantly followed.'

'So did you,' said Roger.

'And the dog had, in point of fact, tracked down Mr Lingfield's body?' said the coroner.

'That is so, sir. Mrs Bradley and I then saw the

body, and—well, the police came up then, and took over.'

'The police came up? Why?'

'They were all over the heath searching for Mr Lingfield, and Mrs Bradley whistled them up.'

'Oh? She could whistle up the police although she couldn't whistle up the dog! Was that it?' asked the coroner, pleased with his own wit.

'The police were more intelligent than the dog,' said Roger, smoothly. 'They came when called.'

Claudia Denbies was the next witness. She was taken over her previous evidence, but still declared resolutely that the dead man was not Lingfield.

'But you do realize,' said the coroner, remarkably gently, 'that the body has been recognized and sworn to by the chauffeur and valet, Herbert Sim, whom I shall call in a moment, to be that of Mr Lingfield, don't you, Mrs Den—Vesper?'

'I realize it, yes,' said Claudia, 'but my statement——'

'My client's statement,' said Mr MacAdam, smoothing his waistcoat as he rose, 'is also made upon oath, sir.'

'No one was suggesting anything else,' said the coroner, looking prim. 'One of the witnesses is mistaken, that is all. It remains to discover which one.'

'Thank you,' said Mr MacAdam.

'Do you pretend,' continued the coroner, returning to Claudia, 'to know as confidently as his manservant the details of——'

'Mr Lingfield's physical peculiarities,' said Mr MacAdam, rising again, 'were very well known to my client. She nursed him in hospital during the first World War, which you probably recollect, sir.'

'Oh, ah, er, yes,' said the coroner, recoiling from this simple revelation. 'Oh, I see. And during this—er—nursing——'

'Certainly. Mr Lingfield was suffering from——' He ostentatiously flicked open a typewritten folder.

'Yes, yes,' said the coroner. 'I think we can leave that, Mr MacAdam. Nevertheless,' he continued, turning to Claudia again, 'I must ask you (and *not* your lawyer,' he added, glaring boldly at the beautiful solicitor who appeared to be cracking a small joke with Mrs Bradley), 'I must ask you to give me an answer to my question.'

'Yes, I *do* know,' said Claudia sharply, 'and Mr MacAdam has told you why. I know perfectly well that Mr Lingfield had two noticeable scars on the left buttock, and I even know how he got them, because, as a matter of fact, he told me all about it himself. He was getting through some barbed wire when he was poaching rabbits, and he caught his trousers and tore them and his—and himself, too.'

'Poaching? But he had plenty of land of his own!'

'He always preferred poaching on other people's property. My late husband often remarked on it,' said Claudia with an emphasis unmistakable in the circumstances.

Somebody laughed and the coroner coughed a rebuke. Then he asked suddenly:

'*Which* buttock?'

'The—the left; no, the right,' said Claudia.

'Call Herbert Sim,' said the coroner. Sim, his buttons shining and his chauffeur's cap smartly under his arm, looked as though he were going to click his heels and salute the coroner. The coroner regarded him mildly.

'You have no doubt that it was your employer whose body you saw?' he enquired in gentle tones.

'No doubt, sir.'

'Describe the marks of identification which gave you the impression that it was Mr Lingfield who was dead.'

'Scars, sir. On the posterior, sir. Two. About three inches apart. Shaped like you'd tear your trousers, sir, on barbed wire. Bluish, sir. For a dark-complected man, Mr Lingfield had a very white skin.'

'Which side were these scars?'

'On the left, sir. Mr Lingfield was a right-handed gentleman.'

'What has that to do with it?'

'If you'll notice, sir, with very few exceptions a right-handed gentleman will put his left leg through first, sir. Same with getting into his trousers, if you'll notice.'

'I hadn't noticed, but you may be right. You swear to the left buttock?'

'Oh, yes, sir. And, as I say, sir, the marks had

kind of bluish edges, and was raised a bit. The wire was very rusty, I should fancy. He was lucky not to have blood-poisoning, and so I told him at the time I see them first.'

'He doesn't seem to have been very lucky afterwards,' said the coroner, dismissing the witness, whom he privately classed as a scoundrel, although not, in this instance, a liar. He then called Claudia again.

'Mrs Den—Vesper, you will understand why I attach so much importance to these scars. We must correctly identify this man. Now, since you came before me at the preliminary enquiry, I have devoted some thought to the matter, and I want you to tell me, if you can, any *other* reason you had for supposing that the dead man was not Mr Lingfield.'

'I had no other reason. It was just the scars. I'm afraid there was nothing else to go by.'

'And are you still prepared to hold to your statement in view of what Sim has just said?'

'Of course I am. If I really thought it was Harry I should have said so.'

'I am not——' The coroner stopped, and gazed in exasperated enquiry at Mr MacAdam, who had risen in his place and was elevating a handsome nose (not completely of Scottish extraction) preparatory to offering battle.

'Sir!' said Mr MacAdam, in awful tones.

'If you please,' said the coroner, waving him back into his seat. 'I was about to say, Mrs Den—Vesper——'

'Do call me Denbies. I'm so much more used to it,' said the witness.

'Very well, Mrs Denbies. I was about to say that I am not impressed with your evidence of identification. It seems to me much less convincing than that of the valet Sim. Nevertheless, to clear the matter up, as there seems to be this dispute, if you did not believe the dead man to be Mr Lingfield, whom did you suppose it to be?'

'My husband, Vassily Vesper,' replied the witness, creating by this statement such a sensation that, as she caught her lawyer's horrified eye, she involuntarily smiled.

'But,' said the coroner, himself completely taken aback by this disclosure, 'how did you—what made you—why did you not tell me this at the last hearing?'

'If you did not believe me when I told you I did not think it was Harry Lingfield——'

'But the scars?'

'Vassily had similar scars.'

'That is very curious, surely?'

'Oh, yes, very.'

'How do you explain it?'

'I suppose there was some more barbed wire somewhere.'

'Were they—was it——?'

'They were not both climbing under barbed wire at the same time—no. But my husband had his scars first.'

'Can you prove that?'

'No. You must take my word for it. I am still under oath, you know.'

'Mrs Denbies, you must please not to appear flippant. This is a serious matter. You now tell me that to the best of your belief the body you were shown in the mortuary was that of Vassily Vesper, your former husband?'

'Not my former husband. I mean, we were not divorced. The answer to your question is, yes I do. I know quite well that it was.'

'Although you cannot remember on which side Mr Lingfield had his scars?'

'I'm no good at right and left, but if you'll get the clerk or someone to stand and turn round—oh, thank you, Mr MacAdam!—I can assure you that Vassily's scars were on *this* side.'

She pointed to Mr MacAdam's perfectly clothed and elegantly rounded posterior.

'Oh, on the left, were they?'

'If that's the left, yes, they were.'

'I think you know that the scars on the body were also on the left.'

'Of course I know. That's what I'm trying to point out. Harry's were the opposite side.'

'But Sim disputes that,' said the coroner.

'I never knew you were married to Vassily Vesper!' said Lady Catherine, annoyed that she was disregarded. She remained so, however, except for the coroner's irritated click of the tongue.

'You know that for certain?' he demanded. 'You seemed very doubtful just now. Was Mr Lingfield a left-handed man?' He was still addressing the witness.

'I can't remem——Oh, yes, I can, though! I think he must have been right-handed. At least, he used to shoot right-handed. Still, it might be awkward not to, so that wouldn't prove much, would it?'

'It would depend upon what you wanted to prove,' said the coroner. 'Call Inspector Lucas, again.'

The inspector made way for Claudia, and the sergeant gallantly handed her a chair.

'A bow and arrow?' said the coroner, when the inspector had answered his first question. 'Oh, I see. That's the kind of shooting Mrs Denbies had in mind. I suppose that makes rather a difference.'

'Our submission, sir,' continued the inspector, 'is that the deceased was killed by being shot through the throat or the jugular vein by an arrow, his head being afterwards removed.'

'But it's only a theory?'

'Nothing but a theory, sir, of course. And, at that, we owe it to Doctor Lestrange Bradley, sir,' he added handsomely, 'who was the first to make the suggestion. We thought of a gun.'

'I see. That was why the head was cut off?'

'That again is only theory, sir, of course, but there would be need to disguise the actual means of causing death.'

'It might be worth your while to look into it. I can see that. But why a bow and arrow? I believe that was mentioned before. Ah, yes! I have it here in my notes about using the right and left hand.'

'The house-party were apt to practise archery, sir. It was one of the pastimes provided for the guests by Mr Lingfield. I believe he was himself a good archer.'

'Call Hector MacIver,' said the coroner.

MacIver was short and squat. He had a small scrubby beard which made him look a good deal older than he was, and the childishly candid eyes which are not often set in brachycephalic skulls. He was sworn with a solemnity and a frightening importance which he himself involuntarily created by calling for the Roman Catholic instead of the Authorized Version.

'Your name?' asked the coroner.

'Hector James Andrew MacIver.'

'You are an engine-driver?'

'I am so.'

'Will you describe your experiences on the night of Thursday, the 29th of March?'

'I will do that. We were a wee thing late, ye ken, and I was not just easy in my mind that we would run to time. There is being just a bit anxious I was, but not greatly.'

'There was nothing else troubling you, Mr MacIver, except that the train might be late?'

'Och, now, no, there was not anything troubling me at all, at all but that same. I will be a man wi'a record, ye ken.'

'No domestic worries?'

'Och, that!'

'Your wife was expecting a baby.'

'Och, aye. And we have him, aye, and he's bonny!'

'I'm glad to hear it. You were naturally a little anxious about your wife on that particular night?'

'Och, aye. She's no very bonny at siccan times, ye ken. But a's well. Aye, and the wean's fine!'

'I congratulate you. But—well, never mind, Mr MacIver. Go on with your story.'

'Aye. Well, we would have been running up the gradient before ye win to the level crossing we ca' Stump's Gallows, and I was thinking I could see a body across the line. So I put on the brakes and pulled up, and then I was thinking the body had nae heid on him. It was an awfu' thing, that. Man, man, but that was a gey awfu' thing! I will have seen it several times in the war, and I dinna wish to see it again. Guid sakes, but I couldna thole it!'

'You had a bad shock?'

'I did, so. But I needna hae fashed mysel' at that, for there was naething across the line at a'.'

'You believe that?' asked the coroner, very sharply. 'You did not believe it at the time! Do you really believe it now?'

'Och, aye.' The childlike gaze was rested on his. 'Och, aye. Why for should I not be believing it? Isn't it myself has the gift, bad luck to it for a mournful thing and a black handicap to a man's peace, so it is, so it is!'

'The gift?'

'Och, aye. Hae ye never heard tell of the gift?'

'You mean, I take it, that you suffered from a—from a hallucination?'

'Ye may ca' it that!'

'But haven't you ever been medically treated?'

'Aye.'

'Well, what did the doctor say to you?'

'He said, "Ye're fine. Dinna do it ony mair, ye gowk!"'

'He said——?'

'I had drink taken, ye ken,' explained Mr MacIver with the flicker of a smile. 'Hooch. I was very ba-ad. Very ba-ad, so I was, indeed. That was in Germany I was, I was so ba-ad.'

There was a rustle. The coroner quelled it with a glare which he then switched on to the witness, only to find its fierceness rendered impotent. Mr MacIver clearly expected sympathy and not censure. The coroner gave in.

'The—this experience left you, no doubt, with some—er—after-effects, Mr MacIver?' he suggested, abandoning his attempt to discredit the witness's sanity.

'I dinna ken,' replied MacIver, very gravely.

'Did you know the dead man, this Mr Lingfield?'

'Sir,' said the witness mildly, 'I put it to ye with a' possible respect, but ye should pay mair attention to the leddy.'

'To the——?'

'To Mrs Denbies,' said MacIver quietly. 'She tellt ye ye're chasing after the wrong deer, and ye dinna care to heed her. It's an awfu' mistake. Och, aye!'

'Answer the question!' said the coroner wrathfully. 'You are not here to direct me what to do.'

'I kent Mr Lingfield verra well, och, but verra well. A' that I am after telling ye the now is that the leddy is right, and Mr Lingfield, in *my* opinion, isna deid.'

'Oh, you think that, do you?' said the coroner. 'Well, I don't think we need that opinion. You had better stand down. Call Mr Hoskyn again.'

Roger, looking bored and feeling empty, went back to the chair which served as a seat for the witness giving evidence.

'Now,' said the coroner, 'take your time, Mr Hoskyn. On the day of the deceased's death you saw him alive at some time during the afternoon.'

'I don't know.'

'But I understand from the report that you saw him!'

'I don't know, really. You see, I've never met Mr Lingfield, so I don't know whether the man I saw——'

'Oh, you *did* see somebody? Who was with him?'

'The word is "were",' said Roger. 'The man I saw was accompanied by Mrs Denbies and by a boy, George Merrow, Mr Lingfield's nephew, I believe.'

'The man *was* Mr Lingfield,' said Claudia's solicitor. 'There is no argument against that, sir.

My client admits that she was with him. She even admits she quarrelled with him.'

'Thank you, Mr MacAdam,' said the coroner. 'No more of your shuffling, young man!' he added, addressing Roger ill-temperedly. 'Now then! You saw these three people together?'

'Yes.'

'At what time?'

'I don't know. Half-past five, I should say.'

'Then you saw one of them alone?'

'Yes, the boy, George Merrow.'

'What did you conclude from that?'

Roger involuntarily grinned.

'Oh, that they'd managed to get rid of the kid,' he answered, 'and go off riding by themselves.'

'After you had seen this boy ride past, it appears that you went to Whiteledge, the dead man's home. What made you think of going there?'

'Oh, I didn't *think* of it at all. The house happened to be a sort of outpost of civilization, and we'd lost our way, so we went and knocked to see whether they could tell us where we'd got to.'

'And in this house you saw Mrs Denbies and the boy, but not the man you had seen with them on the common. Did that not strike you as odd?'

'No. And even if it had, it needn't have. It was all explained very soon.'

'I should think so, too,' said Lady Catherine, who was tired of being ignored. 'Thirteen at table, of all unconscionable things! That's what Harry had done for George's party! But Harry never did have the very slightest thought for other people! I have

often told him so myself. I was never afraid of
Harry, no matter what people have told you!'

'Ah, yes, Lady Catherine,' said the coroner. 'You
were responsible for inviting Mr Hoskyn and his
fiancée to your—to this house. Now, if I might just
finish first with Mr Hoskyn——'

'I don't know any Mr Hoskyn,' protested Lady
Catherine. 'There would never have been any
question of Mr Hoskyn but for Harry's ridiculous
behaviour. And it's all nonsense for Claudia to tell
you that he rode away and left her like that. They
couldn't have quarrelled! I don't believe a word of
it! They were head over heels in love, and who
can blame them? Do you blame them? You may
not look intelligent, but I cannot think you would
blame them. I did not.'

'In just a minute, please, Lady Catherine!'

'Nonsense! It doesn't need swearing on a Bible
that Claudia met him after midnight. Everyone
knows that she did. Bugle knows, Sim knows, I
know. Even Mrs Bradley knows, although I swear
on the Bible I did not tell her.'

'Oh, hell!' said Roger, under his breath. There
was another stir in the courtroom, and the reporter
in the back corner scribbled vigorously, his tongue
at the corner of his mouth.

'Really, Lady Catherine, you must not interrupt
me or the witness,' said the coroner, very severely.
'Now, Mr Hoskyn, please attend to me closely.
You were in the train, I understand, driven by the
witness MacIver on the night of Thursday, March
29th, when the train was stopped near—er—he

consulted his notes—near the level crossing at Stumps Gallows. Is that so?'

'Oh, yes,' said Roger. 'I was on the train all right.'

'Do you identify the driver?'

'Yes. Mr MacIver drove the train.'

'Do you identify anyone else who was on the train?'

'Yes. I can see the guard and the fireman—I don't know their names, but there they are. There was also my companion, Miss Woodcote.'

'Will you describe what happened?'

'Nothing much. It only took about ten minutes. The train stopped and I got out. The driver thought he had seen a body on the line, and we—that is, the guard, the fireman and myself— looked about, but there was nothing out of the ordinary.'

'What do you mean by that?'

'No body, no head, no blood. Nothing that one would expect from such an accident. We looked all the way along the train and back along two hundred yards of the track.'

'To what did you attribute the driver's strange aberration?'

'I thought at first he must be tight.'

'I protest,' said the railway company's solicitor. 'You must not say that an employee of the Company was drunk in charge of a train.'

'And you, sir,' said the coroner with spirit, 'must not presume to give orders in my court.'

'Then let me urge, sir,' said the solicitor, 'that you suggest to the witness to alter the form of his answer.'

'As to that,' said Roger, 'I was going on to say—well, anyhow, I knew the man wasn't drunk. He knew what I thought and he told me to smell his breath. I did, and he hadn't had a drop. Well, then I was told he was worried about his wife, so I just thought it must be a sign of nervous strain, this headless body on the line. I mean to say——'

'Havers!' said Mr MacIver. 'I hae the gift, I tell ye. It's no a thing to boast about, and I wouldna be confessing to it if I wasna very sure that it is true.'

'Yes, I understand now,' said Roger, 'but at the time, you see——'

'You ascertained to your own satisfaction, then, that there had been no fatality,' said the coroner: 'All right. And now, Lady Catherine . . .'

'I beg your pardon,' said a rich and beautiful voice, 'but Lady Catherine Leith is not in a fit condition to give evidence in this or any other court. It is only fair that you should know that before you begin to question her.'

'Madam?' said the coroner, amazed.

'I support that contention,' said a stout man of vaguely Jewish aspect, rising from his place in the middle of the room, and speaking in a thin and unconvincing voice. 'I am Doctor Beni Yusman of Santiago.'

'Well, really, this is most disconcerting!' said the coroner. 'I had been counting upon Lady Catherine's evidence to throw some light on the matter——'

'I should think so, indeed,' said Lady Catherine good-humouredly. 'Mad I may be, and poor Mary,

too, but that's no reason why he should be kept
out of his grave like this. It's quite disgraceful,
and nobody knows what they suffer. Lucidly,
then, she went out in her car in the very early
morning, and only Sim knows when she came back
because her car was left out on the gravel. I only
know that because I am a Boy Scout and look at
tyres.'

'Thank you very much, Lady Catherine,' said the
coroner hastily. 'I don't think we need go into all
that. Now, Mrs Denbies——'

'No!' said Claudia's lawyer, speaking violently.
'My client admits nothing more! This witness is
quite mischievous, as you have just heard from
the two distinguished alienists who are present.
No account whatever can be taken of anything
that Lady Catherine says.'

'But I admit the truth of what she says,' said
Claudia calmly. 'And I thought the alienists were
for Mary Leith, not Lady Catherine. I would like
to make a further statement if I may.'

'Come up here,' said the coroner.

'I did leave the house that night—or, rather, very
early next morning,' stated Claudia, disregarding
the expression of helplessness and dismay on the
countenance of Mr MacAdam. 'But I did not go
to meet Harry—Harry Lingfield. I went to meet
my husband, Vassily Vesper. I know now that it
was a hoax, and that I was never intended to see
him, but—I went.'

'No, no!' moaned Mr MacAdam, almost wringing
his hands in his distress.

'I can't have Lady Catherine called a liar and a madwoman in public when she isn't either,' went on Claudia, throwing up her splendid head. 'I prefer to offer this voluntary statement.'

'Go on!' said Roger, *sotto voce*, but scarlet in the face with resumed love and dreadful anguish. 'Go on! Go the whole hog, you beautiful, adorable fool! Tell him you took your bow and arrows!'

'You admit, then,' said the coroner, 'that you met a certain gentleman at this rendezvous, and you assert on oath that it was not the deceased but another man of whom the court has never heard, that you went to see?'

'If you please, sir,' said the inspector, very drily. 'Things are beginning to come out, sir, which will hardly serve the work of the police, and may even hinder them in the execution of their duty if gone into closely at this early stage of the proceedings.'

The coroner, by this time nearly as red in the face as Roger, looked with some hatred at the inspector and proceeded to read, at a fast gabble, more or less what everybody had said. Condensed, there could be but one conclusion to draw from it. That he did not draw this conclusion was unforeseen but a great relief to everybody.

'I find,' he said, 'that Harry Lingfield, deceased, was murdered, by a person or persons unknown and by decapitation or other means, on the early morning of Good Friday last, March 30th, and I should like to add——'

'These damned riders,' said Mr MacAdam loudly

to Mrs Bradley. Mrs Bradley cackled. The coroner abruptly swept his papers together.

'You don't suppose Lady Catherine did it, do you?' asked Roger, struck by a not unpleasant thought, as he and Dorothy strolled out into the sunlit garden and went and stood idly by the pond.

'She did her best to put it on Mrs Denbies. Of course, it's the transport question, and the head being missing,' said Dorothy, 'that make the whole thing such a puzzle. It's all horribly mad, and yet horribly sane, too, if you know what I mean.'

'None better. I've tried to work it out until my skull feels like splitting with sheer frustration. *How* did the head get cut off? It couldn't have been a train, could it? I mean, for that, the body must have been placed right across the line as MacIver said. The neck must have rested on one rail. The driver couldn't help but know he'd run over it, I should say. After all, there's no black-out now, and wouldn't one feel the bump?'

'They'll try to find a driver who did know, and who hasn't said anything,' said Dorothy, shivering. 'Fancy knowing you'd done a thing like that! I think I'd come forward at once, if only to get the weight off my mind. Wouldn't you?'

'And then there's the head. Where is it? Of course, there was that fellow in the play who carried one about with him in a hat-box.'

'There are the clothes, too. It isn't easy to get rid of clothes.'

'Perhaps the murderer wears them. Or, of course, there's always the black market. I shouldn't think they ask many questions.'

'Well, I hope the police soon clear it all up, because, unless they do, there is only one thing that can happen.'

'You mean—Claudia Denbies?'

'I don't see anything else. And the coroner thinks so, too. I wonder, really, how many lies she told?'

'Do you think she went to meet Lingfield? Or do you believe that yarn about her husband?'

'Goodness knows. Anyway, who else is missing except Lingfield? That's the point.'

'That might be a thing that only the murderer knows. I suppose it *couldn't be the husband?*'

'You know, I can imagine, with anybody like Mrs Denbies, a husband might possibly be a nuisance. Could she and Mr Lingfield be concerned in it together?'

'Thompson and Bywaters, you mean? That's always possible. Crimes of passion—I prefer that description to anything which actually suggests sex, don't you——?'

'Infinitely. Passion is a tactful sort of Victorian, anti-macassarish word, isn't it?'

'So different from lust, lewdness, fornication and adultery, you mean?'

'Roger, what *is* a crime of passion? Are there really such crimes? It doesn't seem as though anti-macassars ought to lead to murder. They don't go together a bit.'

'Don't they, though? What about Adelaide Bartlett? What about the Seddons? What about——'

'But I don't know anything about any of them.'

'Oh, well! Anyway, that was a very odd line for Claudia—Mrs Denbies—to take, although particularly noble, I thought. You know, refusing to shelter behind the fact that Lady Catherine is cuckoo.'

'I don't know,' said Dorothy, frowning a little. 'It may have been noble, but, at the same time, if you see what I mean——'

'Well, come on! Out with it!'

'Well, I like her, of course, but—she's rather too intelligent, don't you think, to put a rope round her neck when there were Mrs Bradley and that man able and willing to say that no notice need be taken of Lady Catherine?'

'Talking of that, what an eye-opener! I can't say I'd have spotted it. Would you?'

'Yes. But, look, stick to the point.'

'Don't know that I want to,' said Roger, with a slightly shame-faced grin. 'No, hang it, you're perfectly right. One ought to face the facts. And I do see what you mean. At least, I think I do.'

'Yes. I mean that for some reason Mrs Denbies didn't want Lady Catherine to be discredited. The point is—what is the reason? Do you think she'd have liked to take it back when Lady Catherine mentioned the car being left out?'

'I don't know. It would account, though, as I

was going to say just now, for all that business of thirteen at table when there were only twelve.'

'What would?'

'Her being—well, not quite right in the head.'

'Oh, she may not be very good at counting up.'

'I think personally that she was unconsciously counting Lingfield all the time.'

'What do you suppose will happen next? Do you think the inspector will arrest Mrs Denbies at once?'

'I don't think there's much doubt about it.' Roger kicked the stone basin moodily. 'Somebody will be arrested, and, unless something startling turns up, it's almost bound to be Claudia. I should say she dished herself completely by that last statement she made. Besides, that lawyer of hers is scared stiff. He knew that if he let her open her mouth she'd put her foot in it. Bit of a fool, I should imagine. That fellow, I mean. He might have known that a woman—especially a red-haired woman—won't put up with having somebody jump down her throat every time she wants to say a few words.'

'You mean, then, that although you're determined to think she's innocent, you really believe that she's guilty.'

'Well,' said Roger, dislodging a piece of gravel with the toe of his shoe and kicking it viciously on to the well-kept lawn, 'you might put it like that, I suppose. But, if she's guilty, *what did she do with the head?* And who changed the burnt-out car for the wrecked one? And if the wrecked car was used to carry the body from the railway to the copse, why weren't there bloodstains inside it?'

'Perhaps there were.'

'No, no. The inspector would have taken it as Exhibit A if there had been. Instead of which, he's left it just where it was. Oh, well! School tomorrow! I ought to have gone back today, so there's something gained, I suppose. Still, term doesn't start until tomorrow. I say, you'll write to me, won't you?'

Chapter Fourteen

'God Lyaeus, ever young,
Ever honoured, ever sung,
Stained with blood of lusty grapes,
In a thousand lusty shapes,
Dance upon the mazer's brim,
In the crimson liquor swim;
From thy plenteous hand divine,
Let a river run with wine:
God of youth, let this day here
Enter neither care nor fear.'
JOHN FLETCHER, *God Lyaeus*

ROGER WAS not given to brooding during term-time, except in so far as he entertained occasional thoughts of vengeance upon certain childish miscreants; but he was disquieted more than he realized at first by the events of the Easter holiday and by his own apparently narrow escapes from injury and possible death.

He saw now, in the invitation to the Stone House at Wandles Parva, that Mrs Bradley had summed up the danger accurately and was determined to put him upon his guard. That he had, at the time, been insufficiently grateful for this kindly concern for his health and safety troubled him not at all, but what did trouble him was the continual, and, so far as he could see, insoluble mystery of all the abortive attacks which he had suffered. He still could not see that he possessed any knowledge which might prove dangerous to anyone else, and he racked his brain to find a clue to the puzzle. A minor mystery, but one not a bit less baffling, was the fact that the attacks upon him had been, comparatively speaking, so mild. It scarcely seemed as though his death could be the object of the encounters. He wondered whether someone was merely trying to frighten him; but, even so, he could not see any reason for this. He tried hard, when once school opened, to put the matter from his mind and devote himself to his little boys. Things were ordered otherwise, however. One fine day near the end of April had been set aside by the headmaster for a school journey. It happened that the Reverend Ashton Clinton had a passion for what he was wont to refer to as Old London—a passion which he desired his boys to share. Accordingly, he had arranged for Roger and another of the junior masters whose name was Parkinson to take some of the boys to Waterloo Station, and on to Westminster Abbey, the Tower of London, Saint Paul's Cathedral, and to anything of historic interest which fell between these major spectacles.

The expenses of the trip were to be defrayed

by the headmaster himself out of School Fund, a convenient and remarkably large nest-egg which was the result of various money-making pursuits such as school fines for minor breaches of the peace together with the profits from concerts, jumble sales and such other parochial knaveries as the headmaster and his staff were accustomed to permit from time to time for the purpose of adding to the takings.

The London outings, known to the school as Dekkers, were extremely popular with the boys; not nearly as generally so with the masters. To Roger, so far, they had been anathema, but this time, as he was to go with Parkinson, who was only two years his senior, and not with one of the elderly gentlemen who generally took a junior master in tow, the thought of a day out of the classroom was welcome.

The boys were to be provided with sandwiches; so were the masters. This was the general rule.

'But it will be hard,' said Parkinson, with a slight smile, as he pouched his portion of food with his mackintosh and a guide book, 'if we cannot give each other a breath of freedom during the hours of licensed victualling, Hoskyn, my man.'

Roger, who, on his previous Dekkers, two in number, had consumed stale sandwiches upon a bench outside the British Museum and had finished with a drink of water out of a small metal container at a public fountain, felt his heart warm still further to the expedition, and also to Parkinson, under whose auspices the outing, he felt, would prove to be blithe and bonny even beyond expectation.

Thirty boys were to be of the party, his own fifteen, whose average age was ten and a half, and fifteen out of the twenty apportioned to Mr Withers, the Sixth Form master. These boys were almost fourteen years old, and would normally proceed to their Public Schools at the beginning of the autumn term. The theory was that a thirteen-year-old should partner each ten-yearold and assist him to understand the beauty and grandeur of all that he would see in London.

To the Reverend Ashton Clinton a day in London was a full day. No time was to be wasted, and an elaborate and detailed Time Sheet was supplied to each boy on which to record what had been seen and noted, and, as the staff rather sensitively perceived, to act as a check on the masters, and to ensure that the boys had really been taken through the whole programme drawn up by the Head for their benefit.

Roger and Parkinson had 'got together' over the Time Sheets, and had had them filled in in their form rooms on the day preceding the journey. This labour of hoodwinking the headmaster had been possible owing to the fact that Mr Clinton had caught a cold and was not in school that day.

The idea itself had occurred to Roger, but not its logical application.

'I say,' he said to Parkinson, meeting him in the corridor at the end of morning break, 'I'm stuck

with my devils all day long today. I do call it just
a bit thick!'

'Same with all of us; no change of classes while
the old man can't take his subjects,' said Parkinson.
'Just have to lump it, that's all. Let 'em read their
library books. That's what I always do. Anyway,
you're luckier than I am. I've got the Sixth dumped
on me because my form have to visit Stokes' Farm
with Heathers. They've been promised it this last
fortnight, and the old man won't send me because
I'm going out tomorrow. He doesn't believe in too
many treats at one time!'

'Don't fret. It's a bit of luck for me that Heathers'
gammy leg won't stand a day of it in London.
Besides, I thought, if you agree, that we could get
the Time Sheets done.'

'Eh?' Parkinson began to smile.

'Well, I suppose we shall visit all the perishing
places that are down, so the kids might just as well
push a pencil over the spaces in class as waste time
licking their leads in public. What do you say?'

'I say you're a genius, my man! Save time? You
bet it will save time. We can miss out the Abbey
and give the boys some notes on it instead. That
ought to save us at least three-quarters of an hour.
We can also miss out either the Tate or the National
Gallery—I suggest the Tate. Then——'

'We'd never get away with it,' said Roger.

'Of course we would!'

'The kids have to write an essay, don't forget.'

'They won't know what they've seen and what
they haven't. The only thing they really like is

the Tower. They can spread themselves on that in the essay. We can remind 'em to mention the Abbey.'

'He'll probably set them some questions. Besides, the Sixth will have been before. They'll all know what to expect.'

'All right, all right. But get the Time Sheets filled in, anyway. It's the scheme of a life-time, my man!'

'I say,' said Kirby to Healy-Lunn, 'how about you and me going for a river trip on the *Sunbelle* instead of the Tower tomorrow?'

'How can we, lunatic?'

'Well, we've filled up our Time Sheets, haven't we? There's nothing else to worry about.'

'We'd be missed at once.'

'If we were it wouldn't matter. It's only Roger and Nosey.'

'We'll be shadowed by two of Form Three. Catswhiskers thinks we're going to look after the lousy little swine.'

'What a filthy idea! It won't come off. It can't! It's enough to ruin the day! One of them's my kid brother! We must repug—repudiate them.'

'*What* them?'

'Ignore their existence, fathead. Act as though they weren't there. Hang it, we're not their mothers.'

Healy-Lunn giggled.

'Jolly funny if we were,' he remarked. 'All right, then. What'll we do if we're missed?'

'Swear we got so interested in the White Tower or somewhere that we didn't notice the rest had gone on. Be yourself, for goodness' sake!'

'Well, I've never been to the Tower. I had measles last year. Remember?'

'You can have my last year's notes. I've got my worm-casts in them.'

Waterloo Station, although not crowded, was in its usual state of stir, activity and noise. Roger and Parkinson, having managed to separate their charges from the train which had brought them in to London, led the way out from the platform and, outside the gates, counted heads and then paired up the innocent-looking lads in meek, polite couples ready for the march through the streets.

By the time the party was out of the station and fairly launched on its hair-raising journey towards Westminster Bridge, Kirby and Healy-Lunn had contrived to get the two masters into the van by the simple expedient of twice leading the line down side-turnings and once into the side-door of County Hall.

'I'm sorry, sir,' said Healy-Lunn, aggrieved. 'But I thought we had come to the Abbey.'

'The Abbey, you oaf!' shouted Parkinson. 'You knew jolly well it wasn't the Abbey! Didn't you come to the Abbey last year with Mr Donaldson?'

'No, sir, I had measles.'

'Mr Donaldson didn't explain it to us as well as you and Mr Hoskyn will, sir,' put in Kirby. 'I've almost forgotten the way myself, so I'm not surprised——'

'Dry up! Perhaps we'd better lead the way, Hoskyn. Now you jolly well stick to our heels, do you understand, or I'll let you know what for when we get back to school.'

'Very well, sir,' said Master Kirby. 'I'm really very sorry, sir.'

'I suppose one of us ought to keep at the back to chivvy the line along,' suggested Roger, who had had this method explained by the senior masters, and had discovered that, with himself in the van and the senior master as whipper-in, it had really answered rather well.

'Oh, that be blowed! If the little horrors get lost, it's up to them,' replied Parkinson, firmly. 'Come on. I hate this poisonous parading of kids through the streets as though we were a couple of blasted ushers!'

'Well, aren't we?' said Roger, falling into step beside him. It was at this point that the line behind them executed a neat, precise manoeuvre which brought all the Sixth Form boys together, and their juniors thrust at the back. The column then continued to march breast-forward.

There was some loitering on Westminster Bridge to which the two young masters (who, far from holding their charges in the detestation which might have been expected from their way of referring to and addressing them, were really rather attached to the devil's brood they were supposed to educate), turned a blind eye while boats, tugs, barges, a dredger, launches and skiffs were passed in review by the boys.

At last the pilgrimage over Westminster Bridge was accomplished, and the boys, having had the Houses of Parliament pointed out to them, were marshalled to cross the road at the end of the Embankment. At this point one Percifer, a child of ten, was moved to demand that he should be permitted to set foot on Captain Scott's ship, which he understood was moored alongside the Embankment on the further side of Charing Cross Station.

Parkinson was inclined to favour the idea. By judiciously leaving out certain items of the headmaster's programme they would leave themselves plenty of time. He nodded, said, 'Round to your right, then,' and prepared to fall in in front of the line once more. Immediately the words were out of his mouth, however, his herd stampeded. Joyously they commenced to tear along the broad pavement of the Embankment towards their goal, visible at the moment only to the eye of faith.

The masters had a straight choice: to tear after them, or to stroll in their wake. Roger's instinct was to adopt the former policy, and smack all the heads within reach as soon as he could catch up with them. Parkinson, it appeared, had other views.

'Well, that lets us out for ten minutes,' he said contentedly. 'The cuckoos can't get on board, in any case, until we catch them up.' He thereupon produced cigarettes, and the two young men stood still to light them and then strolled casually in the rear of the boys.

The sunshine was pleasant and rather warm. The ancient river was a never-failing source of interest. The plane trees, not yet sooty, were brilliantly green. There was in the air that sensation of sparkle and excitement which London has the secret of conveying to her admirers, especially in the spring. Roger, smoking his cigarette, walked along gaily and without care. Parkinson, beside him, holding his cigarette between two thick fingers, hummed the stave of a seventeenth-century drinking song and seemed equally happy and at ease.

There was by this time no sign of the boys, for the scurrying business people and the holiday loiterers along the Embankment, having been washed slightly out of their course by the onrushing tide of the children, had lapsed into position with the effect that they now screened the route.

Parkinson had been in error in supposing that the boys would have to await his arrival before they could get on board. He had judged their minds correctly in believing that no boy would part with threepence of his own money, but he had not realized that in Master Kirby there were the buds of Napoleonic power.

'Our beaks have the money,' Master Kirby had said to the Sea Scout on duty, after the boys had swarmed joyously over an ingenious little stone stile and had hastened along the landing-stage towards the ship. 'They're just behind us. Thirty boys and

two masters.' As there were thirty school caps to
be counted, and other visitors to come aboard,
the Sea Scout nodded and the schoolboys took
possession of the ship.

Roger was relieved to find that everything had
settled itself except for the mere matter of payment,
but Parkinson, rather to his surprise, was somewhat
perturbed.

'I hope the little hell-hounds aren't going to
take matters too much into their own hands,' he
complained. 'That's the worst of bringing the Sixth
out. Cocky little devils! Do them good when they
leave us and become less than the dust for a bit
at their public schools. Kirby is going to Rugby.
Little blight!'

He spoke severely to Master Kirby when he met
him. Kirby was contrite.

'I'm awfully sorry, sir. We just thought it would
save you trouble, that was all. I didn't dream you
wouldn't like it, sir, really! Please be fair to me,
sir!'

'You jolly well stick to us in future.'

'Very well, sir.' He then stuck to them so faithfully
that he almost precipitated Parkinson down a steep
and narrow companion-way on to the deck beneath,
and then got jammed with Roger, Healy-Lunn and
a score of co-mates, in the chart-room until no
one could move either into its narrow passage-way
or out.

'And for God's sake get out from under my feet
and *stay* out!' snarled Roger, when this Black Hole
of Calcutta had been emptied.

'Very well, sir,' said Master Kirby, with an injured expression. 'But I thought Mr Parkinson said——'

'To hell!' said Roger, to the surprise and disapproval of two old ladies who were being shown over the vessel. By dint of the superhuman exertions of himself and Parkinson, who took it in turns to round up the boys and guard the queue of boys already rounded up, they contrived, at the end of nearly an hour, to collect their charges and get them off the ship.

Master Kirby, feeling that he had placed himself sufficiently in the public eye for the time, stood at the head of the queue and assisted the masters with his advice.

'You ought to go through the galley and head them off there, sir,' he said helpfully. 'I don't see how Mr Parkinson is ever to get all those little Form Three boys together. I think the ship is very interesting, sir. Did you see the bunks in that—in the saloon, sir? It reminded me of *Treasure Island*. We read it in the Fourth Form with Mr Simmonds. I should think it is very seldom that one has the opportunity of examining a large sailing vessel, sir. I feel I know this ship inside out. Shall *I* go and help Mr Parkinson to collect up the little Form Three boys, sir?'

'Oh, shut *up!*' said Roger, feeling that there was a good deal to be said, after all, for going on school excursions with one of the senior masters.

The thirty boys were all accounted for at last, but so much time had been lost that it was decided to entrain the mob at the Temple District Station and go immediately to Mark Lane for the Tower.

'If we have to leave out St. Pauls', we do,' said Parkinson. 'We must describe it to them in the train coming home, or while they sit having their grub.'

The thought of the Tower was sufficient to effect an almost instantaneous change in the behaviour of the party. From appearing to act rather more like the herd of Gadarene swine than those unaccustomed to small boys would have believed possible, the cortège assumed (under the leadership of Kirby and Healy-Lunn) an almost funereal decorum, and entrained and detrained without incident.

Master Kirby and Master Healy-Lunn were missed very early in the tour of the Tower. It occurred to Parkinson that it might be a good idea to count heads upon leaving the White Tower. This was known to be the prize piece, as it were, of the excursion; and the boys were delighted with it, although not, perhaps, for the reasons their headmaster would have chosen.

'Bet you,' said one Burnett to his friend Sawleys, 'I can get my head out through that embrasure, or whatever it's called.'

'What do you say we have a shot at climbing up the chimney?' said one Pullin to his opposite number, Sellingford. 'I bet you could get a jolly long way up if you tried.'

'Bet I can climb higher than you can,' Sellingford replied immediately.

'Wonder what would happen,' enquired one

Kingsford of his partner Mapping, 'if we shoved a fist into the middle of the Battle of Waterloo?'

'Can't think why they stick a thing like that in the middle of the Tower,' complained Mapping, who had not yet learned to despise the steep ladder of learning. 'What's it got to do with the Normans?'

'Oh, don't be an owl,' responded Kingsford. 'What have the Normans got to do with *it?* I bet the Battle of Waterloo was far more important, anyway.'

'That's not the point, you ass! In any case, they were important in different ways. Don't look now, but here's the keeper.'

The thirty were at last divorced from the lower floor with all its attractions, and were persuaded to go across to the staircase (which, fortunately, they had not had time to discover for themselves) and ascend to the little Norman chapel. It was after they had descended a long staircase to the well, and, having been wrested thence, were once more in the open air, that it occurred to Parkinson to count heads. Twenty-eight boys were present.

'Oh, damn!' said Parkinson. 'Who's missing?'

'I'll go and round them up,' said Roger. 'It's Kirby and Healy-Lunn, isn't it?' He returned to the White Tower and searched it faithfully. There was no sign of the truants. The truth dawned on him as he disgustedly rejoined the party. 'I bet they cut their stick at the entrance as soon as we'd counted up and taken the tickets,' he said. 'Goodness knows *where* they are now! They may be anywhere.'

He applied to the custodian at the gate, but

received no comfort. Several schools were visiting the Tower that day, and the attendants had been kept extremely busy. Roger took a feverish walk round, but, apart from an abortive chase of two school caps which proved to be different from those of his own boys, as he perceived as soon as he got nearer them, he had no encouragement in his search. He returned to Parkinson.

'I think they must be outside somewhere,' he said. 'Probably thought they'd be bored. They came last year, I believe. At least, Kirby did. I suppose they've gone off on a toot.'

'Better give chase, I suppose, then,' said Parkinson gloomily.

'O—oh, *sir!*' said twenty-eight reproachful voices.

'Aren't we going to see where the Princes in the Tower were murdered?' demanded Kingsford.

'And where Sir Walter Raleigh's ghost walks?' enquired Mapping. 'I think I'm psychic, sir.'

A babel broke out, during which Anne Boleyn's head and Colonel Blood were mentioned by the disappointed boys. Roger, receiving a resigned and acquiescent nod from Parkinson, strode away back to the gate, and the others went onwards towards the Bloody and Beauchamp Towers.

Once outside the Tower precincts it dawned upon Roger that Kirby and Healy-Lunn were not entirely the perishing little nuisances he had supposed them. The sun was shining, the Thames, so near Tower Bridge and Saint Catherine's Dock, was full of life, and he was freed for a time from his little charges and their incessant questions and chatter. Keeping their fingers off the polished armour, too, had been more than one man's work, and he felt fatigued. To be alone, even for five minutes, while he hunted the two stragglers, would be restful and refreshing, he decided.

His own tastes urged him to the river. He argued, too, that this was the way the boys would have taken. There was a river steamer about to leave the small pier. She was just casting off. Roger stood a moment to watch, and then began to run. On her deck, leaning over the rail to watch operations, were Kirby and Healy-Lunn.

He was almost thrown on board by willing hands, and told to get his ticket from the master. The screw began to revolve, the pier to back away, and the steamer set her nose eastward, reversed her engines and began to gather speed for her trip.

Roger was no sooner aware of all these facts than he began to think he had done a foolish thing.

'Where do we stop?' he enquired of a woman with three children and some bundles.

'Sarfend, dearie. Least, that's where *I'm* agoing.'

Roger sighed with relief. The steamer would call, then, at Greenwich. Bad enough, but not nearly as bad as it might have been. The two boys were safely tied up. He would have half an hour to himself and then give them the shock of their lives.

It was just eleven o'clock. He went into the small saloon and had some beer. He did not know the rate at which the river steamers usually travelled, but he reflected comfortably that Greenwich was only about five miles from Tower Pier by river and that the steamer seemed to be making good time. From Greenwich a bus, or, at most, a couple of buses, would bring him, he supposed, to Tower Bridge. As Parkinson and his boys would spend about three-quarters of an hour over lunch and in examining the old guns which were parked along the esplanade opposite the watergate of the Tower, the contretemps of Kirby's and Healy-Lunn's truancy would not have wasted very much time.

Roger had a second beer and a cheese sandwich. He filled and lighted his pipe. It was chilly on deck. He might just as well, he decided, remain in the stuffy but snug and cosy atmosphere of the saloon. Besides, the longer he could remain out of sight of the boys, the more pronounced would be the shock with which the sight of him would be greeted, and he was young enough to appreciate this fact.

The steamer threshed on through the Lower Pool and past the entrance of the Regent's Canal. It semi-circumscribed the Commercial Docks and passed the West India Docks and the Isle of Dogs. It passed the Millwall Docks and rounded into dirty, historic Deptford. Along Limehouse Reach it ran, and past the mouth of the Deptford Canal. Then Roger went out on deck.

There lay Greenwich, with the Royal Naval College well in view, but the steamer took no account of this. To Roger's almost open-mouthed horror, she ran on past Greenwich pier and the training ship drawn in under the starboard bank, and swung into Blackwall Reach on her way to Gravesend.

Roger sought the bar-tender.

'Where do we stop?' he enquired.

'Gravesend, Southend, Clacton-on-Sea,' replied the man. Roger ordered a gin and another beer, and then seated himself on a plush-covered bench and leaned back, closing his eyes.

'I say, sir,' said the hateful voice of Master Kirby in the middle of a day-dream—or, rather, a waking nightmare in which Roger imagined himself being dismissed by the headmaster with opprobrium and without a character, 'why don't you come up on deck, sir? Healy-Lunn and I saw you come aboard, sir, and we couldn't think where you'd got to. We wondered whether you were sea-sick. I have an aunt, sir, who is always sea-sick on the Thames. I say, sir, do you think I could ask for a ginger-beer, sir? Or is it like a public house in here? I'm awfully thirsty, sir.'

'Oh, Lord!' groaned Roger, fishing in his pocket for a shilling. 'Here you are. I wish you'd both drop overboard and get drowned!'

'Oh, thanks *awfully*, sir,' said Master Kirby; but whether he was gratified by the gift or the pious wish Roger did not enquire.

He drank his gin and beer, and finished his cheese sandwiches, and then thought longingly of the food he had left in the care of one Munnings, who had offered to carry it for him and no doubt still had it in safe keeping. He dared not order more food or drink until he knew what the price of the tickets

on the steamer would be, and the three return
fares to Tower Bridge. He cursed himself that he
had spent so much already. And what on earth
had induced him to part with a precious bob to
that little swine Kirby, he wondered—Kirby, who,
together with Healy-Lunn, was the cause of all this
trouble and loss of time.

Kirby and Healy-Lunn came up to him.

'Please, sir, we've got our tickets. The steward or
someone came round. We took them to Gravesend,
sir. Shall I go and get yours? And, sir, we've just
passed a dredger. Did you see it? And there's a
tanker coming up, sir. Do come up on deck and
see her!'

The steamer passed Blackwall Tunnel and slanted
round Bugsby's Reach. The Victoria Docks were
far away to port. Woolwich Dockyard approached,
and Woolwich Reach. The river mouth turned
northward, buoyed all along the northern bank
between George V Dock and the Northern Outfall
bordering Barking Reach. Barking Creek went
by, and the eighteen-foot sounding line remained
obstinately along the northern shore.

Halfway Reach and Dagenham Breach—it was
like a madman's poetry, thought Roger. Jenningtree
Point and Erith Marshes, Erith Reach and Erith
Rands, Crayfordness and Dartford Creek, Purfleet,
Long Reach, even Clement's Reach—he knew
them all from the chart and the log of his little
motor cruiser *Sunfleet*—the semi-circular curve
past Blackshelf and the training ships *Exmouth* and
Warspite, the southern slant down to Northfleet on

Northfleet Hope, and so to Tilbury Docks and the Tidal Basin.

Tilbury Fort, and, opposite, Gravesend at last! The steamer rang bells and edged in. There was a crowd of people at the gangway to go ashore, and some were pushing. Roger thrust himself in front of his charges, who remained cheerfully prattling up to the very moment of disembarkation, and began making tracks for the gangway. Suddenly he heard behind him a shout in a childish voice, then a gasping snarl, then he got hopelessly jammed in the wedge at the gangway railing.

'Oh, sir! Please, sir!' cried Master Kirby, as soon as they were ashore and Roger, having demanded of a policeman the way to the railway station, had dragged them away from the dock past a church and along two streets. 'Did you see the man with the knife, sir?'

'What do you mean?' asked Roger, uncomfortably reminded by this question of his previous escapes from injury.

'A man with a knife, sir. Lunn bit him.'

'Bit whom? What the devil are you talking about?'

'He's still got blood on his teeth, sir. Show Mr Hoskyn, Lousy. Perhaps you'd better spit. It might be poisonous.'

Master Healy-Lunn spat vigorously on to a passing cat. Roger glanced behind him. He had a suspicion, founded on past experience, that it was not unlikely that they were still being followed.

'Much obliged, Lunn,' he said lightly. 'And now,

perhaps, Kirby, you'll explain what you're talking about.'

'Well, sir, you know that squash getting off? Well, sir, you know we were just behind you? Well, sir, I don't think the man understood that you were with us. He shoved us aside and then we saw the knife. Like a sailor's knife, sir. Keary has one. The headmaster doesn't like it, sir. He told Keary to put it away. Keary is a Rover Scout, sir. At least, he will be one as soon as——'

'For heaven's sake keep to the point!' said Roger. 'And *hurry!* I don't want to miss a train!'

'The odds against our catching a train, sir, without knowing the time-table,' said Master Kirby, 'are about one hundred thousand million to one, sir. My father worked it out. It is quite mystical—er—mythical to think, sir——'

'Oh, *shut* up!' shouted Roger. '*And get a move on!*'

The conversation was not resumed until they were all in the train. Then Roger turned to Healy-Lunn.

'Well, sir,' said Healy-Lunn modestly, 'it seemed as if the man was going to put the knife in your back, sir. And as I wasn't sure whether he was going to or not, I bit his hand, and he dropped the knife. I bit rather hard, sir.'

'He's the champion biter of the Sixth, sir,' interpolated Master Kirby, who disliked the role of passive listener. 'Last term he bit the end off a riding-crop, sir. You know the little loop that——'

'Oh, shut up!' said Roger. 'Go on, Lunn.'

'I'm afraid that's all, sir.'

'You bit his hand really hard? Which hand? Would you happen to know?'

'Oh, yes. His right hand, sir. I bit him on the Mount of Venus, sir.'

'Where on earth is the Mount of Venus?'

'Oh, *sir!*' said Master Kirby. 'Don't you know *that?* It's hand-reading, sir. I have an aunt who can do it. I know all the mounts, sir. Venus——'

'Oh, shut *up!*' yelled Roger. 'Go on, Lunn.'

'The Mount of Venus is at the base of the thumb, sir. It is fairly fleshy.'

'You mean you may have left a scar?'

'I hope not, sir, but I think so. Do you think I shall have trouble with the police, sir?'

'No, I know you won't have trouble with the police, Lunn. In fact——' He paused, and then added impressively, 'You won't even have trouble with the headmaster over this little jaunt of yours if you can contrive to keep your mouth shut.'

'And Kirby, sir?'

'Oh, blast Kirby!' said Roger pardonably. 'All right, all right. But, mind, Kirby, if you breathe a single solitary word——'

'Oh, I won't, sir! Not a sound! Oh, *thank* you, sir! Oh, sir, you are very, very good to us, sir! I would like you to know——'

'I would like *you* to know that I'll twist your neck if you don't *shut up!*' said Roger.

'So you see,' wrote Roger to Mrs Bradley, 'there seems good reason to suspect that somebody—I suppose the murderer, and it looks very much like Sim—must think I know something against him, although I'm quite sure I don't. Anyway, I am remaining in my digs, after dark every night, just in case, and am not going to the cinema at present. How is Dorothy? And what are the chances of Mrs Denbies' being released without a trial if the police are fat-headed enough to arrest her? And anything might happen after that lunatic inquest!'

He wrote in a letter to Dorothy:

'Mr Clinton wants me to go into residence for the rest of this term. It's a frightful fag, but I suppose I'll have to do it. It means I won't be as free at week-ends, but that can't be helped, and as I'm staying in, anyway, during the evenings, it won't make all that difference. You might write as often as you can.'

Chapter Fifteen

'Why should men love
A wolf, more than a lamb or dove?
Or choose hell-fire and brimstone streams,
Before bright stars and God's own beams?'
HENRY VAUGHAN, Silurist—*Childhood*

AT THE opening of the school term Mrs Bradley
would have been grateful for the decision of the
Reverend Ashton Clinton to make Roger a resident
master for a time, but now that Claudia Denbies
had been arrested and had been sent to prison
by the magistrates, whilst Mrs Bradley and the
police continued, along vastly different lines, to
build up proof, acceptable to a jury, against the
murderer, there seemed less need for caution on
Roger's behalf. At least, that was her reading of the
facts.

Mrs Bradley had used the attacks upon Roger
as a strong argument to show that the murderer
was still at large, for the attacks, particularly the
one threatened by the man with the knife, could

not have been sponsored by Claudia. The fact, too, that the chauffeur, Sim, had disappeared without trace after his attempts to injure or murder Roger, gave the police another good reason—or so Mrs Bradley pointed out to the inspector—for ceasing to suspect Claudia although she did not want her set free.

Roger did not see Mrs Bradley again until his half-term holiday, for, as he had stated, although he would have enjoyed a certain amount of freedom at week-ends in the ordinary course of events, as a resident master he had various duties which prevented his leisure from extending beyond the limit of more than a few hours at a time.

Mrs Bradley had rightly detected in Roger's decision to take up resident duty an ambition to become a housemaster with its consequent increase of salary. She mentioned this theory to Dorothy who had been mildly but unpleasantly shocked at what she concluded (from his letters) to be Roger's puerile regard for his own skin. Dorothy accepted the alternative theory gratefully, and wrote a congratulatory note to Roger on the subject of his wisdom and foresight.

The egregious young man thereupon proposed—off handedly and through the post—and was promptly turned down. This would have occasioned him more mental agony than it did had it not been that his attention was distracted and his safety imperilled by the extraordinary behaviour of Master Kirby and Master Healy-Lunn, who selected the fifth Sunday after Easter on which to make a determined attempt to get themselves expelled from the school and Roger arrested for murder.

It chanced that not so very far from the school was a playhouse of amateur actors. They gave four performances during the week, and a special Sunday night show for the members of their society. The play on this particular Sunday night was by one of the members and was entitled *Blood*. It was, in point of fact, a youthfully morbid study of heredity, but to Master Siggenham, of the Upper Fourth, it represented, when he saw the advertisement in the local paper, such a tantalizing mirage of excitement and gore that he felt compelled to refer to it in class, whilst the form was apparently engaged in working out a problem in arithmetic.

His form-master imposed on him a penalty of fifty lines for talking, and, being a youth of exceptional thrift, he had most of his pocket money left from the previous week, and therefore he repaired to Master Healy-Lunn. Kirby's silent friend's philanthropic custom was to write up a few hundred lines which he was willing to dispose of to customers for a monetary consideration or on terms of barter. Master Siggenham, knowing this, soon purchased the necessary imposition.

'What did you do?' enquired Healy-Lunn, counting the halfpence carefully.

'Nothing much, Lunn,' replied Siggenham. 'I merely said to Hiscock that it was a pity we couldn't all go to see that *Blood* show at the Cockcrow Theatre instead of all that Shakespeare bilge next week.'

'*Blood* show?'

'Yes, Lunn.' And Siggenham explained.

'I see. All right, cut along. And, mind, if there's any query about the lines, you'd cut your thumb and had to do them left-handed. It's practically true, because I did them left-handed myself, and everybody's wrong-hand writing is the same.'

'Oh, yes, of course, Lunn.'

Healy-Lunn sought out his friend.

'I'd like to see this *Blood* show,' he said.

'We'll go,' said Kirby immediately.

'We can't, you ass. We'd get sacked. It's late at night!'

'How late?'

'Well, half-past nine, I think. It won't be over much before midnight. And, anyway, it's the devil of a sweat from here. We'd have to go on our bikes if we went at all.'

Roger usually did visiting rounds on Sunday nights. The boys were sent to bed half an hour earlier than usual on Sundays, this to their disgust. The masters, however, were grateful for the respite, and no amount of pleading or cajoling would gain for any boy so little as ten minutes of extra time. On this occasion Healy-Lunn and Kirby tried the experiment of pretending to catch lice in one another's hair when the visiting master came round, but unfortunately they had miscalculated, for instead of the greenhorn Roger, whom they were expecting, a senior master appeared, and, confiscating the clothes brush (unfortunately long-handled) which they had provided with the laudable idea of adding local colour to the scene of carnage by smacking it down on the imaginary bugs they were collecting, he put them, one after the other, across their respective cots and used the back of the brush to enforce his view that lights out meant lights out, and that little boys who were not under the bedclothes at the proper time must expect some untoward occurrences, of which this was the first and, he hoped, for their sakes, the last. He made the point quite clear.

He then tossed them lightly into their beds, pulled their hair, tucked them up and went out laughing.

'We ought to have had a basin of water, and not that beastly brush,' said Kirby, accepting reverses, as a good general should, merely as the text-book of the future. 'He could hardly have drowned us, could he?'

The smacking had had a soporific effect, and the boys, when the time to break out drew near, would have given a good deal to be out of the business and to have lapsed into comforting slumber. Like older and supposedly wiser persons, however, having committed themselves to the expedition they felt in honour bound to go through with it.

Roger might have known nothing about it at all had it not been for the entirely fortuitous circumstance that a little boy named Thomason was sick in the night, and had to receive attention from the matron.

Kirby and Healy-Lunn, as members of the Sixth, were permitted a room for two. Thomason slept next door to them in a dormitory. He was nine years old, and so were the other three children in the room. Roger, having been brought into the affair by a tousle-headed boy in pyjamas who came to the masters' room at just after half-past nine, went into the two-room to request Kirby or Healy-Lunn to run for the matron who resided in the school sanatorium, distant a stone's throw from the main buildings.

He found the two-room empty and the boys' outdoor clothes gone from their pegs behind the door. Quickly he sent two other thirteen-year-olds for the matron, and then set to work to discover what madness had this time possessed his two blithe spirits.

He had to be circumspect if the headmaster were not to know what had happened, and he was still too near his undergraduate days to want boys to be expelled for what he felt quite sure was a silly prank. He owed this particular pair a debt of gratitude, moreover, for having saved him from injury, possibly from death, at Gravesend—from his point of view aptly named. He resolved to go after the truants and get them back to their room and say nothing to anyone about it.

Leaving the capable matron in charge of the sick child, he went out to the shed where the masters kept cycles and motor cycles, and borrowed Parkinson's machine. The minimum of enquiry had given him a clue. Roger was not a bad psychologist except where girls were concerned.

* * *

The boys, Roger concluded, would have ridden to the theatre on bicycles. A key to the cycle shed hung in the boys' lobby, and was under the guard of a lobby prefect. It was a simple matter, however, for a boy to abstract it when he came to bed, carry it up to his dormitory, and use it after lights-out: simple, that is to say, in theory. The practical difficulty was that as bicycle lamps were forbidden, cycling at night was a breach of the law as well as of the rules of the school.

Roger wondered, as he kicked Parkinson's machine into motion, whether the boys had managed to acquire bicycle lamps, or whether they were running the risk of cycling without lights. Time alone would show.

It was a dark night, and Parkinson's head-lamp made the hedges of the school drive look black, strange and solid. It seemed as though the boys would be already at the theatre unless some accident had prevented this or had delayed them, so he felt little need to keep more than a cursory lookout for them on his way. He turned out of the school gate, which the boys had left wide open, and, once upon the road, he opened up the throttle and made speed.

The trip by day would have been both pleasant and pretty, particularly at that time of the early summer, but in the darkness there was nothing much to look at except the brilliance of the headlight on the road. He roared over a bridge and past a roadhouse, took the straight road into the village, slowed for a town, and then accelerated briskly and was soon touching fifty miles an hour across a common.

He mistook the way after that, having taken a left-hand fork instead of keeping straight on, and he had come to a railway bridge before he realized what he had done. He knew where he was, however, and decided that to keep straight on would be quicker than turning in his tracks.

The road he was following was narrower than the one he had intended to take, but the surface was good, and he did not need to slow down except on a very rough couple of miles across a gorse-covered heath where the road became no more than a track and the surface was very uneven.

He struck a good road after that, and came into another town to find it all very quiet. He stopped to ask a policeman the way to take for the theatre, for he was now some miles out of his way. He was directed, and drove on out of the town towards the village in which the theatre had been made from an ancient tithe-barn.

Roger had no particular plan of action in his head beyond arriving at the theatre and getting the two boys unostentatiously out of it. That this would be no easy task had not occurred to him. The theatre was up a short lane. He saw the lanterns swinging on either side of the entrance, propped up his motor cycle in the only space he could find which was not already occupied by pedal cycles, other motor cycles and cars, and went up to the entrance of the barn.

'Ticket?' said a handsome youth in a pink shirt, orange trousers and a black tie.

Roger said brusquely:

'I've got two boys inside. I want to get them home.'

'Oh, yes? Their seat numbers?' said a blonde girl, joining the youth and talking through her cigarette.

'I don't know them,' Roger confessed. 'Do you mind if I go in?'

'Well, you might go in at the interval,' said the youth obligingly, 'but you can't interrupt just now. We've just begun the second act, you know.'

'How long does the second act take?'

'Over in three-quarters of an hour—another forty minutes from now. Not long to wait. Have a gasper, won't you?'

'But, good Lord!' said Roger. 'I can't wait forty minutes! I've got to get back with these kids! They've broken out of school!'

'Sorry,' said the blonde, 'but there it is.'

She retired with the pink-shirted youth and they conversed learnedly of the Abbey Theatre, Dublin, the Maddermarket Theatre, Norwich, the Mercury Theatre, Notting Hill, and the Citizen Theatre, Bath, until Roger, in desperation, pushed his way in through a badly-hung door and stood in the auditorium.

He had a self-congratulatory moment in which he believed he had crossed his last fence, but he found that this was not so. The barn seemed pitch-dark except for the light from the stage, for the

box-office from which he had come, although
lighted only by the lanterns, had made his eyes
already unaccustomed to darkness.

It was not going to be possible, as he realized
almost at once, to locate his two truants without
going along all the rows until he found them.
He went back to the box-office. Neither the pink
shirt nor the blonde hair took the slightest notice
of him. They were discussing the Little Theatre,
Bournemouth.

He felt he could not hang about for nearly forty
minutes, so he went back to Parkinson's motor cycle,
started it up, and went for a thirty-minute ride.

At first he went towards Guildford, but suddenly,
before he had covered half a mile, he had another
and a crazier scheme. He would go back, he thought,
to Whiteledge, and have another look at the house
in which so many extraordinary incidents had their
root.

He took the road by Merrow Down and Clandon
Park through the village of East Glandon and out
by way of the two Horsleys as far as Effingham.
He turned off, but, realizing very soon that, in the
darkness, he was not likely to find the house at all
easily, he went past the golf course and as far as
White Hill, and then thought it better to return.

He was in good time, but the interval came at
last, and he went in, collared his truants (who were
very sleepy, rather bored, and looked extremely
frightened when they saw him), gave them a good
start on the homeward road, and then went after
them.

All went well; he let them into school with his own latch-key, saw them to their dormitory, and told them to come and see him in the morning. He interviewed them grimly when they appeared.

'Oh, but sir!' said Master Kirby, at sight of the cane. 'You can't mean to *beat* us, sir!'

'Bend over,' said Roger briefly.

'But you can't *do* this to us, sir,' urged Kirby. 'Mr Simmonds smacked us only last night, sir. With a whacking great clothes-brush, sir, too.'

'What for?' said Roger, who did not much like Mr Simmonds.

'Well, nothing, really, sir. I thought I saw one of those things, sir, in Lunn's hair, and, as he is going home at half-term, I thought it only fair to his people——'

'Oh, *Lord!*' said Roger, putting away the cane. 'Shan't I ever get some of my own back on you two pests!'

The morning papers were delivered to the masters at breakfast. Roger opened the paper two mornings after his night ride, read the sports page, turned to the news, and had his eye caught by a heading.

The body of a man identified as Sim, the Whiteledge chauffeur, had been discovered on a common between Effingham and Little Bookham. His head had been cut off and left beside the body, and the features had been so disfigured as to be unrecognizable, but his brother had sworn to the corpse. Roger noted, with quickening interest, that he himself must have passed the spot on Parkinson's motor cycle, probably within a few minutes of the time of the murder.

The inspector turned up at school at twelve o'clock, and at twenty minutes past twelve the headmaster sent for Roger.

'When you have had your lunch, Mr Hoskyn,' he said, 'you had better accede to this officer's request that you show him our countryside as a contribution to his work on a case of, I regret to say, murder. He states that he has met you before.'

'Yes, headmaster. We met during the Easter holidays.'

'Very well. You will return, I anticipate, in time to take preparation for Mr Parkinson if he deputises for you in the games field this afternoon.'

'Certainly. But I don't quite understand——'

'The officer will explain, and would like, I dare say, to take lunch in the dining hall with the boys.'

'I see.'

'You had better escort him, meanwhile, to the masters' common room.'

'It would be better, sir, if you've no objection,' put in the inspector, speaking with great respect but firmly, 'if Mr Hoskyn could accompany me now at once on our tour of the district.'

'He will miss his lunch,' said the headmaster.

'I shall not keep him long, sir.'

'Very well. You know your own business. Have you any objection, Mr Hoskyn?'

Roger, who knew that he and the inspector would

lunch at a public house and that bread and cheese and beer would be a satisfactory substitute, so far as he was concerned, for the school meal of stewed beef and boiled cabbage, replied demurely that he had no objection at all.

He and the inspector were to make their round by car, and Roger was at no loss to understand the reason for the jaunt. Somebody must have seen him on the previous Sunday night and reported his movements. He did not feel at all nervous. He knew that, subconsciously, he had expected the inspector to turn up.

'I understand you were on the spot, sir, at the time the murder took place,' the inspector observed, as they drove away from the school.

'On what spot when what murder took place?' Roger demanded, his heart thumping most unpleasantly.

'Haven't you seen the morning paper, sir?'

'Good Lord!' said Roger. 'You don't mean——' But it sounded over-done, and he knew it.

The car made a grinding noise as the inspector changed up and the speed increased. They travelled for about another half mile, and then the inspector said:

'Yes, sir, that's what I mean. You were known to be out and about in the neighbourhood just about the time the doctor thinks the man died. The head was cut off a bit later.'

'I saw and heard nothing, I assure you. I can't help you over this, I'm afraid.'

'It's yourself you have to help, sir,' said the

inspector earnestly. 'I've brought you away from the school deliberately, to see if I could persuade you to come across.'

'With what? Speak out, man! I don't know what the devil you're getting at!' cried Roger, hoping that this sounded like the truth, but feeling the rope round his neck.

'Well, sir, the dead man, as you know from the morning paper, was Sim, Mr Lingfield's chauffeur. We know he had a crack or two at you. Now he's found dead under very peculiar circumstances, and *you* were in the immediate neighbourhood at the time of his death. I thought perhaps you'd care to give me, as it were, a friendly account of your movements, sir, that's all, on the night of the crime.'

'Why, you idiot!' said Roger, swallowing hard, and wondering why he had thought that he did not feel nervous. 'You don't think *I* murdered the perisher? Although, if I had, it was no more than he deserved, as you said yourself!'

'That's the point, sir,' said the inspector, gazing stolidly through the windscreen, 'and that's what we've got to clear up. If you had, it would have been no more than he deserved. And we're with you there, sir. You've had a lot to put up with since Mr Lingfield's body was found. Nobody knows that better than the police. Well, sir, there was you in the offing of *that* murder, and there's you in the offing of *this* murder——'

'Look here,' said Roger, 'what exactly are you getting at, damn it!'

'This, sir. If it was in self-defence, I'd advise you to say so at once.'

'Get it into your fat head that I know absolutely nothing about Sim's death except for what I read in the paper this morning! As for the other murder, you know I've told you nothing but the truth.'

'I hope you'll reconsider that statement, sir. All I want——'

'All you'll get is a thick ear,' said Roger wrathfully. 'Hang it all, I was simply chasing two kids who'd broken out at night to go to a show. A dozen men might have been murdered. I still don't see that you've any reason whatever for trying to fasten anything on me.'

The inspector, who had been driving all this time towards Godstone, did not reply until he had turned in to the courtyard of the fine old sixteenth-century inn of that place.

'Let's have some lunch, sir,' he said, 'and after that we'd better track out your movements on the night in question. Any objection to that programme?'

'None, so long as you don't keep calling me a murderer.'

'Such was not my intention, sir, as I think you know. But I'd be glad of a full explanation.'

'All right. We'll call an armistice. I could do with a drink, couldn't you?'

They had some beer, and then had steak and kidney pudding, some more beer, and an apple tart.

'And now, sir——' suggested the inspector,

when he had smoked a pipe and Roger a couple of cigarettes.

'Look here,' said Roger, recalled by this elliptical remark to the exigencies of the situation, 'perhaps I'd better tell you just what happened.'

He described in careful detail his night's work.

'And the boys would support this account, sir?'

'I suppose so, but you'd have to promise to keep it dark from the headmaster.'

'That could no doubt be arranged, sir. And now, as to where you went, and the time you took——'

'So you don't believe me? All right. Suit yourself. My story is true and I stick to it.'

'Very good, sir, though I don't know that I'd say very wise. Still, you must please yourself.'

So the car was driven into Guildford and beyond it, past the half-timbered cottages of East Clandon, past the elms of West Horsley and the fine front of West Horsley Place, past Effingham, and then to where Roger had turned the motor cycle and returned to the theatre and his boys.

'And where exactly was the body found?' he enquired, feeling that he was entitled to some information in return for that which he was supplying to the inspector.

'That's neither here nor there, sir,' the inspector imperturbably replied. 'I must congratulate you, sir, on being either a very cool customer or on knowing as little about Sim's death as you say you know. We have now passed the spot twice, and I noticed very particularly that you never turned a hair.'

'Oh?' said Roger, unimpressed by this dubious compliment. 'And what the devil do you want with me now?'

'Particulars of your acquaintance with Mrs Denbies, sir. The whole thing seems to us to hang on that.'

'But I haven't any acquaintance with Mrs Denbies! You know that as well as I do! I had never set eyes on her until——'

'Maundy Thursday, sir? How came it, then, that you confessed to knowing her, and that in front of witnesses?'

'When?'

'When you arrived at Whiteledge House, I understand, sir.'

'Well, but——hang it all, Inspector, I expect I said I'd seen photographs of her in the illustrated papers. After all, she is a celebrity, isn't she?'

'There is that, sir, but your subsequent actions——'

'Eh?'

'Well, they were remarked upon, sir. Lady Catherine herself——'

'Lady Catherine my foot! What on earth are you getting at? Are you trying to suggest that that weak-minded old woman has been leading you up the garden?'

'I suggest nothing, sir. But from what I heard——'

Roger was both baffled and furious.

'You heard nothing that could have any bearing,' he said, 'on——'

'Yes, on what, sir?' The inspector drew up the car at the entrance to the school grounds. 'Bearing on what?'

'On the murder of Lingfield, of course!' said Roger, savagely. 'If you ask me, Lady Catherine did that herself! She's crazy enough to do anything!'

'Now you're talking, sir,' said the inspector. He drove gently in at the school gates and pulled up on the gravel path outside the headmaster's house.

Chapter Sixteen

'Little boy, pretty knave, shoot not at random,
For if you hit me, slave, I'll tell your grandam.'
ANONYMOUS (16th century)

KIRBY AND Healy-Lunn were greatly impressed by the inspector. He had asked Roger, in the presence of the headmaster, to lead him on to the cricket field and introduce him to a couple of intelligent boys, and Roger, who understood the hint, at once went out with him and found him the two he wanted. Roger went back to an empty common-room, and wrote to Mrs Bradley.

Mrs Bradley was sympathetic. She wrote in return long and soothingly, giving comforting hints of her own activities and conclusions in the matter of the two murders, and suggesting that Roger should not worry himself unduly, even if he were arrested. She added a postscript to the effect that, once he had been cautioned by the police, he was not to say anything at all about the murders.

Meanwhile the inspector had had Roger's story

confirmed not only by Kirby and Healy-Lunn (who begged him not to betray them to the headmaster 'because, you see, it would get Mr Hoskyn into no end of a jam'), but by the pink shirt and the blonde at the theatre.

'He went off for about half an hour, but he certainly came back all right,' said the pink shirt. 'And if he told you we were discussing the contemporary theatre, well, of course, quite actually, we were. And he certainly collected two boys. I saw them go. Chrystabel can confirm.'

This Chrystabel did at once. In response to the inspector's next question she said that she would certainly have noticed blood on Roger's clothes. 'Our play was *called* "Blood," and you see the connection?' she added, looking at the inspector as though she felt sure that he did not.

This evidence, coupled with that of the boys, convinced the inspector that unless there was a flaw in the time scheme which had not yet made itself evident, Roger was not very likely to have been the murderer of Sim.

'One thing strikes me, too, sir,' said the sergeant. 'How far from the railway was the body?'

'Yes, I know,' said the inspector. 'The whole thing's the spit and image of the murder of Mr Lingfield.'

'If it *was* Mr Lingfield,' said the sergeant.

It was very shortly after this that Dorothy was invited to spend the Whitsun week-end at

Whiteledge. As this week-end coincided with Roger's half-term, she scarcely knew whether to accept the invitation or not. She did not, after his proposal, want to meet him, but, on the other hand, it seemed unkind to put herself entirely beyond his reach. The thought, however, that at Whiteledge she might be in a position to find out more of the mystery than she would be able to do by remaining outside what now seemed to her the magic circle of that place, tipped the scale and persuaded her to accept the invitation.

It had come from Mary Leith.

'We saw so little of you,' wrote Mary, 'and should like to have seen so much more.'

This was flattery of the wrong sort, but, to Dorothy's pleasure, the first person she met at Whiteledge was Mrs Bradley, this on the lawn in front of the house. The archery targets were in position, and Mrs Bradley, clad in a bilious green woollen pullover and a heather-mixture skirt of an almost incredible hairiness, was practising with bow and arrows and had scored, it appeared, a gold and two reds, a total of twenty-three points.

She walked up to the target and withdrew her arrows before she greeted the girl. When she did, it was with none of the usual formulae. She said merely:

'That's how it was done, and that's why the head was removed. But the questions still remain of who did it, and where is the head, and who enticed Mrs Denbies out of the house that night, and where she went. We must endeavour to find

out which members of the house-party understand
how to use a bow and arrows. Do *you* understand
their use, child?'

Dorothy laughed.

'You can hardly expect me to say that I do,' she
replied. Mrs Bradley cackled, and led her towards
the house.

'I have requested that you should occupy the
bedroom they gave you last time,' she said.

'Are *you* responsible for my invitation here?'
Dorothy enquired.

'Yes, child.'

'But what about Roger?'

'He must amuse himself for today and tomorrow.
After that you can meet him if you like. Are you
afraid of ghosts?'

'N-no.'

Mrs Bradley cackled again at the expression of
indecision on the girl's face. They walked into the
house together, and Mrs Bradley handed her bow
and the sheaf of arrows to Bugle. He received them
with an inclination of the head, thumbed the bow
knowledgeably, and then said:

'Phoebe should be here, miss. She will show
you.'

Exactly what pretext Mrs Bradley had made
for getting Mary Leith to invite her to the house
Dorothy did not discover. She realized at once,
however, why Mrs Bradley had insisted upon her
having the bedroom she had been given before.
The broken architrave over the mantelpiece was
now completed with a remarkably good likeness

of Captain Ranmore which certainly had not been there before.

'Yes, poor Harry did it two years ago,' said Lady Catherine, when Dorothy referred to it at dinner. 'It is very fine, is it not? Of course, Harry would have been a famous sculptor if he had not indulged his guilty passions.'

'What guilty passions?' Mrs Bradley enquired. Dorothy had mentioned the sculptured bust to her and had been requested to refer to it in public.

'Well, I cannot particularize in front of George,' Lady Catherine replied. 'You are a woman of the world, surely.'

'Yes, but not of the half-world,' Mrs Bradley meekly answered, accepting a nut which Captain Ranmore had cracked for her.

She invited herself into Dorothy's room that night to look at the bust.

'Does it come down?' she enquired. 'Or is it, perhaps, cemented into place?'

Dorothy, slender and childish in silk pyjamas, said that she did not know. She got into bed, leaving Mrs Bradley staring thoughtfully at the likeness.

'I think it must be,' Mrs Bradley muttered. 'I ought to take it away. One can hardly expect you to sleep with it in the room.'

'What is it?—a bomb?' enquired the girl. Mrs Bradley brought a chair and stood on it. Then she extended her yellow arms, short-sleeved in her dinner frock, gave a sudden heave and a jerk, and had the head between her claws.

'Look out! You'll drop it!' cried Dorothy.

'Exactly what I intend to do,' Mrs Bradley imperturbably replied. 'Are your nerves strong enough to stand the noise?' Upon this enquiry, and without waiting for an answer, she deliberately dropped the bust on to the edge of the fender, where it smashed into pieces, some large and others smaller.

'Oh dear, oh dear!' she remarked, as she climbed from the chair and stepped daintily over the débris. 'Stay where you are, child! We don't want this trodden about.'

Dorothy, sitting up in bed, was half aghast and half tickled at the incident.

'*Now* you've done it!' she said. 'I wonder who will come along to see what has happened?'

Mrs Bradley snatched the quilt from the foot of the bed and spread it out evenly and smoothly on the floor.

'Stay where you are,' she said, as Dorothy began to get out of bed to help her. Watched by the fascinated girl, she began to gather the broken pieces into the quilt, whose four corners she brought together, as soon as she had finished her task, to make a commodious receptacle. She acknowledged Dorothy's interest with a grin. 'There!' she said. 'Now, as you rightly point out, we must expect that someone will have noticed that it made a noise in falling. Fortunately——'

To Dorothy's amused surprise, she went over to a built-in cupboard and produced a newspaper parcel whose contents proved to be broken pieces of china. These she shot gently upon the area of the floor from which she had recently removed the portions of the smashed bust, and, picking up the laden quilt very carefully, she put that in the cupboard in place of the newspaper parcel. Then she folded the piece of newspaper and placed it tidily in the empty fireplace. She then went down on her knees.

There came a discreet tap at the door. Mrs Bradley rose from her knees and called:

'Come in!'

'Her ladyship thought perhaps you rang, madam.'

'I've made a mess,' said Mrs Bradley, brushing the front of her skirt and leering at the maid. 'You had better leave it now until the morning.'

'Very good, madam. Good night, madam. Good night, miss.' She withdrew.

'She'll know, in the morning, what you *really* broke,' said Dorothy. Mrs Bradley shook her head.

'I doubt it, child,' she replied. 'I come prepared for every contingency. It would surprise you if you knew all. Well, I have another small errand before I go to bed.' She tucked Dorothy up, grinned balefully, and was gone, leaving the bundled quilt in the cupboard, the pieces of crockery on the floor, and the mystery unexplained.

Dorothy turned over and closed her eyes. A fumbling at the door-handle roused her. She was a little startled, but the door admitted no one but Mary Leith, who switched on the light, and, uninvited, came over and sat on the bed.

'Why did Granny ask to have Mrs Bradley invited?' she demanded. 'I don't like her, and I don't want to have her here. She disturbs the balance of my mind.'

'I don't know anything about it,' Dorothy rather nervously replied. 'And I don't know—oh, Captain Ranmore?'

'Of course. Mrs Bradley isn't here to see *me* again, is she? I don't want any more treatment. I don't like it, and it isn't necessary. It's really for mother, you know. I mean, I don't inherit, whatever people may say.'

Dorothy was caused considerable embarrassment by these questions and facts, and did not know how to reply. She was saved from the necessity, however, by the entrance of Eunice Pigdon, who took Mary by the arm and led her out.

She returned in about five minutes, and took Mary's place on the bed, causing it to creak and groan under her weight.

'You mustn't mind Mary,' she said. 'She's bad again. A nuisance, isn't it? Harry Lingfield's death. A bit of a shock, you know.'

'I'm sorry,' said Dorothy, helplessly.

'Yes. Lady Catherine begged Mrs Bradley to come along and see her, but it does not seem as though anything much can be done. They're talking of a nursing home. I do hope it won't come to that. After all, she's perfectly harmless.'

'A nursing home? Oh, dear! I suppose she needs rest and quiet.'

Eunice Pigdon looked oddly at Dorothy, and then laughed.

'I see you know nothing about it,' she observed. 'Oh, well, get to sleep. I'll see to it that she doesn't disturb you again. By the way, we're having much the same people at dinner tomorrow as we had for George's party. Do you remember? Mrs Bradley's instructions, I believe. That woman runs this house as soon as she gets inside it.'

Eunice got up and the mattress leapt into place. She glanced at the broken architrave over the mantelpiece. 'I see they've taken Granny away,' she remarked. 'Or have you hidden him somewhere? It must have been the last bit of work poor Harry Lingfield did. We found it in his studio in the garden. Quite a good likeness, too, but—— Oh, well, some people have queer tastes, that's all I can say.'

'I didn't like it,' said Dorothy, 'and, besides——'

She hesitated, hoping that Eunice would oblige her by finishing the sentence for her. The knowledge that the pieces of the bust were reposing in a quilt at the bottom of the built-in cupboard gave her a feeling of guilt. Eunice was obliging enough to come to the rescue. This she did by saying, with a hearty laugh:

'Oh, don't apologize! He isn't a general favourite, I'm afraid. I noticed he made a pass or two at dinner.'

Dorothy, who disliked this particular vulgarism, although she could not deny that it described well enough Captain Ranmore's approaches that

evening, did not reply. Eunice waited as though
she half-expected an answer, and then said, as
she strolled across to the window and closed the
shutters:

'Lock your door when I've gone. I've bolted the
shutters. One takes things as they come in this
house, as no doubt you've already discovered.'

'Oh, but,' cried Dorothy, who loathed the feeling
of being shut in, particularly in a strange room,
'I really don't think you need———' Eunice closed
the door and then called softly and eerily through
the keyhole:

'Lock it! Lock it now, before I go! I shall wait
here until I hear you lock it.'

Dorothy did not want to obey, but decided that the
obstinate, heavy-faced woman probably meant what
she said. She got out of bed with great reluctance,
went across to the door and turned the key.

'There you are, then,' she said.

'That's it,' Eunice responded. 'That's one weight
off my mind.'

Dorothy, returning to bed, could not help
wondering what other weights might also be on
her mind. She heard Eunice walk away, and then
she turned over again and tried to go to sleep.

She was not at any time a ready or heavy sleeper,
and at midnight was still wide awake. The wind
rattled the shutters and made her imagine that
someone was trying to get in. Then, from the
chimney, came a faint, persistent crying, as though
a kitten had got lodged in the flue and could not
get down. Dorothy tried to believe that this was

also the wind, but she could not persuade herself of it. Neither could she bring herself to believe that the shutters, which were on the inside of the window, could be rattled quite so violently by a wind from outside the glass.

Just as her nerves were beginning to play the usual trick of persuading her that there was something fearful and unpleasant in the room, she was brought up short by the sound of somebody hammering at the door.

'Fire! Fire! Come out! Come out!' yelled a voice.

Dorothy was inclined afterwards to think that, had she been roused from sleep by such a warning, she might have felt considerable alarm; as it was, however, the human sounds drove her waking nightmares away, and she felt relief.

She got out of bed very quickly, switched on the light, found her dressing-gown and a pair of thick walking shoes, and went over to the shutters and opened them.

Her room looked out on to the garden. Nobody was below. They would naturally make for the front of the building, she supposed, for there were only two main exits and one of these was in the servants' part of the house.

There was no smell of smoke and no crackling of flames. However, she had unlocked her door and was preparing to make the descent when Mrs Bradley came into the room and unwrapped a heavy parcel.

'Do not be in too much hurry. Dress warmly,

child,' she said. 'I think the alarm of fire is most probably false.'

'What are you doing?' asked Dorothy, as Mrs Bradley placed her parcel on the bed and composedly locked the door.

'Effecting replacements,' Mrs Bradley replied. 'Kindly hand me the contents of the parcel as soon as I get up on this chair.'

There was a scurrying sound on the landing and staircase, followed by the clanging of a bell.

'Good heavens!' said Dorothy, unwrapping the parcel and displaying a bust very similar to the one which Mrs Bradley had broken. 'What's this? A conjuring trick?'

She raised it. It was heavy. Mrs Bradley took it from her, placed it in position in the centre of the broken architrave, climbed down, opened the window, opened the cupboard, picked up the quilt and, to Dorothy's astonishment, having tied the four corners together, she lowered the quilt with its contents out of the window and let it fall on to the lawn. She closed the window and the shutters, turned round quickly—all her actions had been neat, deft, speedy—and said:

'Under the bed, and don't sneeze!'

As Dorothy dived underneath, the light went out. Then Mrs Bradley joined her, and they lay on their stomachs side by side. Dorothy's desire was to giggle, but she was too much in awe of Mrs Bradley to dare to do it. Five dragging minutes went by, and then the door opened and the light went on again.

The intruder stood in the doorway. Dorothy could see a pair of shoes not two yards from where she was lying. Then a man called quietly:

'Miss Woodcote! Miss Woodcote! Are you there?' It was Captain Ranmore's voice. He walked away from the bed, to Dorothy's great relief, and crossed the room. She had the feeling that he was going to open the shutters, and if he did she felt certain that he would look out and see the white quilt, dim but distinct on the dark, still pool of the lawn. But he did not open the shutters. After shuffling his feet a little, he went out of the room and left the light on, taking the key.

Mrs Bradley held on to Dorothy to indicate that she must not move, and they waited again in breathless silence. Dorothy felt she must suffocate. The claustrophobic atmosphere began to make her nervous. Then sounded footsteps, this time like a woman's. The newcomer did not do more than cross the threshold, however. The next moment the light was snapped out and the room was in total darkness. The door was quietly shut and they heard the key turn in the lock.

Mrs Bradley crawled out and switched on a torch. She went over to the shutters and flung them open.

'Come out, child,' she said. 'The coast is clear.' She spoke in oddly satisfied tones.

'We're locked in,' said Dorothy. 'What do we do about that?'

'Nothing, at present,' said Mrs Bradley. 'You might as well go back to bed.'

'What will *you* do?'

'Stay here for a bit. Then, when people have realized that the alarm of fire was a hoax and have gone back to bed, I shall find means of projecting myself——' She paused and cackled harshly, 'into the garden and of picking up the quilt and its contents. Altogether a most satisfactory night's work. I think we should be congratulated. It is odd how well Sherlock Holmes' tricks nearly always work.'

'I say,' said Dorothy, struck by a thought. 'Did *you* raise the alarm of fire?'

'Yes, child. Didn't you guess?'

'Did you know that Captain Ranmore would come in here?'

'And rescue the bust of himself? I hoped someone might.'

'The bust? Oh, the new one! The one you put there? It's gone, and you knew it would go!'

'I hoped it might. Of course——' She paused.

'What will happen when he finds it isn't the right bust?' enquired Dorothy.

'We must wait and see, child.'

'Meanwhile, here we are.'

'Yes, I'm afraid so. Into bed you get. I don't suppose it is the least use to suggest that you should go to sleep whilst all this excitement is in the air, but you will be warmer and more comfortable in bed.'

As soon as the girl was settled and seemed relaxed, Mrs Bradley seated herself in an armchair near the bed, and faced the door. She took out a small revolver, and, sitting upright, cocked it and prepared to spend the rest of the night on watch.

She was not kept waiting very long. The door-handle twisted at about two in the morning, and the door began to open. Mrs Bradley knew this only because of the draught which fanned her ankles through the aperture.

She waited without breathing; then she uncocked her gun and cocked it again. She heard a gasp which she interpreted as dismay; then the door shut. She switched on her torch. The intruder had disappeared without trace or clue. Dorothy stirred, murmured, sighed, and was still again. Mrs Bradley went over, keeping the torch from shining on her face, but the child was fast asleep.

At half-past four Mrs Bradley went to bed. She came down to breakfast at ten to find nearly everybody as late as she was herself. The topic of discussion was the night alarm. She ate her frugal breakfast and listened to the conversation, joining in, but merely to make humorous references to the affair. After breakfast she went into the garden. To her satisfaction, but not to her surprise, there was now no trace of the quilt.

She went round to the front of the house. The archery targets had been taken in. She stood for a minute in the pillared portico, looking away over the garden towards the common. The morning air was fresh and pleasant, but not particularly warm, and she was about to go in when Captain Ranmore joined her.

'Very odd,' he said, 'that business last night, you

know. I can't understand it at all. Who raised the alarm, I wonder? I've questioned the servants and all our people, and no one knows anything about it. Did you hear the alarm, or did somebody come and wake you? I didn't see you on the lawn with the others.'

'I heard the alarm, but there seems to have been no fire.'

'Of course there wasn't any fire. Somebody had a bad dream, I should rather think, and woke up suddenly and raised the alarm. Of course, Mary may be responsible. She seems to be in one of her moods.'

'Oh, we'll soon clear *that* up,' said Mrs Bradley. 'It certainly was not Mary's voice I heard.'

Captain Ranmore regarded her in what seemed to be a perplexed way. He then said:

'Are you sure of that? That it was not Mary's voice?'

'Quite sure,' Mrs Bradley replied.

'I suppose you feel, as you have been in such close contact with Mary, that you would know her voice in any circumstances?'

'I would not say that,' Mrs Bradley responded, pursing her mouth judicially. 'But I think I could say that I would know if it were *not* her voice.'

'Yes, I think I understand what you mean. But, surely, if there were no fire, and it was not Mary (whose mentality, we know, is curious) who raised the alarm, does that mean that we have a practical joker in the house? Of course, a boy's voice could sound like a woman's.'

'It could, perhaps.'

'But I should not have thought George would have raised an alarm of fire. If I thought he had——'

'I am sure it wasn't George,' said Mrs Bradley. 'Besides, George is away at school.'

'Oh, yes. Of course. I forgot. That will spoil your dinner party, won't it? Didn't you intend to reproduce the conditions of the last one—the one—well, you know the one I mean.'

'I know the one. It will make no difference at all.'

'You do not then suspect George of having murdered Harry?' He laughed. Mrs Bradley favoured him with a long stare, and then with her reptilian grin. 'But who else could there be?' he continued. 'I mean, to rouse the household like that, last night. We haven't a practical joker in the place.'

'Except present company.'

'Of course I except present company!' He laughed again, but she knew that he knew he had put a false interpretation on her words. 'By the way,' he added, 'I don't remember seeing Miss Woodcote either. Was she out on the lawn?'

'No, she was not. The young, of course, sleep soundly, particularly if they have not guilty consciences.'

'Oh, yes,' said Ranmore. 'You know, I'm very glad you mentioned that. These two people—I can't say I was attracted by that rather weedy-looking young Hoskyn—can't stand minor poets—never could—but, my point is, those two admitted to having seen poor Harry Lingfield out riding.'

'Yes? They did? What of that?'

'Well, I suppose—I mean, accidents will happen, we know—I suppose they couldn't, by any chance, know anything of his death?'

'Why should they, if they haven't admitted that they did?'

'I only advance it as a theory. Poor Claudia! By the way, perhaps you could arrange for me to go and see her. I understand she is keeping quite well. Would that be so?'

'She does keep well, I believe, but I cannot give you any hope of seeing her at present.'

'Cannot? Or—will not?' He looked at her fixedly.

'Cannot, naturally. I do not know her wishes, either, with regard to visitors.'

'Oh, but I thought—— Oh, well!' He stepped out into the garden. 'Let's relax. What about a little archery practice? I'll shoot you for love. What about it?'

Both laughed, and he went off to the little summer-house where the bows, the arrows and the targets were usually housed. He disappeared up the steps and behind some trellis work, and was gone for about five minutes. Mrs Bradley, admiring the fine tall columns of the portico, had one of them between her and the steps up which Captain Ranmore had disappeared when there came the sound of a very loud yell in a masculine voice, followed by a slight scream in a feminine one.

There followed a dramatic pause of perhaps five or six seconds; then a heavy body came crashing against the trellis and brought part of it down. At the same moment Mary Leith appeared at the top of the steps as though she had come from the summerhouse. It almost seemed as though she must have come from there, for in her hand was a bow and on her back was a quiver.

She saw Mrs Bradley, and ran towards her, crying out in an excited but not a panic-stricken voice:

'You're a doctor! Come quickly! He's shot poor Granny! He's shot poor Granny through the thigh! I thought it was Harry come back!'

Mrs Bradley ran with unexpected swiftness (unexpected, at any rate, by Mary Leith) up the steps and towards the summerhouse.

The arrow still stood out from Ranmore's thigh. A bow was on the ground beside him, and near it lay an arrow, the cock-feather broken off short and the point gleaming silver in the sun.

'I am going to hurt you,' said Mrs Bradley firmly. She knelt beside him. 'Mary, sit on his shin and hold his foot.' Mary Leith, her mouth quivering like that of a child who is going to cry, obeyed at once, and turned her back on the proceedings.

Mrs Bradley took the victim's handkerchief out of his pocket, and, spreading it over her hand, picked up the silver-tipped arrow. Before she proceeded with her work she blew three shrill blasts on her whistle. As though they had expected the signal, out from the bushes darted the inspector and the sergeant.

'The summer-house! Quick!' said Mrs Bradley. The inspector returned in two minutes.

'Nobody there, mam,' he said disgustedly.

Chapter Seventeen

'Illustrious idol! could the Egyptian seek
Help from the garlic, onion, and the leek
And pay no vows to thee, who wast their best
God, and far more transcendent than the rest?'
ROBERT HERRICK, *The Welcome to Sack*

MRS BRADLEY'S reconstructed dinner party
lacked, so thought most of the guests, three out
of its four principal figures. In place of Captain
Ranmore, laid low in the local hospital but
in no danger, was Bob Woodcote, present by
special request of Mrs Bradley; in place of Mary
Leith, suffering from shock, was the inspector.
In place of the vivid Claudia Denbies was a
nurse who was there to keep an eye on Lady
Catherine, whose state of mind was no longer in
doubt.

Roger had arrived at four in the afternoon and
had been welcomed by almost everyone except
Dorothy. She avoided him. He was not as much
put out by this as he might have been, however,

because Bob's presence did something to keep him in countenance.

The two young men went out for a walk after tea, and did not return until it was time to dress for dinner. While they were gone, George Merrow arrived from school.

'So you got here?' said Eunice Pigdon, helping him put away his things.

'Oh, yes. Week-end and Whit Monday,' George replied. 'Jolly good, I think, Piggie, don't you?'

'Well, it's nice for us to have you,' said Eunice, with sincerity and irony so nicely mixed that the boy did not even look up. 'Pity Mr Bookham can't be here.'

'Oh, I don't know,' said George. 'I've rather outgrown him, don't you think? I shouldn't think I'd have him again.'

Eunice laughed as though he had said something with which she could agree.

'Here's Miss Woodcote,' she said. 'Have you outgrown her, too?'

George greeted Dorothy, invited her to sit on the bed and then said suddenly:

'Do women unbend the mind?'

'I wouldn't know,' she answered, studying the handsome child intently but without appearing to do so. 'Come and find out. You can put your other collar on in my room.'

George, accepting this handsome offer to extend his social education, went along the passage with her and stared round her room with the liveliest interest.

'Oh!' he said, in tones of disappointment, 'they've taken away my piece.'

'Piece of what?' Dorothy enquired.

'Piece of sculpture. The one I had for my birthday.'

This speech raised doubts and surmises in Dorothy's mind.

'What was it like?' she enquired.

'Like me, of course. Harry Lingfield made it. I suppose you don't know where it went?'

'No, I don't,' said Dorothy. 'The only one in here when I came this time was a bust of Captain Ranmore. Did Mr Lingfield make that, too?'

'Oh, yes, but it wasn't finished.'

'Oh, wasn't it? How much was done?'

'I don't know. He took it to the summer-house to finish it. I am hardly ever allowed in there. He often uses—used—it as a studio. And, of course, there are the bows and arrows as well. He looked after those.'

Mrs Bradley was left to welcome John Hackhurst, who had come (he admitted peevishly) at great inconvenience and at short notice to make this visit to Whiteledge. He had scarcely been soothed, and provided with the whisky and soda which alone, he reported, would restore him after his journey, when Clare Dunley, the archaeologist, arrived.

Unlike the painter, she was thoroughly delighted to have received the invitation.

'This will see me through nicely,' she confided to

Mrs Bradley. 'I am off to Africa next week, and am all packed up and my flat let for sixteen months. I should have gone to a hotel, but I loathe them. Whose bright idea was this week-end? Don't tell me Lady Catherine's. She never entertains from Easter until the autumn.'

'We've met to discuss the last hours that Mr Lingfield spent here,' said Mrs Bradley. Clare Dunley looked at her and then sniffed.

'I guessed as much,' she said. 'Poor Harry! Not a bad sort in his way. I was a friend of his, you know. We met in Syria, as a matter of fact. I did not know him previously in England. That was quite ten years ago. He was able to get some concessions for me out there. To dig, you know. Of course, I don't know how he affected younger women, but I liked him. I liked him very much.'

'You say that with meaning,' said Mrs Bradley.

'About younger women? Oh, yes. That's why I'm surprised he wanted to marry Claudia Denbies. Perhaps there was fellow-feeling! One never knows. Both their pasts were—rather eventful, I think.'

'Was he really a sculptor?'

'I suppose so, although Claudia thought him a very good pianist, too. He accompanied her violin solos quite adequately, I believe. Of course, I myself don't know the first thing about music, and I can't say that the violin would be my favourite instrument if I did. I think it a very strange instrument. There is something quite eerie about it. Do you not think so?'

'I should call the double bass more eerie, and perhaps the saxophone,' Mrs Bradley civilly replied. 'But, tell me, Mrs Dunley, did you ever see anything of Mr Lingfield's work?'

'His sculpture? Oh, yes. He used to work in the summer-house, you know, and occasionally one used to penetrate. Not that he liked to have visitors, especially towards the end of a piece of work. He did a nice thing of young George, though, and was getting on with a bust of Granny—that is, Captain Ranmore. I suppose that will never be finished.'

'Oh, yes. It is finished. I finished it,' responded Mrs Bradley, with what her hearer thought a peculiarly uncalled-for hoot of laughter.

The two young Clandons, George's innocuous twin cousins, arrived at six, went straight up to dress and came down early for sherry. The party was completed by the arrival of the inspector, who entered sheepishly, as though he doubted the warmth of his reception, and placed himself, with devout and obvious thankfulness, under Mrs Bradley's wing, shelter to which he had never previously flown.

When the meal was served, Mrs Bradley took the head of the table and little George Merrow the foot. The last person to appear was the nurse who had been engaged to look after Lady Catherine. Lady Catherine did not appear, however, but Mary Leith did, although she still seemed shocked and dazed by the accident to Captain Ranmore.

TABLE II

Mrs Bradley

————	John Hackhurst
Marjorie Clandon	Clare Dunley
Gareth Clandon	Bob Woodcote
Mary Leith	Eunice Pigdon
Nurse Hopkins	Inspector Lucas
Roger Hoskyn	Dorothy Woodcote

George Merrow

The Dinner Party given by Mrs Bradley for her Own Purposes at Whiteledge on Whitsun Saturday, May 19th.

Thirteen persons at table.

The dinner party, curiously enough (for the company seemed at first to be at odds and ill-assembled) turned out a great success. Mrs Bradley put the nervous guests at their ease and distributed the opportunities for conversation, so that Roger, who had come with very ill grace to the table, found himself recounting in lively vein (so that even Dorothy laughed) the story of the expedition to London with Parkinson and the little boys. Clare Dunley told anecdotes of her archaeological experiences which proved to be both lively and amusing. Dorothy referred to an undergraduate rag of the more subtle and brilliant sort, and Mrs Bradley capped everybody's stories without appearing to do so, a rare social gift which Roger, who was not so equipped, wholeheartedly but enviously admired.

The inspector was soon drawn into the general conversation, and related with gusto (and a very belated sense that he was talking of rope in the house of the hangman) the story of how a colleague of his had traced a murderer by means of a pair of braces. The only mute at the feast was Mary Leith, who, pallid, puffy-faced and apparently half-starving, wolfed food with intense concentration and spoke only to the nurse and once to Roger.

Immediately the meal was over the nurse went away. In less than ten minutes Mary Leith followed her. If anybody present watched with a sigh of relief their disappearance from the scene, it was with an inaudible sigh, and the conversation which, in any case, had suffered only the mildest check, recovered as soon as they had closed the door behind them.

Hackhurst had to catch a train at half-past ten, and departed soon after dinner. Bob had to return to the office, and the Clandons to town in their two-seater. Roger and Dorothy were to stay for one night, and so was Clare Dunley. The inspector's plans were unknown except to himself and Mrs Bradley, but he got up almost as soon as John Hackhurst had gone, and was heard to drive away from the house.

Those left were therefore few, and, from their own point of view—except for Mrs Bradley, whom they now watched nervously, and Roger, who never decried his own intelligence and charm—comparatively insignificant. Dorothy, after the events of the previous night, thought that she might have some glimmering of an idea of what Mrs Bradley had planned, and Eunice Pigdon, who sat with her intelligent little eyes fixed on the girl, seemed to be awaiting a cue, and so did Clare Dunley, reclining in a large armchair but really much more watchful than she seemed.

The magic word came from Roger.

'Good heavens!' he cried. 'It's just dawned on me! We sat down thirteen at table!'

'Yes,' Mrs Bradley replied in placid tones, as she gazed benignly round the small drawing-room to which the party had repaired. 'We sat down thirteen at table.'

'Didn't anybody notice? I've only just thought of it myself!' said Roger. 'Was there method in the madness?'

'If anybody did notice, that person did not mention it to me. There was no particular method in the madness,' Mrs Bradley replied.

'I noticed,' said Clare Dunley and Eunice Pigdon, speaking in unison.

'I noticed, too,' said Dorothy. 'But I thought you had done it on purpose. Who got up first?'

'It was the nurse. That was arranged,' Mrs Bradley replied.

She spoke reminiscently, as though she were watching the scene again, but there was something in her tone which made the sensitive Dorothy Woodcote glance at her sharply. Mrs Bradley caught her eye and cackled. Nothing more was said about thirteen.

'I think we start with Miss Pigdon,' said Mrs

Bradley, when the general conversation had died down. As she said this, the inspector inserted himself half-apologetically into the room as though fearful of disturbing the conference.

'How do you mean—start with me?' asked Eunice. 'What do you want me to do? Is it a new kind of game?—because I'm no good at games, you know.'

'I want to get a picture of the household just before George's birthday party,' Mrs Bradley replied.

'But you know as much about it as I do! You were staying in the house at the time.'

'Yes, but I had only been there for one day, and I am only one person, with one set of ears and eyes and one point of view. It would be valuable to have the reactions of other people, starting off, please, with your own.'

'I see. Well, where do I begin?'

'Begin, if you please, with the invitations. I imagine that you and Mr Bookham realized, sooner than anybody else (except for Lady Catherine, who was responsible for making up the table), that the party would number thirteen.'

'Lady Catherine didn't make up the table,' said Eunice Pigdon, almost unwillingly. 'She told me to invite the people who would fit in.'

'Then why did you make the number thirteen?'

'Well, I was not going to count Humphrey and myself. It is true that we usually dined with the family, but on such a special occasion—George came of age, you see, that day, and, by the way, he ought to be in bed!—you know you ought, George, you rascal!—I did not know quite what Lady Catherine intended, especially as you, Mrs Bradley, and Mrs Dunley, who, after all, was not Lady Catherine's but Mr Lingfield's friend, would be at table.'

'That all seems to account very nicely for the number thirteen,' Mrs Bradley agreed with a slow, discomforting smile. 'By the way, what about Mr Bookham? Perhaps we ought to have had him here with us tonight.'

'He was only a holiday tutor,' Eunice Pigdon replied. 'We have him—have had him, perhaps I should say—for all the major holidays. Neither Harry Lingfield nor Granny really cared about boys.'

'But Mr Lingfield went swimming with George.'

'How did you know that?'

'I told Mrs Bradley he did,' said George, speaking up from his corner. 'I helped her to identify Mr Lingfield's body, didn't I, Great-Aunt Bradley?'

'How could he? He didn't——' exclaimed Eunice.

'He didn't attend the inquest? Perfectly true. But he had seen the scars. Moreover, he had seen them on the left side.'

'I thought——' interpolated Roger.

'So did many people, child,' said Mrs Bradley in hasty interruption. 'That is why I have staged this party. Speak freely, therefore, all of you. I am more than prepared for any surprises you may spring.'

There was silence. Her hearers exchanged some uncomfortable glances. Mrs Bradley broke the silence, speaking with her usual cheerfulness.

'I know everything now,' she said. 'I want proof for a jury, that's all.'

There was another pause, which Clare Dunley broke by stating that she did not understand how proof for a jury was to be obtained if Mrs Bradley, knowing everything, still could not point to the murderer.

'I did not say I could not point to the murderer. Miss Pigdon has partly explained why thirteen people were to sit down to dinner that night. I do not wholly accept the explanation, if Miss Pigdon does not mind my saying so. I think that the first confusion about the numbers arose because Lady Catherine 'forgot' one of her guests. I would even hazard the statement that I know which one it was. At least, I know that it must have been one of two.'

'Which two?' asked Dorothy Woodcote, thinking of herself and Roger Hoskyn.

'Either myself or Mr Lingfield. I'll explain that when Miss Pigdon has told us what happened up to the time that Mr Lingfield and Mrs Denbies went out for their ride with George.'

'Describe my day, do you mean?' demanded Eunice.

'Yes, please, and don't leave out anything.'

'Well, I don't know that I should be able to leave

out anything, because, so far as I can remember, I did so very little that I'm sure I'll remember it all.'

'Why, you did everything, Piggie!' exclaimed George. Eunice Pigdon laughed.

'Everything didn't amount to much, then,' she retorted. 'I got up at eight, had breakfast at nine, went through the plans for the day with Lady Catherine, mended a photograph album for George, took the dogs for a run, had lunch, read a book, first to myself while Lady Catherine had her afternoon nap, then aloud to her——'

'What was the book?' asked Mrs Bradley.

'Oh, a detective story. I remember being rather provoked because I had got on much farther in it than she had, and it was rather boring to re-read aloud the part I'd already read to myself. I wanted to get on to the solution. What has the book got to do with it?'

'Every detail helps,' said Mrs Bradley, 'and so far you have not given us many details.'

'I see. It was all so ordinary, except that lunch was a rather slight meal as we were having the big dinner in the evening.'

'Ah, now perhaps we come to something, Miss Pigdon. Can you tell us which people were at lunch?'

'But you know as well as I do. You were at lunch.'

'No. If you remember, I lunched with George in Guildford. We went so that he might select a birthday gift.'

'Which he jolly well did,' said George, in reminiscent triumph. 'I thought it was frightfully good of you when you'd only just come to the house. It was then that I decided to make you my great-aunt, wasn't it?'

'It was, George.'

'Oh, no, you weren't at lunch,' said Eunice. 'I'd forgotten. Well, let me see, then: Lady Catherine, Granny, Harry, Claudia, Mary, Humphrey and myself. The Clandons did not get here until four, John Hackhurst arrived at four-thirty and wanted tea—China tea, and Cook hadn't a lemon and had to send into Dorking to get one——'

'So that's who they were,' said Roger.

'Who were?'

'I mean we met them.' He grinned and looked across at Dorothy. 'Do you remember?'

'Yes. But I shouldn't have thought they could get there and back in the time.'

'Say on,' said Mrs Bradley. 'This fills an all-important gap.'

'But you came across the hills and the Common,' interrupted Eunice Pigdon. 'And it wasn't *they*, surely? We only sent Sim in the car!'

'Sim? Oh, these two were women. We made sure they'd come from here. It was they who directed us to the station, and we came upon this house after we'd lost our way.'

'Wait a minute,' said Mrs Bradley. 'This certainly begins to look like proof.'

'Proof? Proof of what?'

'Of Sim's complicity in the murder.'

'But that doesn't matter now Sim is dead.'

'Does it not? Ah, well! There is one more thing. When Mr Hackhurst made this inconvenient demand for lemons, Mr Lingfield and Mrs Denbies had already gone out for their ride.'

'But Sim did go out for the lemons,' said George. 'I know, because I saw him go.'

'Tell your story, child,' said Mrs Bradley, perceiving that he wanted to speak. 'And then you must go up to bed. There will be no dénouement tonight, so you won't miss any of the fun.'

'Well, when you and I came back from Guildford, I heard Mr Lingfield and Mrs Denbies arrange to go out for a ride. Then I asked whether I could go with them, and I don't really think they wanted me, but Piggie said, "Take him, for goodness' sake! It will be plague enough getting through the rest of the afternoon without having him bothering round!" You did say so, didn't you, Piggy?'

'I suppose so, George. Go on.'

'Well, we went out on the Common and galloped, and then the others said it was getting late and I'd better get back in case I missed the beginning of the party. That's all.'

'Bed, then, George, and thank you for a lucid exposition. Now, Mr Hoskyn, it's your turn.'

'Oh, but I've told all I can,' said Roger, very much surprised at being challenged. 'We saw Lingfield (I presume), Mrs Denbies and George. Then we saw George. Then we saw Mrs Denbies when we got to the house. We did not see more of Mr Lingfield. That's all I know, except that after we had knocked at the door here to ask our way, we were asked in (we thought by mistake) and were given a jolly good dinner.'

'That wasn't quite all, though, Mr Hoskyn,' suggested Mrs Bradley.

'Well, no. As a matter of fact'—he looked across at Dorothy— 'we had another rather queer experience on our way home. I—we—well, what happened was this: You all know the story of Benjamin's sack?'

The company, not unnaturally, looked wooden and non-committal—the usual reaction on the part of English people to any reference to the Bible, their national book—and Roger glanced, for encouragement, at his questioner. She nodded, and he continued.

'I found my tips—they weren't large ones—returned to me. It seemed to me rather queer.'

Encouraged by Mrs Bradley, he told the story of the money he had found in his haversack. The company was suitably interested.

'Then, of course, there was the body on the line,' he added, 'and, further to that, the decidedly rummy business—as I see it now—of Sim's turning up with the car.'

'Ah, yes,' said Mrs Bradley. 'Sim and the car. Sim might almost have been the murderer himself instead of the murderer's accomplice. No doubt you can all guess now who the murderer was.'

'I'm sure *I* can't,' said Clare Dunley.

'I am *not* so sure. When dinner was over, what happened to Granny?' asked Eunice Pigdon suddenly.

'He drank port with the other men. I do not know anything else that he did.'

'He listened to Claudia's recital, did he not?'

'Oh, I suppose so, yes. But so did the rest of us, didn't we?'

'True. We did. Meanwhile Sim had been sent to the station.'

'Yes. He came back, though,' said Eunice Pigdon. 'Then he went out again later. Bugle came and asked me about it.'

'Yes, I know he did. Why did he?'

'Granny was cross. He said that Sim should have taken these young people home, and told me to send him after them.'

'He was cross. Meanwhile Mr Lingfield was dead, his head was cut off and his body was then transported to the copse where it was discovered. The head——'

'Has never been found,' said Eunice Pigdon.

'Oh, yes, it has.'

'Where?' enquired everyone at once, except for Dorothy Woodcote. She spectacularly fainted.

'Too intelligent,' said Mrs Bradley sympathetically. 'Lift her on to the settee. Yes, just a little brandy, I think. All this is rather a shock to a sensitive child.'

It was Bob who picked Dorothy up, snarling evilly at Roger as he did so. Dorothy recovered almost before he had laid her on the settee. She sat up immediately, apologized, and then told the story of the fire alarm and the bust. At the end of this recital Mrs Bradley nodded.

'Yes,' she said, 'that is what happened. I myself raised that alarm of fire on purpose. It had interesting repercussions.'

'And where are the bones now?' enquired Eunice Pigdon, who appeared unaffected by the narrative.

'In the keeping of the police,' Mrs Bradley responded. 'This is where the inspector takes up the story.'

'There's little to tell,' said the inspector. 'We had our suspicions. Well, it seems as if we were wrong. As for the bones, Mrs Bradley was right about them. She said it was an old trick, in that she'd met it before, but I'm free to admit that it would not have occurred to the police.'

'It wouldn't have occurred to me,' said Roger. 'What bones exactly are we discussing?'

'The bones of the dead man's head. They were in the bust which I dropped on the fender in Dorothy's room.'

'In the bust? Then—but——'

'I know. We cannot prove who put them there, however great our suspicions may be. Still, we do know one thing. A second bust, which I had placed in the gap left when I broke the first one, was claimed and carried off during the alarm of fire.'

'Who claimed it?' demanded Eunice Pigdon. 'Not——'

'Yes, Captain Ranmore burst in and took it away. That doesn't prove anything, of course.'

'I should have thought it did!' said Roger. 'Isn't it

a maxim that a person picks up the most precious things he possesses? If Ranmore is the murderer, and had hidden the head in this rather peculiar, cold-blooded sort of way, wouldn't he naturally make a bee-line for it.'

'I think it could be shown with some success that it was not the bust he desired to save from the fire,' said Mrs Bradley, grinning horribly.

'What?' said Roger, going very pale and then becoming flushed. He looked at Dorothy.

'Yes,' said Mrs Bradley. 'I told you at the beginning of these revelations that I wanted proof to lay before a jury. Well, I regret to say that the majority of persons on a jury would prefer to believe that a handsome, courteous, fatherly, middle-aged man such as Captain Ranmore, would naturally rush to the rescue of a young, pretty, charming, delightful child such as Dorothy here. You even prefer to believe it yourself, my dear Roger,' she added, favouring the so-far luckless suitor with a ferocious leer.

'I'll break his bloody neck,' said Roger, in low and savage tones.

'Mind your own damned business,' said Bob, glaring at Roger across the room.

'Bob, too,' said Mrs Bradley, clicking her tongue. 'Will no one spare a fancy for the bones?'

'Mary Leith,' said Eunice softly. Mrs Bradley glanced at her.

'What do you mean?' enquired Clare Dunley. 'I shouldn't have thought poor Mary knew about the bones.'

'She saw poor Granny shot in the leg,' said Eunice Pigdon, betraying her own state of mind. 'I understand everything now.'

'More than I do,' muttered Roger. Mrs Bradley transferred her gaze to him.

'What would you like to understand, child?' she enquired.

'First,' said Roger belligerently, 'I'd like to know why Mrs Denbies was arrested. If you didn't really suspect her, why should she have been put to all that loathsome inconvenience?'

'She was very strongly suspected,' said Mrs Bradley, replying to the question although it had not been addressed to her but to the inspector.

'And with reason!' said Clare Dunley very dryly. All the company looked at her. She smoothed her silk skirt over her knees and looked down at her strong hands as she performed the action. She did not attempt to meet their eyes. 'If ever any woman had cause to murder any man, I should say it was Claudia Denbies.'

'Did he treat her very badly?' asked Bob. 'I daresay she deserved it. Women usually do.'

'Speak for those you know better than you know me!' said Dorothy; but Roger, looking curiously at Clare Dunley, said:

'Go on.'

'Oh, I needn't enlarge,' said Clare, but still with her eyes cast down. 'You all know the sort of thing I mean. Time for her one day, and no time the next. Broke engagements, left her flat—oh, not

once or even twice, but time after time. I don't
know why she stood it.'

'Oh, they weren't married, you know,'
said Mrs Bradley. 'Did you think they were?
You should have been present at the inquest.'
The effect of these words was alarming. Clare
Dunley sprang up, and so did Eunice Pigdon.
They stood, with clenched hands, glaring at one
another as though only lack of practice in such
matters prevented them from springing on one
another.

'You—you——!' began Eunice Pigdon.

'How—I—I——' said Clare Dunley. Then both
flushed hotly, looked foolish, and while Clare
resumed her seat and prodded the edge of the
fender with her shoe, Eunice got up and went
towards the door.

'Begging your pardon, Miss Pigdon,' said the
inspector, 'but if you wouldn't mind, just for ten
minutes——' He motioned towards the chair she
had left, and Eunice Pigdon obediently returned
and sat down.

'I suppose I've given myself away nicely,' she
remarked. She spoke quietly, as though she were
making a not uncharitable remark about someone
else, someone whom, perhaps, she did not know
particularly well.

'Yes. We've both been fools,' said Clare Dunley.
'I'm sorry, Eunice. We're both in the same boat,
I suppose.'

'I never thought it was Claudia,' said Eunice
Pigdon. 'I knew her pretty well, and, although I

was glad to see her taken up, I never thought the cap fitted.'

'Interesting,' remarked Mrs Bradley. 'And you, Mrs Dunley?'

'Oh, I didn't know. I didn't care. He was dead. That was all I cared about.'

'Do you still?' asked Eunice Pigdon. The two women suddenly seemed to have become reconciled, as though to have exchanged murderous rivalry for friendship were the obvious and normal thing for them to have done.

'I suppose so. I don't know,' Clare Dunley answered. There was a long silence. The inspector looked at his watch. As he did so, there was the sound of a car outside. He got up.

'If you will excuse me, ladies,' he said.

'Thank goodness!' said Dorothy involuntarily, the moment the door closed behind him.

'I don't know. There is worse to come,' said Mrs Bradley. 'You see, Mr Lingfield isn't dead.'

Clare Dunley went red and Eunice Pigdon white. Nobody else looked surprised, much less taken aback, by this pronouncement. Roger felt, now that the statement had been made, that he had known it for a very long time. Dorothy, too, saw it now as a foregone conclusion.

'Then he is the murderer,' said Roger, 'and Claudia was right when she said—and stuck to it—that it wasn't Lingfield's body that she saw.'

'I never thought it was,' said Mrs Bradley.

'What about the proofs, though?' said Bob. 'Didn't you say you couldn't prove it?'

'Well, Mary Leith is prepared to swear that it was Mr Lingfield who shot Captain Ranmore in the leg to keep him out of the summer-house. The point is to find Mr Lingfield. Once we can produce him alive the deed is done. The trouble is that the police can't find him, and, although Mary Leith is convinced that he is alive, she doesn't know where he is.'

'But——' said Bob and Dorothy together. 'He must surely be off to South America by now,' concluded Bob, who had filled and lighted his pipe, and was smoking placidly. Roger grunted but did not speak. He had been struck by a brilliant but, he suspected, a foolish idea.

'Well, I'll say good night,' said Eunice Pigdon.

'Good night,' said Clare Dunley, going with her to the door. Roger leapt up to open it for them, but as he got there the inspector turned the handle and came in.

The three started back, but the inspector waved a large, pale hand and gave an indulgent smile.

'Quite all right, ladies and gentlemen,' he said. 'Just a little spot of bother with Lady Catherine, but the nurse can cope nicely now. All we want to complete the party is Mr Lingfield.'

'You can't find him?' exclaimed Mary Leith, appearing in the hall just behind the inspector's shoulder. 'What can you prove against him when you do?'

'Nothing at all at present, miss,' the inspector cheerfully replied. 'But we *would* like to ask him why he allowed us to hold an inquest on him, and what he can tell us about the body that wasn't his!'

He stood aside, and the two women who were in love with Harry Lingfield went to their beds. Roger saw Clare Dunley take Mary Leith by the arm and compel her upstairs. Eunice Pigdon followed.

Mrs Bradley looked at Bob, who rose awkwardly, scowled, and said good night. When he had gone, she smiled at Roger and Dorothy and waved a yellow claw.

'The inspector and I want to talk things over,' she said. ' "Lovers to bed! 'Tis almost fairy time." By the way, I found out about Benjamin's sack. Now we are alone—you won't mind the inspector, I know!—I can tell you about your mysterious seven and sixpence.'

'I wish you would,' said Roger.

'It did not come from Bugle and Sim, as you supposed, but was a present from Lady Catherine. I got it out of Bugle, although with some difficulty. He seemed to find her point of view indelicate. I pointed out to him, however, that there is either nothing or everything indelicate about marriage. It depends on the point of view.'

'Marriage?' said Roger. 'Good Lord! The price of the licence! I suppose,' he added, 'Mary Leith looks careworn because she's been Lady Catherine's keeper for so long.'

'And had been doing her best to keep Lady Catherine's mental condition a secret,' said the inspector. 'Yes, sir, you've guessed it in one. And she's now on the verge of a breakdown.'

'There's another thing I've guessed,' said Roger carelessly. 'Why don't you look for Lingfield in London?'

'The Yard have been on to that for weeks, sir. If *they* don't find him, *we* can't!'

Chapter Eighteen

'See, see, the Sun
Doth slowly to his azure lodging run;
Come, sit but here,
And presently he'll quit our hemisphere:
So, still among
Lovers, time is too short or else too long.'
JOHN HALL OF DURHAM, *The Call*

'WE'VE GOT this, then, mam,' said the inspector.
'As soon as we get hold of Lingfield he'll have
to explain away the inquest. He can't pretend he
doesn't know of it. It's been in all the newspapers,
and the local papers had a very full account. Then
he's got to explain away the murder of Sim——'

'Can you charge him with the murder of Sim?'
asked Mrs Bradley.

'I reckon we've got it pretty well weighed up,
mam. Sim blackmailed him all right, I'll take my
oath. I've just had word that Mrs Denbies has been
released. My bet is that she knows something more
than she's said, although there's nothing to hold

her for if—as the Yard has advised us to do—we accept your view of her innocence. She did go out that night, and she did go to see Vesper. He was only just out of jug, we find—or, rather, the Yard found for us—and it seems to have been his own suggestion that they should meet very secretly, so as not to prejudice her with her public by allowing it to be known she consorted with criminals. We found the letter among her things.'

'Why didn't she produce it in court?'

'It appears—we've confronted her with all this and challenged her to deny it—the sergeant was handy there, him having the grand passion for her—not as that's very suitable in a police officer, but there it is, and there isn't any arguing with emotions—it appears that she thought from the first that the letter was phony, and really came from Lingfield. She came across with that, and it's contributory evidence in support of your tip that Lingfield isn't dead. We made her—at least, the sergeant did (he don't want her hanged!)—we made her swear to the date Lingfield tore his trousers, and then put the doctors on to that. The scars on the corpse were years older! The bet is that Lingfield had had the murder planned for years!'

'I see. She's been shielding Mr Lingfield?'

'As far as she could. There's no doubt she was in love with him, I should say.'

'And, in his way, no doubt, he was in love with her,' said Mrs Bradley. 'He committed murder to remove her husband, it appears, and even went to the length of lacerating himself on barbed wire in preparation for the deed. Well, well!'

'It's a strange thing, in a country like England,' said the inspector, 'that love—if you can call it that—is responsible for more murders than any other motive murderers have. It don't seem to go with a steady and God-fearing nation, somehow, mam. Now take my sergeant, as I say—though, mind you, he's had his uses! There's a young fellow as sensible as you could wish in the ordinary way, but what does he go and say, the minute we've fixed it all on Lingfield and have only to get him to put him where we want him?'

'He probably said it was a pity,' said Mrs Bradley.

'His very words, mam! "It seems a pity, don't it?" he says, looking more like a piece of cheese than any sergeant of mine has a right to look. "After all the poor feller went through to get her, it seems a pity that we should be after him like a couple of condemned bloodhounds." Told him off I did, good and proper, and finished up by telling him to think of the lady's good name, and not to be wishing a double murderer on her for a husband. "Besides," I said, "we haven't caught him yet."

'He looks at me as if he could cry. "Think of the lady! I only wish as how I *dared* think of her!" he says. Now, I ask you, mam, if that's any way for an ambitious officer to talk. And got brains in his head, mind you, at that. It was him found out that your chauffeur, George, hid the young lady in your garage while Miss Menzies, your secretary, mam, took Mr Hoskyn out of the murderer's way. They were Sim's prints on that spanner.'

'Ah, yes, Laura prefers the lively, picturesque method of achieving her effects,' said Mrs Bradley. 'I heard of the pyjama-trouser hunt. My French cook, who played a small part, enjoyed that affair immensely.'

'Pretty nearly dished the whole issue, though, not foreseeing as the yokel would have his revenge,' said the inspector with a chuckle. 'One thing, thanks to the trip-wires and Mr Hoskyn—I shouldn't care to meet *him* on a dark night if he was feeling kind of tough, mam, for all he looks like a minor poet or something——'

'He *is* a minor poet,' said Mrs Bradley.

'——well, as I say, mam, be that as it may (and my sergeant writes poetry, too, and at the end of his official notebook at that!) the fact remains that he handled his man a treat, by all accounts, and we ought to be able to find the marks if only we can nab his lordship—I refer to Lingfield—soon enough!'

'The little boy who bit the hand was quite clever, too,' said Mrs Bradley. 'I suppose Mr Hoskyn trained him.'

'We've tracked the two cars, mam, and your idea worked out correct again,' said the inspector, handsomely spoken as usual. 'It was Lingfield's own car that had the bloodstains. The wrecked car he bought off a dump-heap just to try and throw dust in our eyes. If he'd had the sense to get some of the blood on it we might have bothered more

about it in the first place, when Mr Hoskyn spotted
it was in the place of that old burnt-out one. The
garage where he bought the wrecked car gave a
description that tallied nicely with Sim. Of course,
it was the wrecked car—but it wasn't wrecked
then—Lady Catherine saw on the gravel. It's the
same make as Mrs Denbies'.'

'You've worked out Sim's programme on the day
and night of the murder, I suppose?'

'Pretty well, thanks to you, mam. But we can't
see when he managed to substitute the wrecked
car for the burnt one. There's witnesses to prove
the burnt one was there the day before the murder.
Mr Hoskyn saw it, too.'

'Lemons,' said Mrs Bradley. She explained. 'It
was risky, of course, and Lingfield had to get rid
of Mrs Denbies to go and render assistance.'

'The quarrel, mam!'

'Exactly.'

'I've got it all now, mam, I think. Sim took the
burnt-out car to bits. He thought Mr Hoskyn had
spotted him, I suppose, that day Mr Hoskyn and
the young lady stopped there on their way to
Whiteledge. That's why he laid for young Hoskyn.
I see it now. A bit of luck, Mr Hoskyn meeting
those two women. I suppose Sim blarneyed them
into going for the lemons instead of him.'

'Then Harry Lingfield went along to help with the
finishing touches and stow the pieces safely in the
holes and behind the bushes of the Common.'

'Then, when Sim was sent to the station with Miss
Woodcote and Mr Hoskyn, he made an opportunity

to tow the wrecked car into position on the way back to Whiteledge. But, mam, I don't see why they went to all that trouble to take the burnt-out car to bits so thoroughly.'

'I have the glimmering of a notion,' said Mrs Bradley. 'Have you still got the pieces of the burnt-out car which the holiday-makers found?'

'Oh, yes, mam. They're up at headquarters.'

'Have you had them looked over for bloodstains?'

'Nothing doing, mam. Not a trace of blood.'

'There's a bit missing, then. You had better put your people on to finding a piece with a very sharp edge capable of being struck very heavily with a wooden mallet or a stone-breaker's hammer.'

'You mean, mam——?'

'They'll find it, but they may have to drag ponds, comb woods and look in hollow trees.'

'Quite a proposition in this county, mam.'

'Yes, but this particular kind of murder could scarcely have been so successful in another type of country, perhaps.'

'As long as it doesn't put ideas in people's heads,' said the inspector.

'By the way,' said Mrs Bradley, 'there might be another explanation of the murder of Sim besides blackmail.'

'Blackmail wouldn't appeal to a gentleman of Lingfield's kidney, mam. He'd soon put a stop to that!'

'I agree. But we don't *know* that Sim was blackmailing him. We do know, however, that Harry

Lingfield was in love with Mrs Denbies, however violently they quarrelled. It is unlikely, therefore, that he would take kindly to the knowledge that Mrs Denbies had been arrested for the crime which he had committed, although he tried to implicate her at the time.'

'You've got something there, mam, I think. You mean he murdered Sim deliberately to take our mind off Mrs Denbies' being out of the house that night.'

'Yes. It's only a theory, of course. First catch your hare——'

'I believe you, mam. You think he'll stay in England?'

'Until Mrs Denbies is safe, yes. Now that you have set her free we shall soon know whether he has a confederate in this house.'

'How so, mam? Oh, yes, I see. One of those you told tonight will tip him the wink she's free, and then he'll try to communicate with her, and then we've got him!'

'If it works out, yes. But I'm bound to tell you, Inspector, out of the depths of my psychological experience and knowledge, that I am very doubtful whether any of the people who know of Mrs Denbies' release are in league with Harry Lingfield or have the slightest idea where he is.'

'Mrs Dunley and Miss Pigdon or the little chap are the only likely ones, mam, I take it. But—wouldn't Lady Catherine know?'

'No. I am quite confident she does not. If she knew, I should have found it out by now owing to the nature of the treatment I have been giving her.'

'Talking of psychology, mam, it strikes me as very queer about that engine-driver, especially as the body could never have been placed on the line.'

'Very odd, and very, very interesting.'

'Can you explain it, mam?'

'No.'

'Well, I'll say good night, mam. We must just see what happens, that's all.'

Weeks passed. Roger returned to school and the term passed into the limbo of Sports Day and cricket, with the promise of the long vacation to come.

Early in July, just before school broke up, Roger was sent for by the headmaster, and entered the presence in some trepidation. Matters had been going well with him. Mr Simmonds, his hated rival, had left for a public school post, and Roger had been promoted (temporarily, he presumed) to the sole charge of athletics and cricket, and had been relieved of his most tiresome classes. He was greatly enjoying the change, and got on well with the boys, for he was a good athlete and an enterprising although by no means a first-class batsman.

With the headmaster was a lady, a handsome woman with a haughty yet adventurous eye. She smiled very sweetly at Roger.

'This is Mr Hoskyn, Princess,' said the headmaster.

'So you are the man who is responsible for the wonderful improvement in my son!' said the lady warmly. Roger felt too much embarrassed to catch the headmaster's eye.

'I—we do what we can,' he mumbled.

'Mr Hoskyn, Princess,' said the headmaster unblushingly, 'is quite the most valuable of my younger men.'

'Well, the endowment is for him,' said the Princess. She held out a firm white hand. 'Do kiss it!' she said. 'I love having my hands kissed, and hardly anyone does it except foreigners, and really they hardly count. Don't, of course, if you'd rather not!'

Roger obligingly rested the hand on his, bowed over it as gracefully as he could, and, pressing the finger-tips slightly, as that seemed to be expected, too, he kissed the smooth knuckles by brushing them slightly with his lips.

'Divine!' said the lady. 'I *must* tell Lousy. He will be so frightfully amused. And his little friend Basil, too. Do you know Basil Kirby, Mr Hoskyn?'

Light dawned on Roger. He had heard, in casual gossip let fall by Parkinson, that Healy-Lunn's mother had recently married into exiled but apparently wealthy royalty, and he realized that Healy-Lunn's gratitude for being saved from expulsion had taken a practical form.

That night he wrote with careful nonchalance to Dorothy:

'A funny thing happened today. One of the mothers rolled up and endowed the school with a new house. Her son and a few selected devils—have I ever mentioned one Kirby?—are to be transferred to it. She's even got a building priority permit! And the queerest bit is this: *I'm* to be housemaster! I can't think what Healy-Lunn could have told his mother. She thinks I have a kind heart and a very nice influence! Let me know what *you* think about that, will you? Better still, could you meet me and come for that walk again? I somehow feel——Oh, well, it wouldn't interest you to know what I feel. I seem to have behaved like an ass, but will you come?'

The day was sunny and fine. The pines smelt pleasantly and the heather was warm to the touch. In place of violets and wood anemones were the long, untidy summer grasses and the hedge flowers—wild rose and bryony, pink convolvulus and the early hops, the trailing clematis and the honeysuckle. The ground was firm underfoot, the clay like stone and the stony paths loose and dry.

Roger and Dorothy were walking hand in hand—the loose, finger-tip conjunction of mutual friendliness and ease. Along the narrow path to which the woodland walk ascended, the hawthorns had lost their may-blossom and showed thick leaf and small, hard, inconsiderable bunches of berries.

The cow-byre came in sight. Its odour, less pronounced than in the spring, still greeted the

wanderers with a pristine, nostalgic scent, and
as they approached the notice-board with its
ineffectual, battered and slightly pathetic hand,
they saw a man at the cow-byre and called out a
greeting as they passed.

The man, a shaggy fellow, tall, wide-shouldered
and thin, hardly looked up at the sound of Roger's
voice. His hat was pulled over his eyes, for the
sun was hot, his shirt-sleeves were rolled above
the elbows and his trousers were hitched round a
slim, taut, horseman's waist with the remains of
an old school tie.

'Now, what do we do?' asked Dorothy, walking
on.

'Do?' Roger stopped to light his pipe. 'I thought
we'd agreed what to do. Aren't we going to make
the pilgrimage to Whiteledge?'

'Yes, but what do we do about Mr Lingfield?'

'Mr——?' He lowered the match, it burnt his
fingers and he flung it down and stamped on it,
cursing a little.

'That was Harry Lingfield,' said Dorothy, affecting
calmness. 'I only said—what do we do? I expect he
waits there, hoping to see Claudia Denbies.'

They walked on, and came to the gate which
seemed to close the path. They took the side turning
which led to the heath, and to the slope upon
which they had rested. Roger sat down, and pulled
the girl down beside him.

'Say it slowly,' he said. 'And tell me how you
know.'

There was no time for this, however. It was

Dorothy who heard the twang of the bowstring. She thrust Roger down so that he crashed flat on his back. The arrow sped past, and grazed her cheek in its flight. Roger, whose head had bumped down hard upon the turf, sat up, feeling his skull. Then he caught with a glance the bright blood streaming from the snick on his companion's delicate, slightly sun-tanned skin. He got up.

'Oh, don't!' said Dorothy. 'I'm not hurt! Don't go!'

He shook her off with berserk impatience, disregard and strength. The bow twanged again as he began to run towards the archer. Without slackening speed, Roger swung out to the right in the beautiful, graceful swerve which had often served him on the Rugby football field. He was in flannels, and had been carrying his jacket, but he had flung it down on the turf. He was therefore at an advantage compared with his muck-encrusted, heavy-booted antagonist. He used this advantage to the utmost, and, with a magnificent flying tackle, of a sort which would have earned stern comment on the field of play, he got his man round the knees and brought him down.

The next moment they were fighting on the ground. Dorothy ran forward. She had not been brought up to believe man to be the master of her fate as well as of his own, and her view was that Roger might well be in need of assistance against an opponent who was already a double murderer.

Roger, however, was not in need of help. A temperamental man and a poet, he had an artist's single-minded thoroughness. His aim was to twist his opponent's head off, and he set to work with a grim zest which had something of religious fanaticism about it.

Had he been informed, as a matter of cold fact, that the sight of a smear of blood on a young girl's cheek would have turned him into a compound of Richard Lovelace and a Commando, he would have accepted this reading of his character with reserve and modest caution. He did not even realize how much he had relished the fight and how much good it had done him, and how many problems it had solved, until it was over.

He got up, wiping mud out of his ear, caught sight of Dorothy's horrified eyes and, limping a little, came, at ease with himself, towards her. He had almost detached a tooth which he presently discovered and spat out.

'That's that,' he said contentedly. The girl recoiled. Roger, who felt like the English equivalent of a million dollars, although rather sore, observed the instinctive reaction, and nodded towards his opponent, who was lying perfectly still upon the turf. 'He'll be all right. He fell soft.'

'You'll—we shall have to get a doctor,' said Dorothy, who wanted to cry.

'You've got one,' said a rich, amused and incomparably beautiful voice. Mrs Bradley, accompanied by the sergeant and followed closely by the inspector, came out of the copse of hazels through which the woodland ride led on to Whiteledge, and walked towards them.

She smiled horribly and knelt to examine Roger's handiwork.

'Did *you* bite him on the Mount of Venus?' she demanded.

'No. That was Healy-Lunn,' said Roger, grinning.

'Better make direct for the station,' said Roger, 'if they're going to take him up to the house. Don't want to barge in there. I can get a wash and brush-up in the waiting-room or somewhere, I expect. I say, you aren't sick with me, are you? I mean, I had to have a go at him, and, having taken him on, to make a do of it. You do see that?' He spoke anxiously, misunderstanding his companion's silence.

'I know,' said Dorothy. 'It was—a bit frightening, that's all. You see, I didn't know you could fight.'

'I can't. Not in the ordinary way. Don't go getting wrong ideas. I mean, I'd be no good on the domestic hearth, poker in hand, *versus* wife.'

'But—it was so horribly scientific.'

'I know. I'm teaching the kids. I think I'll teach you. It's really quite handy to know how to make a proper mess of people.'

She managed to laugh. They walked on again.

'How do you think old Bob will take it?' asked Roger, at the end of half a mile.

'Take what?' But a tell-tale flush completely gave her away.

'Us, chump. Now I've got a house, what's stopping us? You're not going to back out now, are you?'

'I wouldn't know.'

'Good enough.' They walked on amid the gold-green gloom of the hazels. Suddenly Dorothy said:

'I thought you were a poet. I hoped you were.'

'Oh, I am . . . Oh, I see! Well, this is too serious for poetry—my kind of poetry, anyway.'

'Is it? That's rather a pity.'

'I'm sorry. What can we do? Hullo! Who's coming now?' They looked back across the open stretch of the Common. The thunder of hoofs came nearer, and into the space before them swept a horseman. It was the child, George, riding like a Centaur, boy and beast all one. To add to the illusion, the great horse was barebacked except for the boy, and the boy was bare to the waist. His carriage and poise were god-like, and his hair was blown in a breeze of his own creating.

Dorothy gave a slight sigh.

'There you are, then,' said Roger. 'There's the omen. Eros on the wings of the wind.' He turned and took her in his arms. 'But it isn't *my* poetry we need.'

'Whose, then?' She freed herself. Roger kept one arm about her, still faced her, smoothed her cut cheek with a long, strong thumb, leaned forward and kissed her and said:

> *'To our bodies turn we then, that so*
> *Weak men on love revealed may look;*
> *Love's mysteries in souls do grow,*
> *But yet the body is his book.'*

'But Harry Lingfield, who thought so, is to die,' she said, soberly, giving the statement all its due.

'Yes, but he had his fun.'

'Killing people, and being hunted and afraid, and perhaps hungry? And not getting what he wanted in the end?'

'Life's like that. Our generation ought to know it.'

'I don't want my children to know it.'

'You wanted poetry, and see where it's led us!'

'I know. Do you still—like—Claudia Denbies?'

'In a way, yes, I do.' He did not hesitate. Dorothy did not hesitate, either. She gave him a long look and then put her hands on his shoulders.

MORE VINTAGE MURDER MYSTERIES

EDMUND CRISPIN

Buried for Pleasure
The Case of the Gilded Fly
Holy Disorders
Love Lies Bleeding
The Moving Toyshop
Swan Song

A. A. MILNE

The Red House Mystery

GLADYS MITCHELL

Speedy Death
The Mystery of a Butcher's Shop
The Longer Bodies
The Saltmarsh Murders
Death and the Opera
The Devil at Saxon Wall
Dead Men's Morris
Come Away, Death
St Peter's Finger
Brazen Tongue
Hangman's Curfew
When Last I Died
Laurels Are Poison
Here Comes a Chopper
Death and the Maiden
Tom Brown's Body
Groaning Spinney
The Devil's Elbow
The Echoing Strangers
Watson's Choice
The Twenty-Third Man
Spotted Hemlock
My Bones Will Keep
Three Quick and Five Dead
Dance to Your Daddy
A Hearse on May-Day
Late, Late in the Evening
Fault in the Structure
Nest of Vipers

MARGERY ALLINGHAM

Mystery Mile
Police at the Funeral
Sweet Danger
Flowers for the Judge
The Case of the Late Pig
The Fashion in Shrouds
Traitor's Purse
Coroner's Pidgin
More Work for the Undertaker
The Tiger in the Smoke
The Beckoning Lady
Hide My Eyes
The China Governess
The Mind Readers
Cargo of Eagles

E. F. BENSON

The Blotting Book
The Luck of the Vails

NICHOLAS BLAKE

A Question of Proof
Thou Shell of Death
There's Trouble Brewing
The Beast Must Die
The Smiler With the Knife
Malice in Wonderland
The Case of the Abominable Snowman
Minute for Murder
Head of a Traveller
The Dreadful Hollow
The Whisper in the Gloom
End of Chapter
The Widow's Cruise
The Worm of Death
The Sad Variety
The Morning After Death

www.vintage-books.co.uk